N/A

DOUBLE A Blues

DOUBLE A Blues

PATRICK ROCKENBACH

TATE PUBLISHING
AND ENTERPRISES, LLC

Published by Tate Publishing & Enterprises, LLC
127 E. Trade Center Terrace | Mustang, Oklahoma 73064 USA
1.888.361.9473 | www.tatepublishing.com

Tate Publishing is committed to excellence in the publishing industry. The company reflects the philosophy established by the founders, based on Psalm 68:11,
"The Lord gave the word and great was the company of those who published it."

Cover design by Ronnel Luspoc
Interior design by Mary Jean Archival

Published in the United States of America

ISBN: 978-1-62563-794-9
Fiction / Sports
13.06.05

To my wife, Nilda, thank you for always being there for me and supporting me in everything I have ever wanted to do. You are my compass and my rock in a stormy world. I don't know what I ever did to deserve someone like you, but with deference to Lou Gehrig, I consider myself the luckiest man on the face of the earth.

To my son Dylan, thank you for being the first person to read this book when it was just a draft. Your feedback gave me the confidence to keep going and see it through to the end.

To my son Bryan, thank you for helping to shape the characters in the book. Your creativity is inspiring and helped me think outside the box and go places I didn't expect to go.

To my son Adrian, your energy is boundless and served as motivation when I got tired of writing and helped me keep pushing.

This was a team effort, and without all of your love and support I would still be sitting around with this idea stuck in my head thinking, *Hey, I should write a book someday.*

CHAPTER 1

Zach Fredericks always had a plan. Once he had his mind set on something, he did whatever was necessary to accomplish his goal. He had been that way as long as he could remember. One of his earliest memories was of a baseball set he received one Christmas. He had played by himself with that set for months, trying as hard as he could to hit the ball over his neighbor's fence. It took thousands of swings, but one day he finally did it. If he closed his eyes, he could still see the ball sailing over the fence. That was the moment he knew what he wanted to do for the rest of his life. He wanted to be a professional baseball player.

Now, many years later, here he was living the dream. Well, not quite the dream since he wasn't in the majors yet, but he was a minor league baseball player. He played for the Birmingham Barons, and right now he was in the on-deck circle waiting for his turn to hit and staring out at a very tough pitcher that had already gotten him out three times tonight. Funny, Zach had faced him before at a lower level and had hit him pretty hard. That came with the territory. If you wanted to make it to the big leagues, you had to put in a lot of work and beat the best along the way.

The road to the big leagues was not an easy one, and it got harder every year. It seemed like just when he started to figure everything out, something changed; he got a new manager, new players joined the team, or sometimes he just got tired and wondered if it was worth it. It was a rough life and even though he doubted himself sometimes, Zach loved it. He just wished that things would move along faster, and although he didn't mind putting in the time and effort needed to succeed, there came a point where he had to decide if his best was going to be good enough.

That is what happened over the winter, before the season started. He had been visiting his friend Manny at his baseball academy in the Dominican Republic when he realized that he might not have the skills needed to make it to the big leagues. He remembered the moment clearly; he saw a sixteen-year-old kid hit pitch after pitch out of the park without breaking a sweat. He knew then that he would have to do something different if he was going to make it. He had changed his workout routine over the winter and added something new. Hopefully it was going to be enough to make a difference.

His plan, as always, was to try to hit the ball back up the middle. He usually got in trouble when he tried to pull pitches and either popped up or grounded out weakly to the infield. He had never been one to change his routine, but he had tinkered with his batting stance all during spring training and had yet to feel comfortable at the plate.

It had been a tough couple of games to start off the new season, and he was anxious to get on base. Maybe a little too anxious, he thought as he swung the bat back and forth while he watched his buddy Joe at the plate. Some guys made it look so easy. Take a pitch or two and smack the ball into the outfield, no big deal.

Sure enough, Joe sent a one and one pitch into the gap in left center and pulled into second base standing up. Amazing. The guy never seemed to break a sweat; he just hit lines drives all over the field like it was nothing. They said some guys could roll out of bed on Christmas morning and hit lines drives. Joe would fit right into that club.

This was Joe's first year with the Barons, but at the rate he was going he would move up to the triple A Charlotte Knights by the end of the season. Who knows, maybe he could even get called up to the big leagues and finish the year in Chicago with the White Sox. It had happened before, a player on the big league club gets hurt and the team needs someone to fill in for a few weeks. For some guys that became their only chance. For others, they made the most of the opportunity and stayed up for good.

Yeah, one way or another Joe would get his shot. He could even play multiple positions, and that always helped. He was more seasoned than Zach, after all, Joe had spent two years at the University of Arizona. He was selected by the White Sox in the third round of the draft three years ago. He wasn't exactly a blue chip prospect, but some guys just had a way about them. Some would call it cocky, but it was really just confidence. Yeah, Joe would make it someday because talent always got you a shot. Sometimes injuries would sidetrack even the best players but if you at least got a chance anything could happen.

A chance is all that Zach wanted. It had been a long five years in the minors already, and here he was stuck in Birmingham again. Unlike Joe, he didn't go to college and wasn't selected until the twenty-first round of the draft. He didn't receive a big signing bonus and had to struggle to make ends meet in the off season working a regular job. He still lived at home with his mom, not the most exciting prospect for a twenty-three-year-old man. But most guys he was drafted with were already out of the game, so he had already beaten the odds to get this far.

It was a funny business. Even though you were teammates, there was always that underlying competition that made things a little tense. Sure, you wanted everyone to do well because you wanted to win, but it always stung a little bit when you saw someone get called up before you. This was going to be Zach's third year with the Barons, and if he didn't move up a level this year it meant his development had stalled and he could end up getting released. He tried not to think about it, but the pressure was starting to get to him.

Too much thinking, now it was his turn to hit. This was always the hardest part of the game, that long walk to the batter's box. It was a pretty good crowd for early in the season, and Zach could feel the weight of a few thousand eyes on him as he approached the plate. The crowd was getting anxious. The Barons had not won a game, and in fact hadn't even had a lead yet this season.

Stick to the plan. The score was tied at two. Joe was on second base, and there were no outs. This would be a nice spot to get a hit and drive in the go ahead run, but at the very least he needed to move Joe over to third base. Even a groundout to the right side would do it and set up the next hitter to get the run in with a fly ball. Sometimes you had to give yourself up for the good of the team. It didn't help your individual stats, but Zach thought of himself as a team player and the coaches had just spent all of spring training drilling that concept into their heads.

Zach took a quick look down the line to see if there was a play on before he stepped into the batter's box. The third base coach was Jimmy Riggs, a former National League All-Star and pretty nice guy. He had been with the Barons the past five years and had always been good to Zach. He had positive things to say and didn't make him feel dumb if he missed a sign.

It was easy to miss a sign. It seemed like Jimmy touched every part of his body, but nothing mattered until he touched his left ear. That was the indicator sign and if he did that you really had to pay attention to find out what you needed to do because it could be one of few different things. Hit and run, bunt, take a pitch, swing away, each represented by a different part of Jimmy's body. But this time, he seemed to touch everything but his left ear, so that meant hit away.

Zach did the same thing every time he came up. He held the bat in his right hand, and with his left hand he made the sign of the cross as he stepped in from the left side of the plate. He tapped the plate with his bat, again with the sign of the cross, since a little divine intervention always helped. He then settled into a crouch, kept the bat level and looked out at the pitcher.

He got you out on fastballs the first two times up, so be on the lookout for something different this time, Zach thought. *Look for something to pull, try to get Joe over to third base.* The pitcher took a look back at second base and then came to the plate. The ball looked like it was floating in slow motion, and Zach's eyes seemed to jump out of their sockets at what looked like an easy pitch to hit.

Looks can be deceiving, and that was case this time as the ball dropped out of the strike zone at the last minute. Zach couldn't make the adjustment fast enough and swung and missed at a breaking ball in the dirt. Looking for another breaking ball on the next pitch, he stared at a fastball for strike two without taking the bat off his shoulder.

Great, he was behind in the count again. He knew better than to swing at junk and let fastballs go right by him. He stepped out of the batter's box to clear his mind. He found that it was best that he hit with an empty mind as he tended to overanalyze things. His frustration must have shown on his face because he saw that Jimmy was trying to get his attention.

No signs this time. Jimmy wanted to talk so Zach asked the umpire for time and stepped out of the batter's box and walked up the third base line. This was not good; it felt like he was in trouble and on his way to the principal's office. Nobody liked to get called over to talk the coach at this level. Maybe back in little league, but he was a professional ballplayer. Why didn't he just give him a sign like before?

"Take it easy, Zach," Jimmy said when he got close enough to talk. "We don't need you to drive in the run; just get him over to third base. You missed the bunt sign, so now you need to make contact and hit the ball to the right side."

"I missed a sign?" Now Zach really felt like he was in trouble. "I never saw you touch your ear."

"That was last year, Zach," Jimmy replied with a sigh. "We changed it in spring training. Now the indicator is when I touch the bill of my cap."

"You're right. I can't believe I forgot that." Zach made a mental note to ask Manny to go over the signs with him tonight. "I won't miss a sign again."

"Don't worry about it now," Jimmy said. "Keep your head in the game and get the runner over. I don't feel like extra innings tonight." With that, he walked back to the third base coach's box.

No pressure, Zach thought as he walked back to home plate.

"Everything clear now, son?" the umpire asked as Zach crossed home plate.

"Yes, sir," Zach replied. He was embarrassed enough, the last thing he needed was an unhappy umpire.

"Then let's play ball!" the ump said as he pointed to the pitcher.

Zach held the bat in his right hand and with his left hand made the sign of the cross as he stepped into the box. He tapped the plate with his bat, again with the sign of the cross and settled into a crouch, kept the bat level and looked out at the pitcher. Just get the runner over.

This time he recognized the pitch as it came to the plate. It was a fastball coming inside, the perfect pitch to pull. He shifted his weight and opened up his shoulder to get out in front of the ball, but he didn't expect what came next. It wasn't a fastball. It was a slider, and it was breaking away from him.

They say baseball is a game of inches, and that was certainly true right now. He didn't have time to adjust his swing enough and ended up off balance just a fraction. The ball hit the end of the bat and bounced directly to the third baseman, who looked the runner back to second base and easily threw Zach out.

Walking back to the dugout was never fun, especially when you didn't get the job done. Zach pulled off his helmet and put it in the cubbyhole at the end of the dugout. He could feel the disapproving stare of his manager, Tom Powers, as he found a seat at the end of the bench. It had been a long night, and it wasn't getting any better.

Tom had been the Barons' manager for the past two years. He had played in the big leagues for 14 years, been an All-Star for six, and was a two time World Series champion with the Marlins and Cardinals. He was known around the game as a tough manager who didn't tolerate mistakes and he was expected to have a long career as a manager in the big leagues.

But now, he was just like Zach, putting in his time in the minors trying to work his way back up to the show. Funny how things came full circle. You start out as a player in minors, work your way up, and then have to start all over again as a manager. It was the same for everyone, even a former All-Star and World Series champion. It had to be hard for him too, he must have felt stuck in Birmingham, just like Zach.

Tom had what it took to be successful; even Zach could see that. He emphasized the fundamentals: don't give away at-bats chasing bad pitches, make the routine plays in the field, pick up your coaches when you are on the bases and move runners over with no outs. Which is exactly what he didn't do right now. Zach buried his face in his hands and shook his head. Maybe it was his imagination, but he could feel Tom's stare from across the dugout.

"Don't worry about it, man. It happens to all of us. We'll pick you up," Doug Garrison said as plopped down next to Zach.

Leave it to Doug, who always had something positive to say. Even though he was a pitcher he stayed in the dugout during the games to cheer on his teammates. He wouldn't be doing anything to help them win tonight, he couldn't hit even when he was in the game, but it made Zach feel a little bit better.

"I know," Zach replied. "I can't seem to do anything right this year."

"We all go through slumps. I haven't had a hit it two years. You don't hear me complaining," Doug said with a smile.

"But at least you can pitch," Zach said, which was an understatement. Doug was a first round draft pick two years ago and got a $2.1 million signing bonus. It was just a matter of time before he made it to the big leagues.

"Amen to that. This arm is taking me all the way, baby. You just wait and see." Doug patted him on the shoulder and walked back to the other end of the dugout.

Like Joe, Doug also went to college, but at the University of Texas where he almost single handedly carried them to the College World Series title in back to back seasons. He could probably get major league hitters out right now and in fact was coming off a very successful spring training with the White Sox. He had even started the final exhibition game against the Cubs at Wrigley Field a couple of weeks ago.

The team had decided to bring him along slowly, but word on the street was if the bottom of the rotation didn't perform over the first few months of the season he could be called up by the All-Star break. All he needed was a few good starts down here with the Barons, then a quick move to Charlotte and finally Chicago. He had been outstanding in his first start, giving up a single run while striking out eleven with no walks. Unfortunately, the Barons were shut out, so it went down as a loss for Doug, but it was just a matter of time.

It wasn't good to just sit on the bench and feel sorry for himself; that was one of Tom's pet peeves. He would give you a minute to compose yourself, but you could expect a private word after the game if he saw you sitting on the bench for too long. Always support your teammates he would say; you are only as successful as the team. Easy for him to say, he needed to show that he could be a leader and a winning team was his indicator of success. Zach needed to make a name for himself, winning was nice, but he also needed to contribute.

In the few minutes it took Zach to take a seat and have a few words with Doug, the Barons had a rally going. The pitcher who was so rough on him all night had suddenly lost his control and walked the next two batters. The excitement on the bench snapped Zach out of his fog, and he joined his teammates on the top step of the dugout.

A few base hits later, and the Barons took a lead that they would keep for the rest of the game. *Funny how things can turn around so quickly,* Zach thought, but Doug was right. His teammates had picked him up. Zach made it a point to high five every guy that came back to the dugout and even started to think he might get another chance to hit.

A couple of one, two, three innings later, and the game was in the books. Zach grounded out again in his last at-bat, but he had made a nice diving stop of a ground ball at second base in the ninth inning for the final out. At least he felt like he had contributed something tonight. He was an excellent infielder with great range and an above average arm. Unfortunately, good fielding only took you so far, so if you wanted to get to the big leagues you needed a glove and a bat.

Zach had always been a good if not spectacular hitter. His success at the plate was based on discipline; he had a good eye and seldom swung at pitches outside the strike zone. He didn't have a lot of power, but he could hit the ball into the gaps and drove in his fair share of runs. His first year with the Barons he hit .282 with 11 home runs and 57 RBIs.

He had regressed a bit last year, hitting .263 with eight home runs and 42 RBIs. Maybe the pitching got a little bit better, new guys were always coming up, or his bat got a little slower, but he never felt right at the plate. After a rough spring training and a 0 for 11 at the plate to start the new season he was starting to get nervous. Baseball was a competitive sport and you were always looking over your shoulder. The team expected you to get better every year, not to go backwards. A lot of guys spent years in the minors, bouncing around from team to team. Zach didn't have that kind of time; he needed to get there fast.

As the team lined up for the traditional hand slaps and hugs at the end of the game, Zach took a look around the stadium. It wasn't the big leagues, but it was a start. It wasn't time to panic yet, he still had a little time left. Maybe the changes he made over the winter would kick in soon, then if he could just stick to the plan, he would make it; he could feel it in his bones. Now with the game over, the real work for the night was about to begin.

CHAPTER 2

Zach never really liked the locker room. Maybe it was because he was an only child and never had to share anything with a brother or sister. He was getting used to having roommates in the house that he shared with three other members of the Barons. But here in this cramped space with twenty-four other men, it was just uncomfortable.

He always tried to get a locker as far away from the shower as possible. That was a high traffic area, and some of his teammates were not very considerate in how much they chose to wear, or not wear. Zach was pretty conservative and always tried to at least wear a towel as he walked around. He couldn't say the same for everyone; in fact, some of his teammates could pass for nudists. He always found it odd that even as a professional athlete it had not changed much in locker rooms since his school days.

The first time he had to dress out for gym class was way back in the sixth grade. There were almost fifty kids in that class and they barely had five or six minutes to change before they had to be on the field. Then, after thirty minutes of exercise they returned to the locker room to change. No time for showers, just an extra layer of deodorant and back to class. Fortunately Zach always seemed to have gym during one of the later periods, so he didn't have to walk around all day smelling of sweat and extra deodorant.

High school was a little better because at least they had the opportunity to shower. It was always uncomfortable though, and you had to follow the unwritten rule, look straight ahead at all times, don't look down. Pity the poor kid that had his eyes wander around the shower. More often than not he would end up face first in a toilet bowl.

That was the other odd thing about high school; none of the stalls had doors. It must have been set up that way in an effort to prevent some poor kid from getting dunked, but it actually made it easier. Kids could be rough sometimes; that's why he kept to himself most of the time. He had a few friends but spent most of his time working out and practicing.

As he made his way through the minor leagues, the locker rooms got a little bit better, but not much. At least here there was a common area removed from the showers where the post game meal was laid out. They also had a couple of TVs that were usually turned to ESPN and served as a constant reminder of where everyone wanted to end up. All in all, it wasn't too bad, but if he had his choice Zach would prefer the semi–private dressing and shower area the coaches shared.

His post game ritual was always the same. Make a run for the food table and try to get something to eat. Imagine a dinner table with a large, hungry family and multiply it by a hundred. Despite what people may think, minor league ballplayers do not make a lot of money. The team provides a limited dinner after games, usually some type of sandwiches and the occasional hot item, but it's not much with twenty-four hungry men around. On the road they got a small food allowance that basically covered one of a number of fast food options.

You would think with the amount of money that they had invested in some of the players they would provide better nutritional options. In reality, the minor league teams were more like independent businesses and not funded by the major league teams. The players came and went so fast they didn't get a chance to build a fan base and the teams had to squeak by on what they made in attendance and concessions. It was rare that a player would spend three years with the same minor league team. That usually meant that their development had stalled, and they ended up getting traded or released.

It really was a cut throat business. Every year there was a new group of can't miss prospects coming up from the lower levels. The good news was that once you made it to double A you had a one in three chance of making it to the majors. If you could make it to triple A, your odds improved to three out of four. Triple A players also saw a significant bump in salary from the $1,300 a month Zach earned now to about $2,200 a month. From there if you got your shot in the big leagues the minimum salary was almost $500,000 a year.

Some players like Doug got big signing bonuses and didn't have to worry about off-season jobs. Zach couldn't afford to live on his minor league salary full-time, so he still lived at home with his mom when he wasn't playing. A part-time job at the batting cage helping to coach the local kids helped pass the time and gave him some spending money. He also got the chance to work out and hit year round. Not the most glamorous life, but it would do for now.

Looking back, Zach was lucky he was even drafted. He had always been a solid, if not spectacular player. He usually made the All-Star team in little league and was even all-league during high school. Physically, he just didn't fit the traditional mold of a high level prospect. He stood just five feet ten and weighed about 175 pounds. He was basically a line drive hitter with a little power and he played an excellent second base, but the scouts were not looking for players like him. He didn't even have an offer to play college ball, not that his grades would have been good enough to get into a top tier school anyway.

He did have the good fortune to play on a team with one of the most talked about pitchers in the state. Javier Martinez had it all and the scouts were lining up to see him. There were usually a couple around at every game he pitched. He had outstanding stuff and tossed three no-hitters in his senior year, including one in the state championship game. He was drafted by the Brewers and had already made his major league debut at the tender age of twenty-one.

Zach would never have had a chance to get drafted, but he got hot at just the right time during the run to the state championship. He had been hitting well during the last few weeks of the season but it was the final three games where he made an impression on the scouts. They had all come to see Javier, and even though he tossed a no-hitter in the final game, there had been almost as much talk about Zach's performance. In fact, Zach ended up as the tournament MVP. He had gone ten for twelve with four home runs and fourteen RBIs in the three games. Add in a few acrobatic plays at second base and he caught the attention of Bob Samuels, a scout for the White Sox.

It was quite a shock to get drafted, and Zach would have taken whatever the White Sox had offered. His only other option was trying to walk on at the local community college or maybe an independent league. He had seen Bob around the field and he had even spoken to him a couple of times after games but he was given no indication he was going to be drafted. Sitting at his kitchen table with his mom and signing that contract was one of the best days of his life. The fact that they only offered him a $20,000 signing bonus, a pretty small amount, didn't matter. He would have signed for nothing for the chance to play.

"Hey, are you just going to sit there all day staring at your locker or are you ready to go to work?" said a voice from behind Zach.

"What?" He replied as he turned around to see Manny Dominguez, his best friend on the team staring at him.

"I know how you get when you have a bad game. You relive every pitch and start to get all philosophical on your life. Sometimes you just have a bad game, let it go. You've been sitting there with that sandwich in your hand for the past twenty minutes," Manny said as he plopped down at the locker next to Zach.

"I didn't realize it had been that long," said Zach.

"Well, you did move around for a little bit, but you've been a zombie for a while now. What are you thinking about?"

"Everything," Zach replied, and it was true. Bad games really played on his mind. Especially when it was a couple of bad games in a row. "But you're right it's time to get to work. Have you got anything for me?"

"Well, you don't see as much from down in the bullpen, which is where I was tonight, as if you cared," Manny said with mock disgust as he started to get dressed. "But I've already loaded up our at-bats to your iPad. It didn't take as long tonight, as I didn't play you know."

Zach was well aware that Manny had not played tonight, or in the first few games of the season. At least he should be happy that he had a chance to play. Manny must be getting frustrated.

"I know you didn't play again, and I'm sorry. I'm sure that Tom will get you in tomorrow," Zach said, trying to be positive.

"He already told me I'll be starting tomorrow, no pressure, huh. I'm batting zero for the year so there is nowhere to go but up." Manny immediately lowered his head and then turned back to Zach. "Sorry man, I didn't mean that in a bad way. I know you're like zero for nine, right?"

"That's zero for eleven, but who's counting?" Zach said as he tossed the rest of his sandwich into the trash.

"Only Tom, all the coaches, the reporters, other guys on the team," Manny said with a smile. "Oh, and the entire Chicago White Sox organization. You know the difference between them and you?"

"If you are trying to cheer me up, it's not helping," Zach said with a big fake smile, "but what's the difference?"

"They all know that you are going to hit. You're the only one who thinks you'll go hitless for the season. Now go take a shower. I don't plan to spend the next hour with you smelling like that."

"All right, but don't wipe out the rest of the food. I may want to eat later, and I'm tired of Taco Bell." With that Zach headed toward the shower.

"Oh, and don't stand there thinking about your life. We're in a drought," Manny called out as Zach walked away.

A hot shower after a bad game always made Zach feel better. Unfortunately, since he was the last one in the shower today, the water was lukewarm at best. Well, that's what you get when ring up your third consecutive donut. Three for four, you get a hot shower and a good meal. Zero for four, you get a cold shower and Taco Bell for dinner.

Manny was right; it was not time to panic yet. It had only been a few games, and he usually started out the year slowly. It was usually around the end of April that his bat started to heat up. For some reason, this year seemed a little different; he couldn't quite put his finger on it. There was more pressure to perform. Maybe it was because the White Sox just signed a new second basement to a four year multimillion dollar contract. They also had a hot young second basemen at single A Winston-Salem. He was getting squeezed on both sides. He needed to do well and move up, or else he would have to catch on with another team and that would really be starting over.

Why couldn't he be more like Manny? He had been at this much longer than Zach, but things just seemed to roll off his back. This was also his third year with the Barons, but it was his fourth organization. At twenty-six years old his time was running out, but you could never tell by looking at him. He was the most positive guy Zach had ever met. He was popular in the clubhouse and loved by the coaching staff. His only problem was that for a big man, he was six foot four and 235 pounds; he was basically a singles hitter. As a catcher, he was expected to have at least a little bit of power but even Zach had out homered him each of the past two years.

Manny was from San Pedro de Marquis in the Dominican Republic, which was basically a breeding ground for major league players. He had two brothers, one older and one younger who were currently playing with the Mets and Marlins respectively. Signed by the Dodgers at the age of sixteen, Manny had spent three years at their baseball academy and had been bouncing around the minors ever since. From the Dodgers he went to the Mets then the Pirates and now finally the White Sox. His reputation was the same everywhere he went; pitchers loved him, solid defense, great clubhouse guy, but not enough power for a big man.

Married with two kids, Manny was nearing the end. Either he picked up his game and took it to the next level or he would be released again. He could try to hook on with another team but at this point that was pretty doubtful. He would probably end up going back to the Dominican and manage the baseball academy his brothers had set up. Zach had been down there in the off season, it was a nice place and Manny would be great with the kids, but Zach knew his heart was really set on getting to the majors like his brothers.

"Dude, seriously!" he heard Manny calling out from the shower entrance. "Finish up already; we don't have all night."

"Sorry, my mind was wandering again," Zach replied as he turned off the water and made his way back to his locker.

"Well dial it back in again and let's go. It's going to be one a.m. by the time we're done, and you know I don't like to miss any of my beauty sleep."

"We don't want you to get too good looking or it will go to your head," Zach replied.

"Not your problem, my friend, it's genetic. Every time I close my eyes I get better looking," Manny said as he stared at himself in the mirror.

"Careful, it may crack," Zach replied, "and you can't afford seven years of bad luck."

"No worries, I'm not superstitious."

"Really, what about that ritual you go through every time you bat. I think you adjust your wristbands more than anyone I've ever seen. You look like Nomar Garciaparra up there. No wonder the games are longer when you play." Manny was the most superstitious player Zach had ever met.

"You're one to talk. Do you have to make the sign of the cross every time you step out of the batter's box?" Manny asked as he imitated Zach's batting stance.

"I need all the help I can get," Zach replied.

"Amen to that, we both do, so let's get to it."

"Deal, let's see if we can figure out what's wrong with my swing," Zach said as he picked up his iPad.

Technology was something else. The game had only been over for a couple of hours and Zach already had video of his four at-bats loaded on to his iPad. With a wireless connection to the locker room's TV he could watch himself and try to understand what went wrong. The Barons had views from both center field and above the batter's box. One of the benefits of being with the same team for a couple of years was that the clubhouse guys all knew Zach and Manny and gave them immediate access to their video. Not all of the guys on the team had the same dedication to studying video but Zach found it very helpful.

He would sit with Manny after every game, and they would review each of their at-bats. They had copies of previous games loaded on to their iPads and could compare different at-bats to see if there were any mechanical changes to their swings. Zach's at-bats usually looked the same; his main issue was recognizing pitches and adjusting his swing accordingly. He tried not to get into the pitcher's head and guess what they were going to throw but when he wasn't hitting he would fall into that bad habit. Next thing you know, he was thinking fastball and swinging too early or thinking breaking ball and getting blown away by a fastball.

Manny was just the opposite. He could recognize pitches very early. He was a catcher after all, but he just couldn't pull the trigger fast enough. He didn't miss by much, but baseball was a game of inches, and Manny usually missed by a hair. They called it warning track power. Manny would either pop up or send the outfielder to the fence to catch a long fly ball. That potential for power was the thing that made four different clubs take a chance on Manny, power hitting catchers with good defense were hard to find. But at twenty-six years old, Manny's time was running out.

They would sit together in the locker room after every game trying to understand both the good and the bad. If they found something they would stay and look at more video and even head over to the batting cages to try something out. With the exception of the coaching staff and clubhouse attendants they were usually the last ones to leave after a game.

The coaches noticed the extra effort and would sometimes sit with them to look at video and offer suggestions. Some guys could get by on their natural ability and they didn't have to work too hard to stay sharp. Zach thought that all of the work and dedication he showed would give him an edge when it came down to getting a little extra playing time. That and putting the team before yourself were things that this coaching staff preached. Failing to move the runner over in tonight's game was as bad as making an error in the field or missing a sign.

"When did we change the bunt sign?" he asked Manny.

"The second week of spring training," Manny replied, "Why? Did you miss one today?"

"Yeah, in my last at-bat. That's why Jimmy called me down to talk. See the disgusted look on his face?" Zach pointed to the TV, which showed him talking to Jimmy.

"He doesn't look disgusted to me," said Manny, "I think you are reading into things too much."

"Maybe, I just don't like to make mistakes." With all of the video reviewed, Zach closed his iPad and turned off the TV.

"Letting yourself off the hook early tonight? We haven't gone over too much yet," Manny said as he stood up and stretched. "Either you're really frustrated or hungry."

"Actually, a little bit of both. I'd love to go hit the cages for a while, but I have a feeling you won't let me. It is Friday night, and you know what that means," Zach said as his slipped on his jacket.

"Day game tomorrow?" Manny asked.

"And?"

"Taco Bell!" Manny said with a big smile. "I thought you forgot."

"You would never let me. Especially since you are starting tomorrow. You need your energy."

"Chalupa power! I can taste it already. Let's get out of here," Manny said and walked to the door.

Zach looked around the clubhouse one last time. Even though he knew that Manny and he were the last two people around he thought he heard someone in the training room. Oh well, they'd find their own way out. He didn't have time to worry about anyone else. He had a hungry roommate he needed to get home. You would think a guy from the Dominican would have better taste in food, but he loved the stuff. Zach hit the lights and walked out the door.

CHAPTER 3

The parking lot was empty, so it wasn't hard for Zach and Manny to find Zach's car. Even if the lot had been full, it wouldn't have been hard. Zach had bought the 2004 Ford Taurus from a local car rental place back home, and since rentals tended to be nontraditional colors, the dark purple made the car stand out in any lot. Even though it had over 200,000 miles on it, Zach never had to do much other than change the oil, add brakes, and replace the tires once in a while. Someday, when he made it to the big leagues the first thing he planned to do was buy a new car. It didn't really matter what kind of car it was, as long as it was new.

"I can't believe you still have the purple beast," Manny said as they approached the car.

"All I know is that it runs. There must be something special about rental cars. You can drive and drive them, and they never break down," Zach replied.

"I've never even owned a car," Manny said as he opened the door. "Not much need for them back home. We walk everywhere. That's the thing about growing up on an island: cars are a luxury."

"We weren't a new car kind of family," Zach said as he started up the Purple Beast. He really liked that name. Cars had personality, and the Purple Beast fit.

Zach never remembered having a new car as a kid. Since his mom worked from home, she really didn't need a car so she still had the same Toyota Corolla since he was a kid. His dad always drove a truck, American made of course, and his Ford F150 was his pride and joy. He spent every weekend washing and waxing the truck and never even allowed you to bring food inside. Maybe if he had spent more time with his family on the weekends he wouldn't have fought so much with his mom.

Rarely a week went by without a fight. At first Zach didn't understand why his parents argued so much, but as he grew older he noticed that it was usually centered on drinking and money. His dad wanted to go out on the town with his friends to the local bars, and his mom wanted him to stay home. Money was always tight so she couldn't understand how he could go out and spend the little they had on drinking when they could barely put food on the table. Eventually it got to be too much, and they ended up divorced when Zach was ten.

He rarely saw his dad much after that. Eventually he remarried and moved to another town. The once a month visits and two weeks in the summer ended by the time Zach thirteen. His mom did her best to fill the void, but there are times that a boy just needs his dad. His mom never remarried, and now that Zach was out playing ball most of the year he worried about her being alone. She did have a few close friends, but he always hoped that she would find someone new.

The purple beast had served him well all these years. Sure he got teased by his teammates, but that was okay. Money was tight, so you did what you had to do to get by. It was like their regular visits to Taco Bell, cheap and filling. Guys with big signing bonuses could afford better food, but Manny and Zach had to make the best of a bad situation. They tried to eat healthy, but the food in the clubhouse only went so far and stocking up the fridge took too much time and effort. Even if he did, his roommates ended up breaking into his stash anyway. Living with people he barely knew was also a necessary evil. At least with Manny, he knew what he got, and right now that was Taco Bell.

"It doesn't get any better than this, my friend," Manny said as he tore into a chalupa. "I love the food back home, but I can't wait to get back to the states to get some real Mexican food."

"I know you can't be serious," Zach said. "You know this is not real Mexican food."

"Really? I thought it was the real deal," Manny said as he started working on the burrito supreme. "It's so good."

"We need to get you out of the south and to the west coast so you can get some proper food. Living on this fast food can't be good for you," Zach replied. "My mom knows a few great places."

"How is your mom? You haven't talked about her much lately."

"It's been rough for her lately. She may be losing her job soon. I'm trying not to think about it. I don't know what she's going to do if that happens." He really needed to get to the big leagues and make some money so she could retire.

"I'm sure something will work out. Maybe she could get a full-time job as a coach somewhere. You two talk about hitting all the time."

"She's one of the best coaches I ever had," Zach said. "She keeps me focused on what I need to do."

Zach made it a point to text her after every game and call her every few days. He also sent her video of his at-bats since she knew his swing better than anyone. She had been his little league coach more than once while he was growing up. She started out as team mom but after one particularly rough year with an inexperienced coach she gave up and took over a team. Some parents had a problem with a woman coach, but that ended once they saw how quickly their kids improved. Zach had a roomful of trophies at home that could prove to anyone that she knew her stuff.

"Next time, I'm going to let you drive so I can eat," Zach said as he surveyed the empty bag on Manny's lap and the bits of burrito and chalupa on his shirt.

"No can do. I told you I don't have a car and I don't know how to drive," Manny replied. "Back home we walk everywhere, how do you think I stay in such great shape in the offseason?"

"I thought it was just a better diet. I'm sure that Maria feeds you better at home than when you're here," Zach said as he pulled into the driveway of the house that served as their temporary home.

"Nothing like a home cooked meal. I miss her already, and the season's just started," Manny replied with a sigh. "It would be nice if she could come up with the kids but we just can't afford it. Plus, we're on the road so much she'd be alone all the time anyway. At least she has our family at home while I'm away."

"I don't know how you do it," Zach said as they made their way from the car to the house.

"No choice. This is the only thing I know how to do. It's been my dream since I was a kid. Now that my brothers have made it, I have to get there too. We're one big family and we take care of each other, but I need to pull my weight."

"And you are a big man," Zach said.

"Yes I am. Big enough to take on the likes of you, my friend," Manny said with a smile and grabbed Zach, putting him in a headlock.

"Okay, okay, I get it. Let me go before you hurt me. I don't want to show up on some injury report under 'injured in a headlock.' Let's get inside and see how the wonder twins are doing today."

"It's a deal." Manny set Zach free and headed to the door. "I'm sure they are locked in some type of video game duel."

Sure enough, when they walked into the living room they found Doug and Joe standing side by side in front of the TV playing MLB2K on the Xbox. Joe was pitching, and Doug stood by ready to swing. Joe threw him a virtual curve ball and Doug swung hard and missed turning himself in a complete circle in the process.

"This game is just like real life," Manny cracked as he took a seat on the couch. "Even though you are Evan Longoria on screen, you still swing like Doug Garrison."

"No wise cracks from the peanut gallery," Doug replied as he got back into his batting stance. "Can't you see I've already scored six runs?"

"Sure, and I see that Joe has twenty-six runs," Zach called out as he walked to the kitchen. "I hope your next start is better than that."

In the kitchen Zach could see the remains of Joe and Doug's late night dinner. Pots and pans were scattered all over the countertop and their plates remained where they ate on the small dining room table. He dropped his Taco Bell bag on the table and started to clean up. They may be messy, but it looked like they had a better dinner than Zach and Manny. Based on the left over vegetables and dirty wok it must have been some kind of stir fry. Much more appetizing than Taco Bell he had to admit.

It made sense that they were in a better position to prepare a real dinner. Both had signed for very good bonus money and didn't have to live on the monthly salary the Barons paid. He could also see the difference in status by the cars parked outside. No purple beast for these two. Both had expensive cars, a convertible BMW for Joe and a corvette for Doug. They both could have lived in a nice apartment on their own, but for some reason they had agreed to share the house with Zach and Manny. They had even paid the lease for the entire season, so there was no monthly rent.

It was a really nice gesture and very unexpected. Doug had first approached Zach early in spring training and asked if he knew a good place in town to stay. Zach mentioned that he and Manny shared a house with a couple of other guys the previous year, but they had both moved on. Joe was sitting in the next locker and quickly joined in the conversation and the next thing you knew they were roommates. The house had three bedrooms and there were five guys crowded in last year. Both Joe and Doug said they preferred to have their own rooms and that they would split the entire rent for the year as compensation. Zach and Manny had both protested but the guys stood behind their offer.

It was a much better living situation than Zach had been used to in the past. The house was nice, but four grown men living together was still tough sometimes. They already saw each other every day at the field and now they would spend their off hours together too. Zach had never shared a room before he became a professional baseball player. In some ways it felt like taking a step backwards.

Still, it couldn't be worse than his first season in rookie ball. He lived with six other guys in the converted basement of a host family. For the most part the guys were very respectful but as the season wore on a few got a little rowdy and the team's manager had to talk to them to bring them back in line. Zach was really a pretty private person and rooming with strangers was a necessary evil. Manny was the exception to the rule, Zach really like him and he had become a trusted friend.

Now that he had climbed the ladder a bit from rookie ball he had taken on roommates for the past few years. Some had been good, like Manny, but others he would not miss. Time would only tell how things would go with Doug and Joe, but he had a feeling they would not be around long anyway. Both could make the big leagues at some point this year or at least move up a level to triple A Charlotte. He returned to the living room just in time to see Doug swing and miss for the final out of the game.

"And that's the ballgame!" said Joe. "Would you like to go for four?"

"Have you guys already played three games?" asked Manny.

"Three games plus two home run derbies and a skills competition," replied Joe. "And it has been a clean sweep, so it's Doug's turn to clean up the kitchen."

"Don't rub it in," said Doug, "Did you see how bad the kitchen is? I'll be lucky to clean that up in a couple of hours. You're a good cook, but a messy one."

"I already cleaned up," said Zach. "It wasn't that bad."

"Really? When did you do that?" asked Joe.

"While you guys were playing. It's no big deal," Zach said with a shrug.

"Look, we agreed when we all moved in together that we would take care of our own messes. You don't have to be a maid," Doug said as he gave Zach an unhappy look.

"It wasn't a problem," Zach replied. "I'm a bit of a clean freak, so it's hard for me to see stuff lying around."

"That's true," Manny chimed in. "Have you seen this guy's locker? I've never seen anybody so organized."

"Whatever. We're all big boys here and can clean up after ourselves. Just because Joe and I covered the rent for the year we don't expect special privileges. Understood?" Doug said as he stared down Zach and Manny.

"I'm good," Manny said.

"Me too," Zach added. "But just for the record, that's not why I did it. Manny stuck me with Taco Bell again, and I took the opportunity to pull together some leftovers for myself. Doug's right; you are a good cook Joe."

"What do you mean 'Manny stuck me with Taco Bell?' You love Taco Bell," Manny said as he looked at Zach in mock horror.

"I do. Just not every day," Zach replied. "A home cooked meal would be nice from time to time."

"A couple of weeks with some new people in your life, and I don't even know who you are anymore," Manny said as he waved his hands in the air and pretended to look upset.

"Come on. You have to admit, we do eat there every couple of days," said Zach with a look of exasperation.

"But I thought you liked it. You've never said anything before."

"I didn't want to hurt your feelings."

"Look what we've done." Doug said to Joe. "We've broken up the happy couple already."

"Sad, when you think about it," Joe replied. "It must have been there all along, and they just didn't know it."

"They say that the way to a man's heart is through his stomach. I guess Zach's road is paved with vegetables and Manny's is a Taco Bell drive thru," said Doug. With that he and Joe started to laugh.

That was enough to stop Zach and Manny in their tracks, and they joined in with Doug and Joe. Soon, all four were giggling like a bunch of schoolgirls at a slumber party. Zach had to admit it, he and Manny did sound like an old married couple. It's funny, you got to know someone really well when you lived with them. He probably knew Manny as well as his wife did. He spent as much time with him as she did, at least during the baseball season. His first impressions of Doug and Joe were that they were really nice guys, and at least for now that seemed to ring true.

After a few minutes they all caught their breath and the conversation turned to the evening's game. It was interesting to hear their different perspectives. Manny and Doug saw things from the pitcher's perspective and talked about pitch selection and location. Zach and Joe talked about what the batter was thinking and how they addressed various situations in the field.

Even though Manny had not caught Doug's first game, they seemed to have a pretty good understanding of how they would have attacked the opposing hitters. That made sense since the pitchers and catchers met before each series to go over scouting reports on the other teams. Zach got the feeling that Doug didn't really mesh with the Barons' other catcher, Harold Bushing. He was known more for his bat than his ability to call a game. His suspicion was validated a few minutes later by Doug.

"You know, Manny, I really need to talk to Tom about letting you catch for me. We are right on the same page with these hitters," Doug said.

"I'm just following the scouting report," Manny replied. "You did all right your first game, or is giving up one run too much?"

"No thanks to, Harold. At least you read the scouting report. I had to shake him off all night," Doug said. "I need someone who puts some effort into their pitch calling and defense."

"Defense is not Harold's strength," Joe interjected. "His ticket is his bat."

"That may be true," Doug responded. "But my ticket is my arm, and I can't have somebody who has a different agenda catching for me."

"It's not just about you," Joe replied. "We all want to make it to the big leagues."

"I get that, but we are a team first, and if the pitcher and catcher aren't on the same page we are all going to look bad," Doug tried to explain.

"Really? Sounds like you are just thinking about yourself."

Zach could see that this was getting out of hand so he decided to step in. "Look, we all want to do well. I have to agree with Doug. We have to work together. If I have to give myself up for the team to win, I'll do it. That's what the White Sox have us down here for. Tom always says, 'Play for the name on the front of your jersey, not the name on the back.'"

"Zach's right," Manny said. "I'll do whatever it takes to make it. Even if that means that I give myself up in the process. Good things come to those that think of others, my Tia used to say."

"Believe me, I get it," said Joe. "I know what I need to do, and I'm sure Harold does too. At the end of the day we all have the same goal. We just get there different ways."

"I hear you," Doug replied, "I don't want to come across like I'm only thinking about me."

"It's okay to think about yourself. Nobody else is going to. You need to remember that," Joe said.

"You don't really think that do you?" asked Zach.

"Sure I do," Joe replied with a laugh. "You think Tom or any of the coaches really care about us? They want out of Birmingham as bad as we do."

"I'm sure they do," said Doug, "but the better we do the better they look."

"You keep thinking that way, and we'll see who is still around here at the end of the year."

"Well, I hope we are all somewhere else by the end of the season, maybe Chicago if we're lucky," said Doug.

"Amen to that!" said Manny. "And when we make it, the chalupas are on me!"

It was a bad joke, but that broke the tension in the room, and they all shared a laugh. Leave it to Manny to try to bring everyone together again. He definitely had a future in this game, if not as a player as a manager. After about a half an hour of talk about the next day's game, one by one they headed off to bed. It was almost 2:00 a.m., late for a regular guy's workday to end, but par for the course for a professional baseball player.

CHAPTER 4

It had been another rough night. Ever since he was a kid Zach had trouble sleeping at night. He would lie in bed for hours reliving everything that had occurred during the day. For some reason he just couldn't stop his mind from going over ever possible scenario that could happen as a result of a decision he made during the day. Now that he was a professional baseball player the odd hours didn't help. The games would usually end after 10:00 p.m., and by the time he finished his post game rituals and made it home it was usually after 2:00 a.m.

You would think that would actually help since he should be tired but since he didn't have to go anywhere in the morning he just tossed and turned. It didn't really matter what time he got up since he didn't have to be at the field until the late afternoon. But a little extra rest would be nice. He wished he could be like Manny, who was out the minute his head hit the pillow.

He had read a book once about Roberto Clemente, a Hall of Fame player for the Pittsburgh Pirates back in the late 1960s. He had terrible insomnia and struggled to get even a few hours of sleep each night. It was so bad that he tried to make his room as dark as possible as even the slightest amount of light stopped him from sleeping.

Zach had tried everything from sleep masks to ear plugs and noise machines and even yoga to try and relax his mind. Nothing worked, and he basically got by on just a few hours of sleep a night. Well, if it was good enough for Clemente, it would have to be good enough for him.

Last night had been like every other night after a bad game. He went through each at-bat and second guessed every pitch he had seen. If it was a called strike he should have swung. If it was a swinging strike, he should have let it go. If he made an out, he should have done something else with the pitch. Even if he got a hit he should have hit it harder or farther. And if he made an error in the field, well there was really no point in going to bed.

In his mind every bad game would end up with a trip to the manager's office for a discussion about his future with the team. Zach always felt that a bad game would make the big league club reconsider his role in the organization. He was a high round draft pick, and they didn't have a huge sum of money invested in him like they did with Joe or Doug. They could easily cut their losses and let him go. Then he would have to try and hook on with another club and there were no guarantees that would happen.

Of course it never happened the way he imagined. He didn't get called in to Tom's office after every bad game but that was going to change if he didn't start hitting. He was starting to get a bad feeling. Tom was quick to bring up a mistake and he hadn't said anything about him missing the bunt sign. He usually was quick to bring something like that up. They had ended up winning the game but that wasn't the point, his failure to execute could have cost them the game. He was also still hitless and that was beginning to wear on him. He thought about the changes he made during the winter, they had helped for a while and he hadn't planned to continue during the season but he might not have a choice.

Oh well, maybe it was time to stop thinking and just get out of bed and start the day. Maybe a quick run and a shower would help snap him out of this funk. He looked across the room and saw that Manny's bed was empty. Unlike Zach, he was an early riser and usually long gone by the time Zach rolled out of bed. He looked at the clock and saw that it was almost 11:00 a.m. It was time to get going and see what the day had to offer.

When he walked into the living room, it was a repeat from when he got home the previous night. Joe and Doug were in the middle of a baseball game on the Xbox. From the sound of Doug's complaining, it appeared that he was losing again. "Good morning," Zach said as he walked into the room.

"More like good afternoon," said Joe as he sent another of Doug's pitches over the wall for a three-run homer.

"You are quite the sleeper aren't you?" asked Doug.

"Well, I really don't sleep that much. I mostly toss and turn for a while before I finally fall asleep and end up with only a few hours of rest. You guys probably got more sleep than me last night," Zach said as he sat down on the couch. "Have you guys had breakfast yet?"

"Breakfast is long gone. We're thinking about lunch now," said Manny as he emerged from the kitchen. "You missed out this morning, Joe makes a mean omelet."

"It was nothing," Joe said as he threw another pitch by Doug. "There sure is a lot of nothing going on with your game right now," said Joe with a laugh. "I can't believe you are getting shut out."

"I make my impact in real life, not video games," replied Doug.

"What time are you guys heading over to the field today?" asked Zach.

"I was going to try to catch an early movie before heading over," said Manny, "so I wasn't planning on going until about 4:00 p.m."

"Aren't you starting today?" asked Zach. "I would think you would try to get there a little sooner."

"What can I say? Movies relax me, and I've been waiting for this new Katherine Heigel movie to come out for weeks. Nothing like a chick flick to take your mind off your troubles. Want to come?" Manny asked Zach.

"You really have turned into an American haven't you?" said Zach. "Taco Bell and Katherine Heigel movies. What would your wife think?"

"She loves it. I'm the anti macho man she sees every day at home. Women love it when you show your sensitive side. You should try it sometime," Manny said.

"I think we have to find a girl first," said Joe. "Remember, we're just a bunch of single guys."

"No time for that right now," said Zach, "I'm focused on one thing and that's making it to the big leagues. No time for distractions."

"I think you need a few distractions," said Manny. "You can only think of the game so much or it will drive you crazy. That's why you can't sleep at night. I've heard you tossing and turning for two years now."

"I can't imagine you ever hear anything. You fall asleep the minute your head hits the pillow, and you snore all night long," replied Zach.

"Here we go again," Joe said to Doug. "Arguing like an old married couple. Manny's right, Zach. You can't think about things so much. Just go with the flow. It will all work out."

"They can't help fighting," Doug said. "After two years together you start to think alike. Sometimes you even start to look alike, but I don't see that happening any time soon unless Zach adds on about fifty pounds."

"He should be so lucky," Manny replied as he flexed his arms. "Look at these guns."

"More like pop guns if you ask me," said Zach "or have you forgotten that I've out homered you the last two years."

"Home runs are only a part of the game, I bring much more to the table," replied Manny.

"Buffet table maybe," teased Zach. "All that junk food has to go somewhere, and I don't think it's your arms."

"I've got plenty of pop. I just haven't shown it yet," said Manny.

"Soda pop, maybe," said Doug.

"I've never seen someone from outside the U.S. take to the lifestyle so fast," added Joe.

"You don't know the half of it," said Zach. "He could beat all of us in a game of Trivial Pursuit easily. He has spent years gathering piles of useless knowledge about popular American culture."

"You guys just can't let someone enjoy his life, can you. You don't know what it's like growing up with nothing. Before I came to the states, my life was rice, beans and tortillas. I had only seen a TV a couple of times before I joined the academy." Manny tried to hide it, but he was starting to get upset.

"Don't get all serious now. We're just teasing you, Manny," Zach said, trying to dial things back a little. Manny was a very easy going guy, but everyone had their limit.

"Zach's right, Manny, you've overcome a lot to get here and we all respect that," said Doug. "Right, Joe?"

"I don't know," said Joe. "Signed by the Dodgers at sixteen and getting to play ball every day. Sounds like a pretty good time to me."

Doug and Zach shot Joe a nasty look, but Manny just smiled. "Actually, it was pretty nice. I only had to share a room with one person for a change. Back home, there were four of us to a room. Baseball has been very good to my family."

"You mean besibal bean bery bery good to me,'" said Joe in a very heavy Spanish accent.

"Dude, that's not right," said Doug, punching Joe in the arm.

"It's all right Doug," said Manny laughing. "He's quoting Chico Escuela from an old Saturday Night Live skit. Sammy Sosa used to say the same thing back in ninety-eight during the home run chase with Mark McGwire."

"See, I know my pop culture too," said Joe with a smile.

"You guys have too much time on your hands," said Zach.

"We're baseball players, what else do we have to do in our hours of down time," said Joe.

"Spoken by the guy that lives for video games," replied Zach.

"Say what you want, but there's money in gaming. Curt Schilling started his own company after he retired. Have you heard of 'Reckoning'? It's a game his company, 38 Studios put out. Made millions," said Joe.

"My millions are going to come another way," Zach said. "I plan on a long career followed by a bunch of nothing."

"You can't just do nothing," said Manny. "Look at my brothers. They have made some money, but they are also giving back by building our family's academy back home. It's not about just you. It's helping others too."

"I'm all for that, I guess," Zach said, "but I need to get there first, and I'm going to do whatever it takes."

"Just remember," Doug said, rejoining the conversation. "There are no shortcuts. It's all about hard work and putting in the time. I've seen guys try the easy way, and it never turns out well."

"That's easy for guys like you, and Joe to say. Big time players with big time contracts at an early age," Zach said with some resentment in his voice. "Manny and I have to work for everything we get."

"And we didn't?" Joe said. "I for one busted my butt for years to get where I am. I may not have come from poor family in a third world country, but I've sacrificed a lot to get where I am today."

"We all have," said Manny.

"That's not what I meant. It's just a matter of time until you make it. Everyone knows that. You won't even finish the year out here. I don't know if I'll make it to the end of the season on the team." Zach really didn't mean to offend Joe or Doug. They had been nothing but nice to him.

"It sure sounded like it," said Joe, his voice rising. "There are no guarantees for anyone. I could blow out my knee tomorrow. You never know what is going to happen."

"But at least you'll have something to show for your time. Look at Doug. He's already pitched in Wrigley Field." Zach was now letting his jealousy start to show.

"I earned that start," Doug said.

"Yeah, it's not our fault it's your third year in double A," said Joe.

"Hey, let's all take a step back for a minute," said Manny. "We are going to be together for a while, so we need to get along. We all want the same things. There's no reason we can't all get there. Maybe even together."

"Exactly," added Doug. "We're not competing against each other. There is room for all of us."

Zach and Joe looked at each other for what seemed like a long couple of minutes, and the room turned very chilly. "I didn't mean anything by it. I'm just getting frustrated because I'm not hitting," Zach said.

"We always fought each other when I was growing up. Sometimes you say things you don't really mean, but you've got to just let it go," said Manny, trying to keep the peace.

"Tell you what. Let's all go our separate ways for a while and meet up at the field for the game later," Doug said. "I'm leaving at about 4:00 p.m. if anyone wants a ride."

"Fine," said Joe, turning his attention back to the TV.

"I still have time to make my movie, so I'll see you guys there," said Manny as he grabbed his bag and walked out the door.

"I'm going to head over a little earlier for some extra BP, but thanks anyway," Zach said as he headed off to the kitchen to grab a bite to eat.

Wow, that sure got out hand pretty quick, Zach thought to himself as he made himself an early lunch. He usually had the same thing for lunch every day. A turkey sandwich, a bag of chips, a couple pieces of fruit and a Dr. Pepper. It wasn't fancy, but it did the job and he didn't have to put much thought into it. He preferred to spend his time thinking about the game.

He grabbed his iPad and sat down at the kitchen table to eat. He loved having a routine. It made him feel safe and comfortable, especially when things got tense. His roommates over the years had teased him about his bland diet and his boring pregame rituals, but they had served him well. There was something to be said about routines, just look at Wade Boggs. He was famous for only eating chicken before games and he ended up in the Hall of Fame with over 3,000 hits. If chicken worked for Boggs, maybe turkey would do the same for Zach.

Zach quickly scanned a few websites as he ate. It was always good to know what was going on in your profession, and Zach tried to keep up with all the latest happenings in the major and minor leagues.

He paid close attention to the White Sox and all of their affiliates of course, but he also tried to keep up with all of the second basemen in MLB as well. If someone in the big leagues went down it caused a ripple effect all the way down the line. His future was tied to the success or failure of many guys he would never meet. He knew he that he shouldn't focus on other people so much, but he couldn't stop himself.

Nothing too exciting yet. The Sox were off to an okay start with an eleven and seven record in second place behind the Tigers. Zach always felt a little conflicted looking at the standings. On one hand he wanted the Sox to do well, but on the other if they struggled maybe they would feel the need to make some changes and he could get an opportunity to play. Everyone was looking to catch lightning in a bottle. There were many players who made the jump from double A to the majors and made an impact. Sometimes all you needed was a chance. Hopefully, his would come this year.

Next he reviewed his at-bats from the last three games. There was nothing to write home about since he didn't have a hit yet, but he could still learn by watching himself. He found it amazing that other players didn't take advantage of technology like he did. As far as he could tell, Joe never watched video of his at-bats. When Zach asked him about it, he said he preferred to "feel the ball" whatever that meant. Manny was not a big believer in video when they first met but Zach had quickly made a convert out of him and their nightly post game sessions were a now a must for both of them. You could learn a lot about yourself by watching video, and Zach noticed something he hadn't seen last night.

He pulled up some video from last season to check, and sure enough, there it was. He was holding his hands a little bit lower this year. They looked like they were about an inch lower. That must be it. He would hit the cages early today for some extra BP and work on that.

Boy, he loved his iPad. It was such a great tool; he didn't understand why everyone didn't use one. Most guys on the team had them of course, but most used them just for games or to watch movies. They didn't realize the power they had right there in the palm of their hands.

He decided to go for a quick run before heading over to the field. As he walked through the living room he saw that Joe was still playing the Xbox. Looked like Halo now. He was talking on his headset to someone, and he looked like he was working up a sweat. He could see Doug sitting out on the patio with his sketch pad working on a new drawing. He was actually pretty talented. Mostly skulls and snakes, not Zach's idea of art, but he was sure that they would sell for a good price in some Goth store or tattoo parlor.

Zach always found it interesting to see what other guys did in their spare time. He had seen many different ways to kill time over the years. Some players were into gaming. iPods and other hand held game systems were pretty common in the clubhouses. Many players also brought along their Xbox on the road too. He was sure Joe would fall into that category. Others were into music or art like Doug. A few were writers or trying to learn a new language. Spanish was a popular choice since there were many Latin players in the big leagues, and it would help if he went to play in a winter league during the off season.

Zach preferred to work on his baseball IQ. He read everything he could get his hands on about baseball from the history of the game to biographies of players and how to manuals. He lived and breathed baseball twenty-four hours a day, seven days a week. It was all he had ever wanted to do, and there was no plan B. He had to make it, or else he didn't know what he would do.

He changed into a pair of shorts and shirt, put on his running shoes, and did a few quick stretches. He wouldn't push himself too hard today, just enough to get his blood flowing. He didn't feel like sitting around the house since that exchange with Joe had left him feeling a little upset. It took a while to get used to a new roommate, and Joe definitely was going to take some getting used to. He seemed like he had a bit of a chip on his shoulder.

The day had gotten off to a rough start, and he really didn't need any extra stress in his life. He thought about saying something to Joe before he left but decided not to try and press the issue. Maybe he just needed some space. He seemed friendly enough most of the time. Maybe he just woke up on the wrong side of the bed. He walked out the door without saying anything to either Joe or Doug and started his run.

CHAPTER 5

Time passed quickly and by the time Zach finished his run it was time to head over to the stadium. It was a short drive, and as usual Zach was the first player to arrive in the clubhouse. The game didn't start until 7:00 p.m., and most of the players rolled in around 4:00 or so. Batting and fielding practice lasted from 4:30 to 5:30, and afterwards the players returned to the clubhouse for a quick pregame meal. Zach usually got in around 2:00 or 2:30 and spent the extra time going through his pregame ritual.

Part of the reason he came in early was just to enjoy a little peace and quiet. Over the years he had found that he could only take so much of his roommates until they really got on his nerves. Even Manny could overstay his welcome sometimes, and Zach knew that most players wouldn't come in to the ballpark any earlier than they had to.

The Wi-Fi in the clubhouse always seemed to be much faster than at home, so he took advantage of the time to check his e-mails and Facebook page. He tried to keep up with other guys he had played with over the years, and technology sure made that easy these days. Some had moved on to other teams in the White Sox organization, others had been traded, and a few even released, but all generally had encouraging words to share. It was a tough business, but it was pretty easy to create a support network if you put a little effort into it.

He had twelve e-mails to go through today from a variety of people. The first one that caught his attention was from Joey

Daniels, a teammate on the Barons from last year. Joey was a pretty good guy and a solid middle reliever. He had been promoted to Charlotte this past year, and it looked like he might have a shot at a mid season call up. He was a left-handed pitcher with ninety-five mph heat, and the White Sox didn't have many other options on their roster so he was in a good spot. There were many times over the past few years Zach had cursed the genes that made him right handed. There was always room on a big league team's roster for a left-handed reliever that could neutralize the other team's big left handed bats.

Unfortunately for Joey it sounded like he had a rough first outing giving up three runs and five hits in less than an inning of work. It was easy to get down after one bad outing, especially as a pitcher since they didn't play every day. Joey was already worried that his ERA was going to be inflated for a while and that would prevent the Sox from considering him for a role on the team later in the season.

Zach responded with a story of his three hitless games and tried to pump Joey back up by reminding him that one bad outing didn't doom the entire season. The big league teams looked much deeper at your performance than just a couple of games he reminded Joey. Zach fully understood the irony of his e-mail as he typed; he should be telling himself the exact same thing. He tended to be his own worst critic and was harder on himself than any coach.

He ran through the rest of his e-mails and they fell into a few different categories. Some complained about poor starts or lack of playing time, a few wanted to share success stories, others just wanted to check in to say hi, and one offered words of encouragement over his poor start. The last e-mail was from his mother.

Zach forwarded on copies of his at-bats after each game to his mother for her to review so she could help analyze his swing and approach at the plate. Other than Zach himself, she probably had the best understanding of how bad he wanted to succeed. She had sacrificed a lot to help him get where he was today, and their e-mail conversations helped to keep him focused. He only wished she had the opportunity to watch him play more in person, but for now video and e-mail would have to do.

Sure enough, she had something specific to share today. Just like he had noticed earlier that day, she said he was dropping his hands. That confirmed for Zach that had to be it. It seemed like such a small thing and it shouldn't make a difference, but baseball was funny. It didn't take much to throw you off your game. He sent her back a note that he had seen the same thing and promised to call her before they started out on their first road trip of the season in a few days. Now it was time to take this new information and work on a solution.

Zach picked up his iPad and his bat and walked over to the coaches' office to check in with Jimmy. He could always count on Jimmy to help work out the kinks in his swing. Jimmy was the one who had hooked him up with his video contact and often sat with Manny and him after games to review their at-bats. He wasn't in the coaches' office, so Zach headed over to the video room to see if he was there.

Jimmy was reviewing that night's starting pitcher for the visiting Huntsville Stars. He was an expert at breaking down a pitcher's strengths and weaknesses, so much so he probably would have made a very good pitching coach. Prior to each new series he provided the team with a few key nuggets of information on the opposing pitchers. Not everyone on the team followed his advice, but those that did generally did better than the others.

"Hard at work as usual," Zach said as he pulled up a chair next to Jimmy.

"I could say the same thing to you. You're always one of the first ones here you know," Jimmy replied.

"One of the first ones?" Zach said with a smile. "Don't you mean the first one here?"

"I would, but you're forgetting about me. Nobody beats me to the ballpark, you should know that by now.I bet you didn't sleep at all last night did you?"

"I'm sure that I dozed off for a few hours at some point," Zach said as he tried unsuccessfully to hold back a yawn. "But I did find something interesting at breakfast that was confirmed in an e-mail from my mom."

"Well if your mom confirmed it, then it must be true. That woman sure has got an eye for details. She would have been a great hitting coach," Jimmy said as he turned away from the TV and pushed his notes to the side of the desk. "Show me what you got."

"She is a great hitting coach. Best I ever had. No offense Jimmy," said Zach as he opened his iPad and synced it up to the TV with a Bluetooth connection. He then pulled up one of his at-bats from the previous night. "Check out my hands last night. See where they are?"

"Let me guess. You're dropping them again," Jimmy said before Zach could pull up the video from last year.

"How did you know?" Zach asked.

"You fall into the same bad habit a couple of times a year. Have you ever heard of the 'butterfly effect'?" Jimmy replied.

"No. What does that have to do with my swing?"

"It has to do with chaos theory," Jimmy started to say, but Zach interrupted him.

"Wait a minute. Is that from Jurassic Park? I remember that scene in the movie where the guy put a drop of water on the girl's hand and had her try to predict which way it would go. Does this have something to do with dinosaurs?" Zach asked trying to hold back a laugh.

"No. It has to do with the formation of hurricanes," Jimmy replied.

"Are you serious? What does that have to do with my swing?" Zach asked.

"If you ask someone in Florida if there is a chance of a hurricane, they will tell you it depends if a butterfly flaps its wings off the coast of Africa," Jimmy responded.

"I don't get it," Zach said flatly.

"The point is that a small change, like dropping your hands, can make a large difference in something big like your swing. Just like a butterfly flapping its wings thousands of miles away from the coast of Florida can cause a hurricane weeks later." With that Jimmy got up and headed toward the door.

"Hang on a minute. Where are you going?" Zach called out after him.

"To the batting cages to work on your swing. Are you coming?" Jimmy called out over his shoulder without looking back.

They made their way to the batting cages underneath the stadium. It was a familiar walk for Zach, and Jimmy had said they were considering naming one of the cages after him when he left since he had spent so much time there the last two years. Zach couldn't argue with him; he had to admit, he loved to hit. Working at the batting cages in the offseason gave him the opportunity to hit all the time and it had become a habit. Most of the other guys stuck with live BP before the games, but Zach loved the cages.

He started with exactly twenty-five swings on the batting tee and then twenty-five more in soft toss from Jimmy. He concentrated on his hands, checking every time to make sure that they were positioned correctly. Every five swings or so, Jimmy would confirm for him that they were right. Anyone looking at him probably couldn't tell the difference but Zach could feel it. Exactly twenty-five swings on the machine later and Zach knew that he had found the problem. Tonight was going to be a good night.

"Feel better now?" Jimmy asked as they walked back to the clubhouse.

"Absolutely," Zach replied. "I think we found it. I'm going to have a good game tonight."

"Remember, it takes time for an adjustment to stick. Don't think about results tonight. Think about your form and take good swings." Jimmy knew that Zach wanted immediate results and sometimes that didn't happen.

"I know," said Zach, "but you'll see, hitless for the year ends tonight."

"Let's see if you can keep the positive attitude when I tell you this," Jimmy said as they got back to the video room.

Now what, Zach thought to himself, he didn't need anything else on his mind tonight. "What's up?" he asked.

"Tom wants to see you in his office before infield practice," Jimmy said with a smile.

"Are you serious?" Zach sighed. "What did I do?"

"Don't panic. You know our job is to make you better and get you to the Sox." Jimmy had had this conversation with Zach before.

"You should have told me before," Zach said.

"Give me a little credit. I know you too well. If I told you before you never would have found the problem with your swing," Jimmy replied. "Now get out of here. I've got more work to do before the game."

"You're right," Zach said.

"I know I'm right," Jimmy said with a smile.

"Thanks, Jimmy. For everything," Zach said as he walked out the door.

Zach made his way back to his locker and saw that Manny had already started to change into his uniform. "How was the movie?" he asked.

"I have to be honest, I love Maria, but that Katherine Heigel just does it for me." Manny sat back in his chair and sighed. "How can someone be so talented and so good looking? I mean, other than me of course."

"You have got to me kidding me," Zach said "I don't think you are in the same class."

"Speak for yourself. Like LMAFO says, 'I'm sexy and I know it,'" and with that Manny got out of his chair and started to dance.

"Now I've seen everything," Zach laughed and felt the stress he was feeling about taking to Tom start to fade away a little bit. "How can you be so loose before your first start of the season?"

"What is there to be nervous about?" Manny asked. "It's not like I've never played a game before. We have the greatest job in the world, you just need to go with the flow. Now dance with me." Manny pulled Zach to his feet and tried to get him to dance.

"Not happening," Zach said as he pulled away. "I don't even like to dance when there's music, much less with a half dressed man."

"There's nothing like it. Helps you to let go of all that tension you have rolling around in your body." Manny made a few more moves and then sat down in front of his locker. "You really need something to keep your mind off your slow start."

"Thanks for bringing that up again. No pressure now." Zach quickly felt the little bit of tension he lost while Manny danced come back.

"I thought you had that fixed? Didn't you say you found something in your swing today?" Manny asked.

"As a matter of fact I did," Zach replied. "Jimmy and I have already been in the cage and worked it out."

"So what's the problem then?" Manny asked as he pulled on his warm-up jersey.

"Tom wants to see me," Zach said with a sigh. "That can't be good."

"He is our boss you know. He has the right to talk to us. I would be more worried if he didn't want to talk to you." Manny said, trying to reassure Zach.

"Do you really think he likes me?" Zach asked. "I'm not so sure."

"I think you are one of his favorite players. He always uses you as an example of someone that puts the team first. You know he's big on that," Manny said.

"I guess. I'm always worried he's going to tell me that I'm released." That conversation had already occurred in Zach's mind many times.

"Try to think of the opposite. Maybe he wants to tell you that you have been called up. Try to be positive."

"Well, I guess I'll go and get this over with. Wish me luck," Zach said as he got up to leave.

"I'll see you out on the field. I've got to go over the scouting report one more time. You'll be fine. Trust me." Manny flashed two thumbs up as Zach walked away.

Zach was always nervous when he went to see Tom. It was his job to help develop players and every player that he sent on to the White Sox made him look better in the eyes of the organization. He didn't have to do this job; he made tons of money during his career. He must really love the game to start all over again. It must be frustrating to try and deal with all the various personalities on the team, especially when they were all trying to get playing time.

Tom's office was at the end of a long hallway just outside the coaches' locker room. The door was open just a bit, and Zach could hear two voices on the other side. There were two chairs in the narrow hallway and as he took a seat he couldn't help but wonder who was in with Tom and what they were talking about. It reminded him of the times he had been called to the principal's office back in high school.

Whoever was in there with Tom was sure getting an earful. Tom had been going non-stop for about five minutes now and the other person had not spoken yet. He wondered who it could be and what they had done to set Tom off. Oh well, the good news was maybe he would burn himself out before he got to Zach.

Finally the other person spoke, and Zach recognized is voice. It was Barry Thomas, one of their outfielders who had been in triple A last year. He couldn't tell what Barry said, but Tom's words were loud and clear.

"I expect every player on this team to think of the team before themselves. You play for the name on the front of your jersey, not the one on your back. It's a simple idea. You should be able to understand it," Tom said with a great deal of passion in his voice.

"I'm not doing either name any good if I never get the chance to play," Barry replied, his voice starting to rise.

"I have twenty-five guys in this team to worry about. Everyone will get their at-bats," Tom answered and Zach could tell that Tom was trying to stay cool.

"It doesn't look that way to me. It's obvious that you have favorites." Barry was not letting up.

"Frankly you have not been around long enough to come to that conclusion," Tom said.

"I've seen it enough in the past to recognize it pretty quickly," Barry replied, and Zach knew that comment would not go over well.

"Well, it would appear we had two options here," Tom said matter of factly. "You can go back to the clubhouse and get ready for the game, or you can go home."

"I'm not going to make it that easy on you," Barry said disgustedly, "I'll stick around for a while."

"We would be happy to have you," Tom said, his voice dripping with sarcasm. "Just remember, leave the attitude at home. If you are going to be upset, do it on your own time."

Zach didn't catch what Barry said, but he could tell by the way he stormed out of the office he was not happy. Now it was his turn, and Tom was all worked up. That wasn't good. Maybe he could give him a few minutes to cool down before he went in.

No such luck, because a minute later Tom poked his head out the door and said, "What are you waiting for? Grab a seat."

There wasn't much to look at in Tom's office. It had a desk and two chairs and not much else. The walls were pretty much bare other than the team's schedule on one wall and a large whiteboard behind Tom's desk. Zach had never been in a major league clubhouse before but he had to imagine that their managers' offices had to be nicer than this. It was obvious that Tom didn't spend much time in there and hadn't put much effort into adding personal touches. In fact, the only time he really used it was when he wanted to have private conversations with his players.

"So Zach," Tom began. "Jimmy tells me you think you found something in your swing."

"That's right," Zach replied as he sat down in a gray folding chair across from Tom's desk. "I've been dropping my hands again."

"You know, I don't think there is anything wrong with your swing. Sometimes you just have a couple of bad games at the plate. It is way too early in the season to panic," Tom said.

"I know. But I was looking at some old video and noticed it," Zach said. "Jimmy and I worked on it in the cage earlier, and I feel much better now."

"Look, Zach, I'm a big believer in video. It has really changed the game for the better, but part of baseball is just feel. It really is just see the ball and hit the ball. Don't overanalyze things too much or you'll drive yourself crazy," Tom said as he picked up a lineup card from his desk.

"I know. We've had this conversation before," Zach said. "But looking at video helps me."

"I understand that," Tom replied. "And I know a few games without a hit at the start of a season are harder than later in the season. Starting the season hitless is rough."

"I never look at the scoreboard when I go up to the plate," Zach lied. In fact he always looked at the scoreboard.

"Zach, I've had you on my team for two years. I know you better than that," Tom laughed. "I know you look and I know how you can't sleep after a bad game. That's why I called you in here today. I'm making a change in the lineup, and I don't want you to overreact."

That got Zach's attention. Here it comes. He was going to the bench. "Okay," he said, trying to hide the panic he felt building inside.

"I'm dropping you from the two spot to the seven spot. I need more production early in the lineup, and you just aren't getting the job done right now."

"You know I'm a slow starter, but I always come around," Zach said. This was just the beginning. First they dropped him in the lineup. Before he knew it he would be on the bench.

"I know that's not what you want to hear, but I think it's the best thing to do right now. We need to think of the team."

"Okay. I'll do whatever you want me to do," Zach said. If he had learned anything in the last two years and from the conversation he had just overhead, it was not to disagree with Tom.

"Look, Zach. You just need to be patient and let the game come to you. Don't push so much," Tom said.

"I'll try. I just want it so bad," Zach said with a sigh. "This is all I ever wanted to do with my life."

"I know. It's almost time to hit the field. I don't want you to make more of this than it is, so let's cut it off now so you can get out there," Tom said.

Tom stood up, and Zach took the cue and pushed his chair back and got up. "It's going to be a good game tonight. I can feel it."

"I'll see you out on the field." Tom sat down and turned his attention to the pile of papers on his desk.

Zach made his way back to the clubhouse. He was disappointed about being dropped from the two spot, but at least he was still in the lineup. For now anyway. He had been around long enough to know how things worked. Tom would be patient for a while, but he didn't have much time. Either he started to produce, and soon, or his days were limited. The changes in his swing had better work tonight, or else he was going to have to do something drastic and he didn't want to go down that road. The pressure was on tonight, and he hoped he was up for the challenge.

CHAPTER 6

Zach made the short walk back to his locker grabbed his glove and bat and headed out toward the field. This was usually his favorite time of the day, but his conversation with Tom weighed on his mind. The anticipation of the night's game was heavy in the air and he could feel his excitement grow with every step he took toward the field. He was disappointed at his poor start to the season, but he always tried hard to leave the previous night's game behind him and tried to think of every game as a separate entity.

Tom always preached to the team that yesterday's results had no impact on the current day. In one way, Zach agreed with that thought because every game started with no score. But he also believed in momentum, and you always felt better the day after a win than a loss or a day when you had a couple of hits versus a zero for four.

Same thing with hitting, a couple of hits built up his confidence and the ball came in looking the size of a basketball. When he was struggling, the ball looked like a ping pong ball. Every game was different, but they did build on each other, and Zach was determined to reverse his negative streak at the plate tonight.

His talk with Tom had put him a little behind schedule, and he had already missed his first turn in the batting cage. He walked up behind Joe and took his place in line. "How's it going?" he asked as he stretched.

"Cleared two more levels of Halo this morning," Joe said with a big smile.

"I was thinking more about the game tonight," Zach said, wondering how Joe could be so cool and not worry about the game.

"Oh. Shouldn't be a problem tonight," Joe said with another big smile.

"Really, why is that?" Zach asked.

"Didn't you see who was pitching for them tonight?" Joe answered. "Bobby Jensen. I've owned that guy since high school."

"What's he got?" If Joe had seen this pitcher before maybe he tipped his pitches or had an established pattern of when he threw a certain pitch. At this point, every little piece of information would help.

Joe stepped in the cage to take his swings. After every swing he called out something to keep an eye on. "Two seam, four seam." Whack. Line drive to center. "Sad breaking ball." Whack. Hit the left field wall. "Loves to start you with a fastball away." Whack. Another ball off the wall. "Never throws a breaking ball behind in the count." Whack. Line drive to right. "Can't hold runners on." Whack. Line drive to center. "Falls apart when he gives up a couple of runs." Whack. Deep home run to left and then out of the cage.

"Very impressive," Zach said as he stepped into the cage for his swings.

"I know," Joe replied. "It's going to be a very good night."

"Let's hope so," Zach said he stepped into the box. He made sure his hands were back in the new, really old, spot and sent the next ten pitches flying around the park. Not quite as impressive a showing as Joe, but still pretty good. He felt much better at the plate now and couldn't wait for the game to start.

"Not too bad," Joe said as Zach exited the cage. "I see a little more pop in your bat today. I guess your little talk with Tom helped."

"How did you know I talked to Tom today?" Zach asked.

"It's a small clubhouse. There are no secrets," Joe replied with a shrug. "Actually Manny told me. I know you're never late for warm-ups, so I knew something was up."

"He just wanted to give me a heads-up he was dropping me down in the lineup for a few games. No big deal," Zach replied, trying not to show his disappointment.

"That's never a good sign, but I'm telling you we are going to knock this guy around tonight. Trust me."

"I hope you're right," Zach said half-heartedly.

"I know I am," Joe replied and stepped in to take a few more swings.

After a couple more turns in the cage, Zach's group moved out to the field to take grounders and shag balls for the other players. This really was the only time that they had to practice during the season. It was funny; Zach had spent the majority of his time at practice during high school. Actual games took up a small amount of the time he spent playing ball. Now it was the opposite, you were expected to know what to do and didn't spend as much time practicing.

Maybe they got forty-five minutes to an hour on the field and even then they didn't have full situational drills like when he was a kid. Maybe they all had been doing it for so long it had become second nature, and so they only required a little bit of follow up. The coaches did walk around and give suggestions, but most of the game now was mental compared to physical. Maybe that was part of his problem, the mental game, he thought about things way too much.

Well, tonight was going to be different. He only had one thing on his mind, and that was the position of his hands when he got up to the plate. He was confident that was the issue and he could feel it, he would get at least one hit tonight. Hey, if Joe was right and this pitcher was really a stiff, maybe he could get two or three. He finished up his infield practice and moved to the outfield to stretch and shag fly balls.

As he took his place in the outfield he looked around the stadium. It was going to be a pretty good crowd tonight. That was something he noticed about Birmingham, they really supported their team. It had to be hard as a fan to root for them since the players came and went so quickly. In reality, none of the players really wanted to be here, their goal was to make it to Chicago and play for the White Sox. It was kind of an odd situation, like when you liked a girl more than she liked you.

Still, the fans came out on a regular basis and Zach for one always tried to do his best, both for himself and for the fans who were paying good money to see him play. Now that he had been here for two years he had developed a little following. Mostly among some of the older fans, they seemed to appreciate the way he played the game, always putting the team first. An experienced fan noticed the little things like hitting behind the runners and going from first to third on a base hit. He kind of wished his fans trended younger and female, but a fan was a fan and you couldn't be too picky.

He talked with a few of the other players as they patrolled the outfield and tossed balls back to the infield as the rest of the team finished taking their swings. The general consensus was that this pitcher didn't have much going for him and everyone was expecting to tee off today. Personally, that made Zach a little nervous, it was easy to get overconfident. The guy had made it to double A, so he must have some talent. It was more likely that Joe's observations had made the rounds in the clubhouse and now everyone was buying into it.

Still, like he was thinking earlier, baseball was really a mental game, and if thinking the opposing pitcher didn't have the best stuff helped you, then that was an advantage. Zach would study opposing pitchers to better understand what pitches they had and when they usually threw them, Jimmy was partly responsible for that. But knowing your opponent was only half the battle, the rest was really on you and you had to make sure that you were prepared. That's why Zach focused so much on the game and let the personal things go. He had a short window as a player, and he needed to keep the distractions to a minimum, he had the rest of his life for other stuff.

The team finished their warm-ups and left the field to the visiting Huntsville Stars to complete their pregame routines. As Zach jogged off the field he couldn't help but feel a little more excited than usual to get the game started. All the talk on the field about a less than stellar pitcher had gotten into his head and he wished the game would start right now. Too bad he was batting seventh today, he'd have to wait a little longer to get his first at-bat tonight.

He passed the time by studying video of his last few games and then took a look at the daily scouting report provided by Jimmy on the opposing pitcher. It read almost word for word of Joe's description earlier, but without the cockiness. Bobby Jensen looked like a guy in need of a third pitch, a fastball and changeup were only going to take you so far in this game. Zach made a note to himself to lay off the changeups and try and get ahead in the count so he would have to throw a fastball.

"Ready for a big game tonight?" Manny asked as he sat down next to Zach. He had the remains of a sandwich and bag of chips balanced on either leg.

"How can you eat before a game?" Zach replied. He was lucky if he could keep down a piece of fruit or a granola bar.

"Got to keep my strength up. Frank was all over the place in his last start. I'm going to be busy behind the plate tonight," Manny said as he polished off his sandwich.

"Knuckleballs can be like that. I don't envy you back there," Zach said.

"It's okay. It takes a special talent to throw, and catch, a knuckleball. If he can keep it under control he could be valuable to a team, and he'll need a catcher." Manny smiled, knowing that becoming a pitcher's personal catcher was one ticket to the big leagues.

"Very true. But if he can't get it under control, it makes for a long night," Zach said.

"No worries. We're going to score a bunch of runs tonight. Have you heard who's pitching?" Manny asked as he tilted his head back and polished off a bag of Doritos.

"You must have been talking to Joe." It was crazy how fast Joe's assessment had made the rounds.

"I was looking at Jimmy's notes. What did Joe say?" Manny asked.

"Basically the same thing but with some more colorful language. I hope everyone doesn't get too confident," Zach said.

"You can never be too confident. Just go with the flow. It's going to be a good night. Now I got to run. See you out there." Manny grabbed his gear and headed out to the field.

"All right. See you later."

The dugout was starting to fill up, and Zach put his gear away and staked out a spot on the bench. He usually tried to stay within earshot of Tom and the coaches so he could listen in as they talked about the game. This coaching staff had tons of experience and Zach liked to hear them talk through various in-game situations. He took every opportunity to raise his baseball IQ and found that he referred back to things he heard from Tom and Jimmy almost every game.

"Remember, try to get ahead in the count and wait for the fastball," Joe said as he came over and sat down next to Zach.

"Got it. I read Jimmy's scouting report," Zach replied.

"Why? I told you everything you needed to know," Joe said with a surprised look on his face.

"I know, but Jimmy spends a lot of time putting them together so I always make it a point to look," Zach said, feeling like he had insulted Joe.

"You read too many reports and watch too much video if you ask me," Joe said.

"This from the guy who lives for video games," Zach replied with a laugh.

"I admit it. I like to play video games. But I can only take so much of watching video of pitchers or myself. Hitting for me is reaction. See the ball, hit the ball," Joe said.

"Imagine how much better you'd be if you prepared more," Zach said, and it was true, Joe relied only on his natural talent and that would only take him so far.

"Maybe someday. For now, I'm doing just fine," Joe said with a shrug.

"I can't argue with that. You have been on fire so far this year," Zach said with only a hint of jealousy.

"And it will continue tonight my friend."

"I hope so," Zach said just as the stadium announcer introduced a local high school student to sing the national anthem.

A few minutes later and Zach was jogging out to his position at second base. He took a few grounders and tried to keep an eye on Frank as he warmed up. So far, so good. It looking like the knuckleball was moving tonight. That was good news for Frank, but Manny could be in for a long night.

It didn't take long for Frank to work his way through the first inning as he retired all three batters on easy ground balls to the infield. Two had been hit to Zach at second base and it always felt good to get a couple of plays under your belt early in the game. Zach had already grabbed his helmet and bat before he remembered that he wasn't batting second today. He quickly put them back in their cubbyholes and took a spot on the top step of the dugout to take a look at Bobby Jensen.

At first glance there was nothing remarkable about the guy. Average build, nothing eye catching about his mechanics. It looked like he threw over the top, not three quarters or a side arm motion. His pitches didn't seem to have any real movement or pop. Maybe Joe was right, he could be an easy mark, but then again, he was a professional pitcher so he had to have something going for him.

Apparently he could pitch after all, as the first two Barons struck out and the third hit a weak fly ball to left field. It seemed like they were all out in front of the ball. Maybe everyone was just a little too confident and got overanxious, Zach thought. He would make sure he was a little more patient at the plate and lay off the breaking balls.

Frank worked another one, two, three inning, and the Barons were quickly back in the dugout to take another shot at Jensen. Joe was leading off, and since he was the one who put it into everyone's head that this guy was an easy touch, maybe he could show them how it was done.

He must have been reading Zach's mind because Joe quickly got ahead in the count by laying off two breaking balls in the dirt. He stepped out of the box and looked over to the dugout and gave the guys a knowing smile. Sure enough, the next pitch was a fastball, and he lined it into the gap in left center for a double. Sandy Daniels, their right fielder, worked a four-ball walk, and Zach moved to the on-deck circle as Javier Martinez, their first baseman, stepped to the plate.

As Zach waited in the on deck circle, he thought back to what Joe has said earlier. "Can't hold runners on." Once again, it seemed like Joe was reading his mind as he easily stole third base without a throw. Sandy moved to second, and a hit would now bring in two runs. Javier must not have been listening or watching what was going on as he swung at three straight breaking balls in the dirt for the first out of the inning.

Zach walked to the plate and took a look down at third base to see if there was a play on, but Jimmy just held his hands up near his ear to remind Zach to correct the flaw in his batting stance they had been working on earlier. He stepped in the box and stared out at the pitcher. *Stay away from balls in the dirt he reminded himself and keep your hands up.*

Two breaking balls later the count was 2–0, and Zach could hear Joe's voice in his head "Never throws a breaking ball behind in the count." A look down the third base line confirmed the thought as Joe stood on the bag trying to hold back a smile. *I guess they all know what is coming now. I'll look for a fastball because they don't want to load the bases.*

Zach stepped back into the box, made the sign of the cross, and tapped the plate with his bat in the sign of the cross. Jensen went into his wind up, and here it came, a fastball belt high, right over the plate. The pitch seemed to float toward Zach in slow motion, and he had to hold back and try not to jump on it too soon. He waited for just the right moment, shifted his weight, and pulled the bat through the hitting zone. His patience was rewarded as he felt the bat connect, and the ball flew off his bat.

He knew the minute he hit the ball that it was going to go a long way. He followed the flight of the ball as he dropped his bat and started running toward first base. As with every home run, he hit he flashed back to the first time he hit a ball over the fence back home into Mr. McNeslon's yard. This was why he played the game. He wanted to smile, but he had too much respect for the game and the pitcher to show him up. He put his head down and jogged around the bases.

Joe and Sandy gave him double high fives after he touched home plate. Manny was up next and had a big smile on his face as he shook Zach's hand. "It was just a matter of time!" he shouted.

Tom was the first one to greet Zach in the dugout, shaking his hand and saying "Nice job." He shared handshakes and hugs with the rest of the team and took a spot on the bench to take off his batting gloves and watch Manny's at-bat.

Manny sent a deep fly ball to left field, and the guys immediately jumped to their feet, thinking it also had a chance to go out but it died on the warning track. Jensen got the next batter on another fly ball out, and the inning was over.

The crowd gave Zach a nice round of applause as he made his way out to second base for the top of the third inning. Nothing pumped up the crowd like a home run, especially from a guy batting .000 for the year. Now with a 3–0 lead, all Frank had to do was put the Stars down without a run, and they could take control of the game. Tom always preached, "Hold your opponent after you score and you take the momentum."

Unfortunately, Frank's knuckleball decided to take a break, and he walked the first two batters on eight pitches. Forced to rely on his fastball he gave up a couple of hits, and the Stars scored two quick runs. Then, as quickly as it left, the knuckleball returned, and Frank got out of the inning with no more damage.

The Barons batted around in the third inning scoring five more runs and knocking Jensen out of the game. Joe doubled in two of the runs, and Zach contributed a line drive single for his third RBI of the night. The roommates were having a good game, with the exception of Manny, who hit another long fly ball to the warning track in center field and was 0 for 2.

Frank was doing his best to try and keep the Stars under control, but the knuckleball kept coming and going as the game wore on. He was really struggling with his control and making Manny work behind the plate. He put runners on base in every inning, and even though the Barons kept scoring, the Stars refused to give up and the game turned into a slugfest.

Zach came up again in the fifth inning with a runner on second base and lined a double down the right field line for his third hit and fourth RBI of the game. As he stood on second base he hoped that Manny could come through with a hit and join the party. Unfortunately, he popped up to the third baseman, and Zach was left on base. Well, there would be at least one more chance for both of them Zach thought, maybe next time.

Frank made it through six innings before Tom finally pulled him out of the game. The Barons were leading 10–4 at that point so it seemed like a good time to get the bullpen some work and give Manny a break behind the plate. The Barons had some lively arms in the bullpen and the guys had good control so the pace of the game picked up at that point and the teams traded zeroes for the next two innings.

As Zach waited in the on deck circle for his next turn at-bat in the bottom of the 7th inning Manny came up behind him.

"Going for the cycle?"

"What?" Zach replied as he swung a couple of bats over his head.

"You've got a single, double, and a home run, you just need a triple," Manny said. "You know they give $1,000 to a fan if any player hits for the cycle."

"Really? I didn't know that," Zach replied. He knew the team had a bunch of promotions but he didn't really follow that kind of stuff.

"You'll be a fan favorite here for life if you can do it," Manny said with a grin. "If you're lucky, maybe it will be a nice young lady who wins."

"Well, we'll see. I'm just happy to be hitting the ball. I'm not too worried where it goes right now." Zach tossed the extra bats aside and made his way to the plate.

Don't think about what Manny said, he told himself as he stepped into the batter's box. *Hands up, hit the ball hard, don't worry where it goes.* The pitcher went into his wind up, and just like his other three times up tonight the ball just seemed to float toward the plate in slow motion. He felt the bat connect and send a screaming line drive down the first base line. If it got past the first basemen and down the line, maybe he would get that triple.

The first baseman dove to his left and made an unbelievable catch robbing Zach of his fourth hit and local glory for hitting for the cycle. Oh well, he thought as he made his way back to the dugout, he would take a three for four night any time. He gave Manny a shrug as he passed home plate. He hoped the big guy would get a hit as he was the only one without one tonight.

Once again, Manny flied out to the warning track, finishing his day 0 for 4. The Barons quickly disposed of the Stars the next two innings and the game finished in their favor with score of 12–4. The team exchanged high fives at the pitcher's mound after the last out and made their way back to the clubhouse.

As he ran off the field, Zach was approached by the local radio crew to be interviewed for the postgame show. He knew the guys pretty well since he had been there for two years, but he didn't like doing the media stuff. He preferred to just play the game. But it did come with the territory so he would have to delay his postgame routine for a few minutes.

The interview only lasted for about five minutes, and he was asked the same questions. "How did it feel to get your first hits of the season? Did you know you had a shot at hitting for the cycle? How does it feel to be back with the Barons again?" He did his best to smile and answer with the general clichés. "It felt great to contribute. I would have loved to hit for the cycle so a fan could have won the $1,000 promotion but the first baseman made a great play. If I can't be in Chicago, there's no better place than Birmingham."

His commitment over, he made his way back to the clubhouse. The game was over, but as always, the work was just beginning. He couldn't wait to look at video tonight to verify that the change in his hands had made the difference. It turned out that Joe was right; this had turned out to be a good night.

CHAPTER 7

The locker room always had a different feel after a win compared to a loss. The Barons were a happy group tonight, it was a lopsided win and everyone had contributed. Well, everyone except for Manny, he was the only regular that didn't have at least one hit in the game. Zach approached his locker expecting to see Manny feeling a little down, but instead he was greeted with a big smile and a man hug.

"Great game today, Zach," Manny said when he finally let Zach go. "I knew you would break out of your slump."

"Thanks, I wish you could have joined the hit parade tonight."

"That's okay. I got in some good swings. Anyway, hitting is only part of my game, I feel just as good when our pitchers do well and we win as when I get a couple of hits."

"I've got to tell you, Manny, you have such a great attitude. Nothing gets you down does it?" Zach asked.

"I'm not perfect. I get down on myself sometimes too, but I've been around this game a long time, and good game or bad, it's still my dream job. Tomorrow's another day and Tom already told me I'll be catching Doug, so it's all good."

"That's great. You know the Sox keep a close watch on Doug's starts so if he has a good game maybe it will rub off on you." Zach couldn't help but feel a little bit jealous. Doug was a lock for a midyear call up, and management was watching every start closely. A pitcher's results were linked to his catcher, and Manny's profile would rise along with Doug's.

"I just want Doug to get a little more support this time around. I think he could have had a better start last time if his catcher was more on the ball." Manny didn't hold the Baron's other catcher, Harold Bushing, in high regard.

"Well then, I have high expectations for tomorrow," Zach said with a smile.

Just then Joe walked up. "You boys calling it an early night tonight, or are you going to stick around here like usual?"

"You should know us well enough by now," Zach said, "We still have work to do tonight."

"You know what they say about 'all work and no play.' I told you tonight's game was in the bag. No need to go over video, just go with the flow. We should go out and celebrate."

"Why don't you see if Doug wants to do something?" Zach asked.

"He's pitching tomorrow, so he's already gone. You know how pitchers are. They only go once every five days, so they get all tense before each start. Guys like us are used to playing every day so don't get worked up."

"Well, I'd love to hang with you, but I've got to make sure that I followed through on the changes to my stance," said Zach.

"And I'm catching Doug tomorrow, so I've got to go over both my hitting and the Stars lineup," Manny added.

"Okay. Have it your way. I guess I'll go find someone online to battle tonight. I'll catch you guys back at the house later." And with that, Joe made his way out of the locker room, leaving Zach and Manny to their work.

"Some guys just don't get how hard we have to work just to keep up." Zach sighed. It was true that the game came very naturally to Joe and he didn't seem to put in the work that Manny and he did.

"Anybody that makes it this far has had to put in some work. Natural ability will only take you so far. I watched Joe during spring training, and he definitely takes this very seriously. You don't get a body like that just sitting around."

"You've been looking that closely at his body?' Zach teased.

"I look at everyone's body. Including yours. I can tell you've been hitting the weights a little more this year. You've bulked up a little bit."

"Maybe just a little. You know you've got to do a lot just to keep up," Zach said, not wanting to get into details.

"I'd say more than a little. I mean, you are not the physical specimen that I am, but you are getting closer." Manny sucked in his gut and stuck out his chest. "Look at this body. Such a waste to hide it behind all that catcher's gear."

"A *waist* all right," Zach said and laughed as Manny struggle to hold back his large middle section. "Don't hurt yourself. You've got a game tomorrow."

"Don't try to change the subject. I can see the difference. Did you start a new workout routine?"

"Nothing major, just hit the gym a little bit more. I thought I carried too much weight last year. I can't hide my gut behind a chest protector like you do."

Manny finally exhaled and collapsed in his chair. "You don't understand. Catchers need to be bulky. It gives the pitcher a better target."

"If that's the case, then Doug is in luck since you make a much bigger target than Harold."

"You wait and see. Doug will have the game of his life tomorrow. Trust me on that. All he needs is someone to help him get that arm of his under control, and he's got it made," Manny said.

"Seems to me he did just fine in his last start," Zach said.

"You can't just look at the final result. There is much more to it than that. It's just like hitting. There are things you need to look for to make sure your swing is just right. Pitchers are the same way. Doug had a good game, but he was working way too hard."

"I guess all I know is hitting and we've got a lot of it to look at so we better get to work. Are you ready to check out tonight's video?" Zach asked.

"Tell you what. Why don't you hit the showers first. I need to check with Jimmy on tomorrow's scouting report."

"Okay. Meet you back here in a few?"

"Sounds good," Manny said and went off to find Jimmy.

Zach made his way to the shower and then tried to pull together some sort of dinner from the remains of the food left behind by the rest of the team. As usual, he ended up with just a sandwich and a few pieces of fruit. Oh well, he thought, he could grab something back at the house later.

The clubhouse quickly emptied, and as usual Zach was the last one left. He wondered what was taking Manny so long. It wasn't like tomorrow was the first game of the series. They had just played the Stars today. What could change in the scouting report in one day?

"Nice job today, Zach," said a voice from behind.

Zach turned around to see Tom approaching from the other side of the room. "Thanks. It felt good to contribute for a change."

"You should know by now that you can contribute other than by getting hits or driving in runs."

"I know. But still, it felt good," Zach replied. Say what you want. If you were going to be successful in this game at some point you had to generate some offense.

"Why don't you call it a night and head on home for a change?" Tom said.

"I wasn't going to stay too long, and I have to wait for Manny anyway."

"I already sent him home, and it wasn't a suggestion. It was an order. Sometimes you can over prepare. Don't analyze this game too much. Just remember the feeling and let it carry over to tomorrow." Tom was using his authoritative voice.

If he had learned anything in the past two years, and from earlier in the day, it was not to question Tom when he gave an order. He really wanted to stay and review his at-bats, but he could just do it at home and Tom would never know. "Okay. I'll give it a try," he lied.

"Good." Tom started to walk away but turned around and put out his hand. "Just to make sure you are really listening. Give me your iPad."

"What?" Zach asked in disbelief.

"I'm not stupid. If you keep it, you'll just look at the video at home. Hand it over and get out of here."

Zach hesitated for a split second and tried to think of something to say, but it was no use. He handed over his iPad.

"If you want to review tonight's game, it will have to be in your head. My advice is if you are going to think about it, and I know you will, remember the feeling of making contact. Don't worry about your hands or anything else. See the ball, hit the ball. It's as simple as that." With that Tom put Zach's iPad in his bag and walked away. "Good night," he called out over his shoulder as he left.

Zach watched Tom leave the clubhouse. Now what was he supposed to do for the rest of the night? He liked order in his life and his routine provided that for him. Just going home and sitting around watching TV or playing a video game did not appeal to him at all. He had a goal to make it to the big leagues, and he devoted all of his time to that task. There really wasn't much else that he liked to do.

Sometimes he wondered about the life he had chosen. He was so wrapped up in making it to the big leagues he had let everything else go. Even if he made it, who would he share it with? It's not like he had a girlfriend or anything. It would be hard right now of course, but look at Manny, he had a wife and family and he made it work. All he had to think about was the next day's game. Take that away and what did he have left?

Oh well, not much he could do about it now. Tom was probably waiting out in the parking lot to see if he actually went home, so he'd better get going. As he gathered his things and left the clubhouse, he thought about Manny. How was he going to get home? Zach was his ride. He hoped he wasn't trying to walk it. He quickly got his answer when he hit the parking lot and saw a large figure spread out on the hood of his car.

"Hey! Are your trying to crush my car? I need to get home tonight!" he called out as he approached.

"I was wondering what was taking you so long," Manny said. "When Tom kicked me out, he told me you were next."

"I tried to argue, but it was no use so I just gave up," Zach said as he loaded up his bag and got in the car. "Let's just get home and see what Joe and Doug are doing."

"Any guesses?" Manny asked as he climbed into the passenger seat.

"Hmm. Joe on the Xbox and Doug in his room thinking about the game tomorrow."

"My thoughts exactly."

Zach fired up the Purple Beast, and they covered the drive home in just a few minutes. They talked a little about the game, but for the most part it was a quiet drive and Zach used the time to mentally review his at-bats. Overall he felt really good at the plate. Maybe Tom was right and he would just let it go at that. He thought about the home run he hit, and once again his thoughts went back to the first time he hit the ball over his neighbor's fence. It really was a kid's game. Maybe he was making it too complicated.

He didn't have time to finish that thought because they had arrived at the house. They made their way inside and were surprised to find Joe and Doug seated in the living room with the TV off and deep in conversation.

"Wow. This is not what I expected to see when we got home," Manny said as they walked in the door.

"We could say the same for you," Joe replied. "What are you doing home so soon? I thought you were watching video tonight. Forget to charge your iPad?"

"Tom took it away and kicked us out of the clubhouse," Zach said as he took a seat across from Joe and Doug.

"Really? That must be killing you," said Doug.

"You have no idea. Now I'm stuck talking to you guys all night. You seemed pretty deep in conversation when we walked in. What's up?"

"You haven't heard yet? Joey Woodward got popped for steroids," Joe said looking over at Manny to see his reaction. Woodward was the starting catcher for the triple A team in Charlotte.

"You're kidding!" Manny exclaimed. "I would have never thought he would do something like that. What was it?"

"Word on the street says it was Boldenone," Joe said. "According to Wikipedia, it's mostly used in horses. There have been a couple of guys that have been caught using it the past few years.

"I don't get it. Why would you do something like that?" asked Doug. "We all know we get tested all the time now. Why run the risk?"

"He's been stuck in triple A for a couple of years now," Zach said. "Guys get desperate and think they need just an extra push to make it to the next level."

"That's just stupid. There are no shortcuts. You have to put in the work to make it. I hate guys who think they can take the easy way out," Joe said.

"That's easy for you to say. It all comes easy for you. The rest of us have had to work our tails off to get where we are," Zach said. He didn't want to say it out loud but he really did understand why Woodward would try to get any advantage he could.

"Are you saying I don't work hard? I've put in years of practice to get where I am today. Just because I don't spend all night looking at video and obsessing over every piece of my game like you do doesn't mean I don't work hard." Joe's voice was rising, and he stared hard at Zach.

"That's not what he's saying," Manny said, trying to stop an argument before it had the chance to start.

"Don't try to protect him, Manny. He's a big boy. He said it, not you." Joe turned back to Zach.

"I'm not saying 'you,' Joe, I mean, some guys have more natural talent than others and the game is easier for them. For guys like Manny and me, every day is a struggle."

"It sure sounded like you meant me," Joe said. "And just for the record, every day is a struggle for me too. You don't think I have pressure too? I have a contract to live up to, and I take that very seriously."

"I know. I'm sorry if that came out wrong. It's not right what he did, but can't you at least understand why he did it?"

"Sure. It's just like you said. He felt like he was stuck and was looking for an edge. My point is that's not right. He doesn't impact just himself. He impacts every other guy that plays his position. If he gets away with it, he blocks Manny from moving up. That's not right." Joe was trying not to get angry, but Zach could tell he was upset.

"I don't disagree with you, but I guess I can understand why he did it more that you can. If this is your dream, you will do anything you can to make it. We've all had a rough time or two over the years. You can't say you have never thought about it."

"Never. I would never do it," Joe said flatly.

"Me either," Doug said, finally joining the conversation. "If I can't make it on my own, I wouldn't want to make it at all."

"I have," Manny said. "I even had the needle in my hand, ready to go."

"What?" they all said at the same time.

"It was right after I was released the second time, by the Mets. Maria was pregnant; my brother had just signed a big contract. I felt like a failure, and I needed to provide for my family. It's everywhere in the Dominican. I found a guy, got some stuff, and was ready to do it."

"But you didn't, right?" Zach asked.

"No. I never did."

"Why not?" asked Doug.

"It's just like you said. I realized I wanted to make it on my own. If I had to rely on something else to help me, it wouldn't be real. Sure, maybe I would make it, but I couldn't look myself in the mirror knowing the real reason I made it. I tossed the stuff and just started to work harder."

"And you signed with another team, and you still have a chance," Doug said. "And I bet that feels good doesn't it?"

"Yeah, it does. Maybe I make it, maybe I don't, but at least I will know it was me, not some drug that makes me something I'm not."

"I'm glad you're here. I think you're a great catcher, and you'll get there," Doug said.

"Thanks. I appreciate that."

"Look, I'm sure we can talk about this all night, but I've a game to pitch tomorrow, and I need to get my mind right so I'm heading to bed. Manny, you'll need to keep things from getting out of hand." With that, Doug excused himself and went to his room.

"What do you say, guys? Truce for the night?" There was still some tension in the air, and Manny was determined not to let it get out of hand.

"I'm good," Zach said.

"Me too," said Joe.

"Well, you're both lying, but you're grown men so you can figure it out. Despite what Tom said, I brought a scouting report home and I'm going to grab something to eat and take a look. You're on your own. Just don't kill each other. We have a game tomorrow." Manny excused himself and went to the kitchen.

With just the two of them in the room, Zach felt some pressure to relieve the tension that was still hanging think in the room. "I know you work hard, Joe."

"Do you really? Did you know I didn't even make my varsity team in high school until my senior year? Even then, I sat on the bench for the first half of the season. My parents spent a fortune on private lessons for me for years. I worked out every day, even though I wasn't on the team. Then I was a walk-on in college, no scholarship, working two jobs, carrying a full class load and baseball practice. I didn't sleep for two years. When I got drafted and all I had to do was play, that was like a break for me. So, you can see why I resent someone who wants to get where I am by sticking a needle in his arm."

"Everyone has a story, Joe. I've dreamed about playing in the big leagues since I was five years old. My dad left us, and my mom stepped in and was both a mom and dad for me. She coached my teams and made a lot of personal sacrifices to help me to get where I am today. I've played with guys from Latin America that have come from absolutely nothing. Entire families pin their hopes and dreams on them, and if they fail, their family goes hungry. If they can make it by taking a pill or using a needle, they'll do it. I'm not saying it's right, but I can see why they would."

"I know. I've played with guys like that too. I guess I can't identify with them. I have something to fall back on. I just love the game, and I want it to be an even playing field. If I make it, great, but if I don't I want it to be on me, not because someone else had an unfair advantage."

"Me too. Look, I think we both feel the same way. We've got a long year ahead of us, and I don't want to feel uncomfortable. We are not going to settle it here, so let's just agree to drop it." Zach was hoping they could just let it go, they had to live and work together and it was going to be long year if they fought all the time.

"Okay. I'll try to let it go. Hopefully, we won't hear about any more guys and the whole issue just goes away."

"I'm sure MLB feels that way too. Think about all the time and effort they put into testing players each year."

"That's why it's so crazy to even try. We're tested all the time. We just got done testing in spring training. The days of getting away with it are over."

"People will always think there is a way to beat the system and there is always some new undetectable drug out there. Let's just stop talking about it. Tell you what, I'll play you in Halo." Zach figured video games were the only way out of this conversation.

"Seriously? You?" Joe asked with a smirk. "Do you even know how to play?"

"Just because I don't play every day like you doesn't mean I don't know how to play. Set it up and you'll see."

"Prepare to die." Joe laughed. "This will be like taking candy from a baby."

After about an hour of being killed in a wide variety of manners, Zach had enough and decided to call it a night. Joe teased him a bit about his poor marksmanship but let him off the hook. He went online to find a more worthy opponent, and Zach made his way to his room to try to sleep.

Manny had already turned in and was snoring loudly. Zach quickly changed and hit the bed, trying not to disturb Manny's "beauty sleep," as if that would ever happen, Manny slept like a rock. Hopefully after a good game tonight Zach would get some sleep, but first he had some thinking to do.

He went through each of his at-bats in his mind and based on the outcome, he was three for four with a home run, and the "feel', he deemed the night a success. Still, somewhere in the back of his mind there was something bothering him. He knew what it was, but he didn't really want to think about it right now. He closed his eyes and forced himself to keep them shut.

He could hear Joe in the other room talking to an unknown competitor. He wished he could be that relaxed and confident is his game and stay up all night playing video games instead of worrying about what tomorrow would bring. All he had were doubts. He wanted this so bad, and he was always afraid that it would be taken away at a moment's notice.

He thought about the box in his nightstand. He never intended to bring it with him once the season started, but he did. He didn't really need it did he? He had three hits tonight and was going to start hitting. But then again, what if he didn't? Tom had already dropped him in the lineup. It was just a matter of time before he was on the bench. Maybe one more time, that would be the boost he needed to get started again.

He got out of bed and went to the bathroom and locked the door. Inside the box were four small vials and a few syringes. This was crazy, wasn't it? Joey Woodward just got caught for doing the same thing, but still here he was. Well, testing was probably done for the year, so there really was no risk. Maybe just one more time, it could only help. He filled a syringe, gritted his teeth and plunged the needle into his thigh.

Back in bed he tried to force himself to relax, but his mind kept running through a variety of scenarios. How great it would be to make it to the big leagues. How different his life would be when he got there. All the things he could do for his mom. He also thought about being called into Tom's office and getting his release. Would that be the end, or could he hook on with another club? What would he do with his life without baseball? On and on it went late into the night. He tossed and turned as his mind wandered, and finally, after what seemed like hours, he drifted off to sleep.

CHAPTER 8

Zach didn't use an alarm clock. After years in the minor leagues his body had adjusted to the odd hours, and he slept as long as he needed. Having a roommate usually helped. Manny was an early riser, and although he tried to be quiet when he woke up he was a big guy and he usually made a lot of noise. Today was no different, and when Zach looked at the clock on the side of his bed he saw that is was only 8:30 a.m.

"Why are you up so early?" Zach asked Manny as he pulled the covers up over his head to block the morning sun.

"Sorry. You know I always get up early. I was trying to be quiet since I know you were probably up late last night, but I couldn't find any pants to wear."

"So I have to suffer because you aren't up to date on your laundry?"

"You know we've got a road trip coming up, and I can see from the pile of dirty clothes on your side of the room you need to go too. Why don't you get up and we'll get some breakfast and head over to the laundromat?"

"Okay. Give me a few minutes, and I'll get up." Laundry was the last thing on Zach's mind, but Manny was right, they were heading out on a road trip in a couple of days, and he would need to pack. People thought ballplayers had some kind of fancy life, but they needed to do the little things in life like laundry too.

After a quick breakfast at the house, they loaded up their clothes and headed over to the local laundromat. Two men coming in together kind of stood out compared to the women who generally made up the bulk of the people that were there, and they received a few odd glances as they sorted their clothes.

"Do you want to share a machine?" Manny asked as he started to put some things in a washer.

"I don't want my stuff mixed up with yours," Zach replied, shooting Manny an odd glance.

"What's the big deal? It's just clothes. We sleep in the same room. What's the difference?"

"There is a big difference. We don't sleep in the same bed. Why would I mix my clothes up with yours?" They had had this conversation before. Zach was okay with Manny as a roommate, but there had to be a line somewhere.

"Okay. Okay. No big deal. I just thought it would save us some time and money." Manny finished loading up his machines and added in his quarters.

"Time I have, and I'll pay the extra money. Thank you for asking." Zach turned his attention to sorting out his clothes and started up his machines.

"Excuse me," said a voice from behind Zach. "Are you using this machine?"

Zach turned around and saw a young woman with basket full of clothes smiling at him. "No. I just have these three machines here."

"Okay. Thank you," she replied and started to put her clothes in the machines next to Zach.

Zach finished loading his clothes and walked over to where Manny was sitting. Not much to do now but wait for the clothes to finish. If Tom hadn't taken his iPad last night, at least he could have looked at some video or checked his e-mail. The laundromat had wi-fi. He could even had looked up some more information on Joey Woodward's suspension. He was the starting catcher for the White Sox triple A club, maybe there was a chance Manny would be called up to replace him. He was just about to say something to Manny when he felt a punch on his arm.

"What is your problem?" Manny asked as he punched him a second time, but harder.

"Ouch. What are you talking about?" Zach asked as he rubbed his shoulder.

"An attractive young lady tries to strike up a conversation with you, and you just walk away?"

"What? She just needed a machine. That's all." Zach didn't see where Manny was going with this.

"Look around. Do you see all of the empty machines here? She could have gone anywhere, but she picked the ones next to you. She tossed you a soft one and you whiffed."

"You're crazy," Zach said. "You're reading way too much into it. It's just a washing machine."

"I'm sorry to interrupt," a voice said from behind. "Do you have some detergent that I could borrow?"

Zach turned and saw the same woman from before standing in front of him. "Uh, sure," he said, handing her a bottle of detergent, "take all you need."

"Thank you. I'll bring it right back." She hesitated for a moment and then turned and walked away.

Zach felt another punch on his arm. "What now?" he asked as he turned around to see Manny staring at him.

"Are you that clueless?" Manny asked.

"What?"

Manny shook his head in disbelief. "She can buy detergent from the vending machine. She is looking for a reason to talk to you, and you don't get it. That is really sad."

"Really?"

"Man, I know you haven't had a lot of experience with women, but she can't make it any clearer. I bet you she won't bring back your detergent."

"Why?"

"So you'll have to go over and ask her for it, that's why." Manny shook his head. "You really need to get out more."

"Let's say you're right," Zach said, "but I'm not looking for a girlfriend right now. I need to focus on playing ball right now. This is a big year for me, I don't need the distraction."

"Have you ever thought you might need a distraction? It's not healthy to tie up everything you have into the game."

Zach looked across the room and he had to admit she was very cute. "Maybe. No. No, I don't need this right now. What are you trying to do me?"

"I'm trying to help you bring some balance into your life. Look, I dedicated my life to the game when I was younger. When I met Maria, it changed everything. It gave me perspective, and I never would have made it this far without her. Maybe, just maybe, this is what you need to put you over the hump."

"Okay. So assume you're right. What am I supposed to do, just walk over there and talk to her?"

"Uh, yes. It's not that hard. You've had a girlfriend before. I've known you for what, two years now. I've seen you with girls. You know what to do."

"It's been a while. I wouldn't know what to say. I've never gone up to a girl before. I usually meet them through other people."

"Well, you're going to need to figure something out quick because she's coming over. I think I need to go grab a soda. I'll be right back." With that Manny got up and walked away.

Before Zach could say anything, Manny was gone. He turned around just in time to see her walk up. He tried to think of something to say, but the words wouldn't come out. He hadn't really looked at her before, but now that he did he was even more at a loss for words, because she wasn't cute; she was beautiful. She had long brown hair and was casually dressed, but what really grabbed his attention were her eyes.

They weren't really brown, more like a hazel color, and they seemed to draw him in and he felt nervous and excited at the same time. There was something about her that he found extremely attractive, and maybe Manny was right. This could be someone that could change his life if he let her. Wait, what was he thinking, he hadn't even spoken to her yet and she was changing his life. He was getting way ahead of himself.

She smiled at him as she walked up and he could see her mouth moving, but he didn't hear a word she said. He stood there speechless, just looking at her as she said something. Over her shoulder he saw Manny standing by the soda machine gesturing with his hands signaling him to say something.

"Are you okay?" she asked after a minute or two.

"What? Oh, yeah, I'm fine. Just a little distracted for a minute," he said, finally coming to his senses.

"Okay. I just wanted to bring back your detergent. Thanks, by the way. I can't believe I forgot mine at home." She put out her hand. "My name is Sarah."

He took her hand and said, "I'm Zach, nice to meet you." Her hand was soft, and he didn't want to let go.

"I know," she said, "you play for the Barons, right."

That got his attention. "Yeah, how did you know?"

"My parents have season tickets. I go to the games with them sometimes. Can I have my hand back now?"

"Sorry." He let go of her hand. "Like I said, I was distracted."

She looked over her shoulder at Manny, who quickly turned away. "By your friend over there?"

Zach tried to think of something, anything to say. Before he could think about it, he said, "Actually, I was looking at your eyes."

She smiled and looked him dead in the eyes and lifted one eyebrow. "Really? What did you see?"

"I don't know, but I liked it."

Her face turned a little red, and she lowered her head and looked at the ground. "You're good. You know that."

"I'm not that good."

"Sure you are. You went three for four last night with a home run. I'd say that's good," she said, looking back up at him. "I was at the game."

"Oh," Zach said, and he felt his face start to turn red. "I thought you meant."

"I know what you thought," she said interrupting him.

"Are you going to the game tonight? Maybe with your boyfriend?" Zach asked.

"I don't think so. My parents share their seats and don't usually go two days in a row." She paused for a second and looked up at him, "and, I don't have a boyfriend."

"That's too bad," Zach said, quickly adding, "I mean about the game, not the boyfriend part."

"Really? I'm sure you have a girlfriend. Probably one in every city right?"

Zach couldn't help but laugh. "Hardly. I spend all my time practicing, playing or thinking about the game. Manny, my friend over there, was just telling me I needed to get more of a life."

"It sounds like Manny's a smart man. He also calls a good game. You should listen to him."

"I guess you really are a fan. Should I be scared? You're not a stalker are you?" Zach stepped back and raised his hand up. "Are you going to shoot me or something, like in *The Natural*?"

"You're a good player, and I'd even say you were cute, but you're not Robert Redford."

"Ouch," Zach grabbed his chest. "You really know how to hurt a guy."

"I wouldn't hurt a fly."

"I'm not so sure. You look like you might have a little bit of a mean streak in you. I think I need to be careful." Zach found himself intrigued by this girl. She didn't have a boyfriend, was beautiful and obviously liked baseball. Maybe he should ask her out. He was just getting ready to say something when their washing machines came to a noisy stop behind them.

"Well, it looks like my clothes are done. I better move them over to the dryer."

She started to turn around, but before she got the chance, Zach asked, "Would you like to go to the game tonight? I could leave you some tickets."

"I'd like that. Can you get me two? I'd like to bring a friend."

"I think I can arrange that. I'll leave them at will-call. You can pick them up there. What's your last name?"

"Jenkins. Sarah Jenkins. And I know you want to know, but won't ask. I'll be bringing my sister, Julie." She smiled and walked over to move her clothes to the dryer.

Zach stood for a minute admiring her as she walked away. She really was a beautiful girl. He was lucky Manny made him come to do laundry today. He was still looking at her when Manny walked up behind him.

"I told you so," he said, punching him in the arm again. "Did you ask her out?"

"She's going to come to the game tonight with her sister," Zach said, trying hard not to let Manny see the smile on his face. "Apparently, she's a fan. She knew both of us play for the Barons."

"She's not a stalker, is she?"

"No, her parents have season tickets."

"Okay. You can never be too sure. You know the dryers run for a good forty-five minutes. You can go back over there and talk to her some more." Manny pushed Zach toward the row of dryers.

"Hey, you don't have to push. I was going to go. I don't want to look too anxious."

"That's my boy. I knew you had it in you. You know, she did say she was a fan. Maybe I should go and introduce myself to her. Let her know what she is getting herself into." Manny started to walk over to where Sarah was loading her clothes into the dryer.

"No way. You stay over here. I don't need your help," Zach said, stepping in front of Manny.

"I think you do. You would never have talked to her if it wasn't for me," Manny said as he tried to push past Zach. "Excuse me!" He called out to Sarah.

"Stop! I mean it!" Zach said, pushing Manny back. Unfortunately for Zach, Manny was bigger and stronger, and before he knew it he had picked him up and moved him to the side. Zach quickly moved back in front of Manny and after a brief struggle they fell against the row of washing machines and dropped to the floor.

They wrestled on the floor for a minute or two with Manny trying to call out to Sarah as they rolled back and forth. Zach tried to cover Manny's mouth with his hand but it didn't really matter, the minute they hit the floor, Sarah had started to walk over.

"Everything okay here?" she asked as she approached.

Zach and Manny stopped wrestling and were lying in each other's arms on the floor. "Everything's great. Manny just wanted to come over and say 'hi' and we slipped."

"Slipped, huh? It looks like a little bit more than that. Maybe I should leave the two of you alone."

"No!" They both said at the same time.

After they struggled to their feet, Zach straightened out his shirt and said, "Sarah, this is my friend Manny."

"Hi, nice to meet you," Manny said and reached out to shake her hand.

"Nice to meet you," she replied, "you caught a good game last night. You are much better than Bushing. He makes the pitchers work too hard."

Manny turned and looked at Zach. "This one's a keeper."

"I told you she was a fan."

"But not a stalker," Sarah added.

"Well that remains to be seen," Zach said with a smile.

"True," she said with a smile, "maybe I'm just being nice to you to give you a false sense of security, and I'll turn crazy later."

"Hey, that could go both ways. You have to be a little crazy to be a ballplayer." There was something about this girl that Zach really liked.

"Are you coming to the game tonight?" Manny asked.

"I wasn't, but Zach offered me some tickets so I'm going to come with my sister. I just texted her, and she's free tonight."

"Great," said Manny, "I think you're in for a treat tonight. I have a feeling something good is going to happen."

"Like Manny will get his first hit of the year," Zach teased.

"Big talk from someone that was 0 for 11 before yesterday." Manny turned to Sarah. "A guy gets a lucky bounce or two and scratches out a few hits, and all of the sudden he's Babe Ruth."

"Lucky bounce? Did you not see how far that home run went?"

"The wind was blowing out. It got caught in an updraft. Most nights that's a pop fly to the warning track."

"Like all of your at-bats yesterday." Zach always liked to tease Manny about his warning track power.

"Like I said, it was the wind. It always blows in when I come up to bat." Manny turned to Sarah again and nodded toward Zach. "Some guys have all the luck."

"My mom always said, 'The harder you work, the luckier you get,' so maybe I am lucky." Zach knew Manny was kidding him, but after the conversation with Joe last night he was a little sensitive.

"I will give you that," Manny said and turned to Sarah, "all this guy thinks about is baseball. Do you know he wasn't even going to talk to you until I told him to."

"Really?" Sarah pretended to be upset. "Didn't even want to talk to me huh?"

"Maybe he's just a little bit shy," Manny said.

"Professional baseball player, shy? I don't think so. Maybe I shouldn't have come over. What do you think?" Sarah asked Manny

"He really is a good guy. Just stays in his shell a little bit too much. You seem like a nice girl. I wouldn't steer you wrong," Manny said.

"Thank you. Still think I should take him up on his offer to go to the game tonight?"

"Absolutely. I told you, I have a feeling something special is going to happen tonight. I thought it was going to be on the field, but maybe it's just the fact you are going to be there." Manny smiled and gave Sarah a wink.

"You are so sweet. I think I'll go. It will be fun."

What was happening here? How did he suddenly get left out of the conversation? Why was Manny trying to embarrass him? He needed to say something. "So I'll just leave the tickets for you at will-call?"

"That would be great. Maybe we could grab something to eat after the game?"

"He has a pretty set routine after the game," Manny said. "I don't know if he can fit you in."

"That's too bad." Sarah turned from Manny to look at Zach. "Maybe another time."

"What? Sure we can do something after the game if you want to. I mean, I want to. If you do, or we don't have to, it's up to you." Whatever confidence Zach was feeling before was gone now. What was Manny doing to him?

"Is he always this indecisive?" Sarah asked Manny.

"He's a little slow sometimes." Manny shrugged his shoulders. "But he is nice guy. If it makes it easier, I can come along with you."

"That would be nice."

"Great. It takes us a little while to wrap up after the game. How about we meet you at the Waffle House about an hour after the game ends?"

"Is that okay with you, Zach?" Sarah asked.

"What? Of course. That would be great." Somewhere along the way Zach had lost control of the conversation, but maybe Manny had a plan.

"Okay. We'll see you then. Have a good game." She turned to walk away, but before she did she smiled at Zach and gave Manny a wink.

"Hang on a second," Manny said before she could go. "Maybe you guys should exchange numbers. You know, in case we need to call you later if we are running late."

"That's a good idea." Sarah pulled out her phone, and they exchanged numbers. "I'll see you tonight."

After she walked away, it was Zach's turn to punch Manny in the arm. "What was that all about?"

"Just trying to be a good wing man. You know, take the pressure off, make the girl feel comfortable so you look good."

"Wing man? You watch way too many TV shows and movies. I didn't need any help."

"Sure you did. You were crashing and burning."

"How can you say that? She's going to the game tonight."

"But now she's also going out to dinner with you, and you have her phone number," Manny smiled. "That's what a wing man does, my friend."

Zach had to give Manny credit. He would have never thought to ask her out after the game or even for her phone number. Maybe he did need a little help. "Okay. You're right. What should I do now?"

"Once you make arrangements for the tickets, text her to confirm and tell her you are looking forward to seeing her later."

"Got it, and then?"

"Try to do something during the game that's memorable and find her in the crowd and wave at her or toss her a ball." Manny was really getting into it now. "She'll love it."

"Where do you get this stuff from?" Zach asked.

"All those TV show and movies I watch," Manny smiled.

They spent the next hour finishing up their laundry, Manny taking great care to neatly fold and pack away his clothes, while Zach half-hazardly tossed them back in a basket to take home and deal with later. Sarah had moved back to the other side of the room after their conversation and was still putting her things away as they got ready to leave. Zach tried not to stare at her, but she really was a beautiful girl and once again he felt a punch on his shoulder.

"Don't stare. You look desperate and a little scary," Manny said as he picked up his basket.

"I'm anything but scary, and I can't help it," Zach replied but quickly turned away from her. "She is really pretty."

"Yes she is, but you need to stay cool. Don't try too hard too soon. Let it happen naturally."

"Yeah, you're right. It's been a while though, so it's tough." He gathered up his things, and they started toward the door. They passed by Sarah as she stood at a nearby table folding her clothes. Zach smile as he walked by, gave her a nod, and said, "See you later tonight."

"I'm looking forward to it," she said. "Hey, do you think you can get a hit for me tonight?"

"No promises, but I'll try," Zach said, thinking that was the kind of extra pressure he didn't need right now.

"If he doesn't, I will," Manny added as he headed out the door.

"As long as one of you does, I'll be happy." She smiled at Zach and whispered in a low voice so Manny wouldn't hear, "But yours would mean more."

Zach nodded and returned her smile, As he walked out to the parking lot he felt like he was floating on air. Now all he had to do was have a good game tonight. Normally a comment like hers would make him nervous before a game, but oddly enough he felt very calm and didn't worry about getting a hit for her. In fact, maybe he would get two.

CHAPTER 9

The morning passed quickly, and before too long it was time to head over to the field and get ready for the game. Zach had called over to the ticket office to make arrangements for Sarah and her sister earlier in the day. To his surprise, he was able to get them tickets in the row right above the Barons' dugout. He had mixed feelings about it. On one hand it would make him look good with Sarah, but he was afraid it would be a distraction seeing her every time he came off the field.

Lots of guys on the team would leave tickets for family and friends, but Zach really treated the games like a job and tried not to spend time arranging tickets for people. His mom was really the only one who had come to see him play, and that was usually only once a year. Maybe that's why the guy in the ticket office gave him such good seats. He had never really asked for much in the two years he had played with the Barons.

He had to admit it though it would be nice to have someone come out to see him play. He just hoped that he had a good game. He'd felt great at the plate last night, but since Tom had taken his iPad he didn't have a chance to review his at-bats like he usually did. Zach still wasn't too happy about that, but Tom was his manager and he could do what he wanted. Zach was a creature of habit, and not reviewing his at-bats made him feel funny. He had tried to remember how he "felt" last night like Tom had suggested, but it wasn't the same as seeing the video.

The clubhouse was nearly empty when he arrived with Manny, and Zach was pleased to see that his iPad was sitting on the chair in front of his locker. "Well, at least he gave me back my iPad. I thought he might keep it."

"I'm sure he has his own," Manny laughed.

"You never know. He is pretty old school."

"That may be true, but he knows the game. It's not good to get on his bad side."

"I'll be okay as long as I start hitting. Want to look at some video?"

"Sorry, I've got to go see Jimmy and review the Stars's lineup for tonight. I'll see you out on the field later." Manny got up to walk away but turned back. "Remember, you need to toss a ball to Sarah during the game. It will make a big impression on her."

"How am I supposed to remember to do that? This is my job you know. I can't get distracted by some girl."

"You need to find a way, and not some ball from warm-ups. I mean during the game." Manny smiled at Zach and then walked off to meet Jimmy.

Maybe he's right, Zach thought as he sat in front of his locker. It wouldn't be hard to do. All of the guys tossed balls into the stands at the end of each inning. Sometimes it was to a young kid, but more often than not, it was to a pretty girl. He would just need to make the last out of an inning. That wouldn't be easy for a second baseman, but maybe he could catch a pop fly. If he didn't get the chance, he would just grab a ball and toss it to her before the ninth inning started.

Zach shook his head. What was Manny doing to him? He was supposed to be thinking about the game, not some girl. Here he was a few hours before a game thinking about a girl he just met and he hadn't even reviewed his at-bats from the previous game. It was time to get down to business, put her out of his mind and get to work.

He spent the next thirty minutes reviewing video, and he had to admit that he looked pretty good at the plate. His hands looked like they were in the correct position again, and he could see that he made solid contact with each hit. He even closed his eyes after watching each at-bat and tried to "feel" the bat hitting the ball. Tom was a former major league player and All-Star, so it couldn't hurt to follow his advice.

After changing into his warm-ups, Zach walked over to the batting cage under the stands and hit a few balls off the tee. He tried to concentrate, but his mind kept wandering back to Sarah. It had been a long time since he was interested in a girl. He'd had a few girlfriends over the years but most didn't want to be second fiddle to his true love, baseball. It would be nice to have someone to talk to; it seemed to do wonders for Manny.

He stopped himself. *Get back to work, stop thinking about her. You just met her today, it's not like there is anything going on. For all you know she won't even come to the game.* He refocused his attention on the tee and started to swing again, making sure each time to bring his hands up to the correct position. After a few swings he felt he was ready for the game to start. He made his way back to the locker room and tried once again to get Sarah out of his mind.

The locker room slowly came to life as the other players arrived and got prepared for the game. The quiet of the room quickly disappeared and was filled with a hum, and he could feel the energy in the room rise. Someone turned on the music. Today it was late 1980s rock, Doug's choice, since he was the starting pitcher. It was a familiar routine, and since Zach was a creature of habit he quickly fell back into line and forgot about Sarah. After a quick bite to eat he put on his uniform and made his way out to the field for batting practice.

Even though he had been dropped from second to seventh in the batting order, Zach was still part of the first group in the batting cage. He saw that Joe was already there, so he walked up to him and asked "Any insight on today's pitcher?"

"Not today. I've never faced him before. You?"

"Nothing. He is supposed to be some blue-chip prospect though. Pitched a shutout in his first game this year. Mostly heat on the corners according to Jimmy."

"I'll take that any day of the week over some guy that throws junk," Joe replied as he stepped into the cage to take his swings. He effortlessly sprayed balls all over the field and then stepped back out of the cage. "I hear you have a special guest coming to the game tonight."

"Have you been talking to Manny?" Zach asked as he took his turn at the plate. "I told him not to tell anyone."

"Roommates share everything. You should know that."

Unlike Joe, Zach struggled to hit the ball out of the infield and as he stepped back out of the cage he frowned. "I didn't want anyone to know. It's no big deal."

"Say what you want, but when you meet a girl in the morning and she comes to the game that night, something is going on."

"There is nothing going on. I just asked her to the game."

"Did you tell her you would get a hit for her?"

"Maybe." Zach didn't want to get into this right now. He needed to focus.

"That's a great angle. I tried that once last year, but I couldn't get the ball out of the infield. Too much pressure. You should have just told her you'd toss her a ball." Joe could see that Zach was uncomfortable, but he didn't stop. "Where are her seats?"

"You think I'm dumb enough to tell you?" Zach laughed. "It's bad enough that you know she's coming."

Joe stepped back into the cage. "Fair point. I wouldn't say anything either if I were you. But I tell you what, I bet I can guess who she is by the third inning."

"No way, unless Manny told you what she looks like."

"He didn't. But I bet I can tell."

"Okay. You're on. What's the bet?"

"You get a gift certificate to Boot Barn for being on the radio post game show last night?"

"Yeah, it was in my locker this morning." If you were interviewed on the post game show you usually got a $50 gift certificate from one of the team's sponsors. Zach liked it better when it was a restaurant, but anything was nice.

"If I pick her out, I get your Boot Barn gift certificate," Joe said.

"And if you don't?" Zach asked.

"Fifty dollars to Taco Bell. That should feed you and Manny for a week."

"You're on." Zach was confident Joe couldn't pick her out and even if he did, he didn't want boots anyway.

"Remember, I have until the third inning."

"Okay. But you only get one guess." Zach was determined not to drag this bet out for the whole game.

"I'm only going to need one," Joe smiled, "this will be the easiest fifty bucks I ever made."

"We'll see," Zach said, "now please let me hit in peace."

They finished up their swings, and Zach made his way out to the field to take a few ground balls at second base. He was starting to get excited about the game. Manny had been saying all day about how he expected something "special" to happen tonight. Zach could feel a different energy around the ballpark. Maybe Manny was right.

The great thing about baseball was that each game was different. One day you could have a slugfest, and both teams hit the cover off the ball. The next day could be a pitcher's duel, and runs would be scarce.

It seemed like he was only in the clubhouse for a few minutes before it was time to head out to the field for the game. As he walked to the dugout, he wondered if Sarah was there already. Should he acknowledge her right away or play it cool and not look? He didn't want to be too obvious and stare out into the crowd like he was a teenager but he did want to see her again. He decided to wait until after he finished running sprints in the outfield and take a peak before he headed back to the dugout.

He was running in the outfield when Joe came up to him. "Remember, fifty dollars says I pick her out by the third inning."

"I know. I know. Stop bugging me."

"Are we a little nervous?" Joe teased.

"Maybe a little," Zach confessed.

"No worries. You'll be fine. It's just another game right?"

"Right." Zach tried to convince himself that was true, but he couldn't help peeking over at the seats above the dugout. It was almost game time, and he didn't see her yet. He hoped she hadn't changed her mind. She did say she was bringing her sister. Maybe they were just running late. He needed to stop thinking about her and concentrate on the game. He finished up his sprints and headed for the dugout.

A few minutes later he was out at his position at second base watching Doug warm up before the first inning. He had only seen Doug pitch for a short time, but his pitches seemed to have a little more pop than usual. The White Sox had big plans for him, if he did well early in the season he could find himself in triple A or even with the big club before the year was over. Even though he didn't get the win in his first start he had pitched very well, hopefully they could get him a few runs tonight.

Doug made quick work of the Stars, striking out the first two batters and getting the third on an easy pop fly to the shortstop. He seemed to be on the same page as Manny; he didn't shake him off once. That was a big change from his last game where he and Harold didn't agree on pitch selection at all. It was always nice to get that first zero on the board and get a chance to go hit.

As he ran to the dugout, Zach looked up at the stands and saw Sarah walking down the aisle. She was wearing a pair of jeans and an unbuttoned Barons jersey over a tight black shirt. A young girl about eleven or twelve walked in front of her. *That must be her sister*, Zach assumed. He hadn't thought about it but had figured they would be about the same age. Oh well, you never knew, did you?

They made eye contact right before he entered the dugout and she smiled and mouthed the word *sorry* and looked down at her sister. She must have felt bad for being late. He smiled back and mouthed "it's okay." She looked really cute, and he was so distracted by her he didn't notice how close he was to the dugout steps. Before he knew it, he had missed the first step and ended up stumbling into the dugout. The only reason he didn't fall was because Joe was right next to him and caught him on the way down.

"Brown hair in the black shirt and Barons jersey," Doug said. "That will be fifty dollars please."

"I made it too easy for you," Zach said as he sat down.

"I knew you would," Joe smiled. "She's cute."

"Yes she is."

"Now forget about her and let's get Doug some runs."

"You bet," Zach said, but the Barons went down in order in the first inning without a hit. Both pitchers set down the opposition without a hit in the second inning as well, and it was beginning to look like they were in store for a pitcher's duel. After Doug breezed through the top of the third inning, Zach finally would get his turn to hit leading off for the Barons. As he stood in the on deck circle he looked above the Barons dugout and made eye contact with Sarah.

"You owe me a hit," she called out to him.

"I know," he called back. Great, no pressure now. He had only gotten his first hit of the year the night before and now he needed another one? Who was he? Babe Ruth, calling his shot? Oh well, this wouldn't be his only at-bat tonight. He walked to the plate and tried to clear his mind.

He had never faced this pitcher before but he knew from the scouting report Jimmy had put together that he would come right after you with heat. Zach stepped into the batter's box, making the sign of the cross first with his hand then on the plate with his bat. If this guy threw heat, he would be ready for it. The first pitch came in and Zach instinctively backed away as the ball was inside. To his surprise the pitch curved back over the plate and the umpire called strike one.

I guess he has a little bit more to offer than just heat, Zach thought to himself. He better keep an eye out for breaking balls as well. He stepped out of the box and tried to think about what he would try to throw next. Probably something down and away since he had just moved him off the plate. He stepped back in, and sure enough the next pitch was on the outside part of the plate. Zach didn't try to pull the ball but went with the pitch and lined a clean single over the shortstop's head into left field.

As he stood at first base, Zach tried to hold back a smile. He was seeing the ball really well, and his early season slump seemed like a thing of the past. He was also relieved to get Sarah a hit early in the game so he wouldn't feel pressure later on. He took a peek at her sitting above the dugout and could see she had a big smile on her face. He tried to be cool but couldn't resist and gave her a quick wink as he waited for Manny to step in.

Manny was still looking for his first hit of the year, and this would be a great place to get it. He was able to work a full count but then flied out to deep left field for the first out of the inning. Doug was up next and he laid down a perfect sacrifice bunt, and Zach made his way to second base easily. Sandy Medwick, his double play partner, couldn't cash him in though and struck out to end the inning.

The next few innings passed quickly as both pitchers were in total control and neither team could mount a rally. Zach came up again in the fifth inning and singled sharply to right field for his second hit of the night. Manny popped up, and Doug struck out so he was stranded again and the game remained scoreless. After another one, two, three innings in the top of the sixth Zach took a look at the scoreboard as he was running off the field and realized that Doug had not give up a hit yet.

Baseball players tend to be very superstitious, and one of the unwritten rules of the game was that you never talked about a no-hitter. In fact, players went out of their way to avoid a pitcher between innings just so they wouldn't be the one responsible for jinxing him. The Barons were no exception, and everyone, except for Manny, had started to avoid Doug. Even Manny spoke to him only briefly before moving to far end of the bench near Zach.

"Nice hitting today," Manny said as he sat down. "You know you only promised her one hit, so two makes you look like a stud."

"Just lucky today. These guys are really dealing. You know what's going on right?"

"Don't say anything," Manny said, turning serious. "I mean it."

"Okay. Okay. My lips are sealed. I hope we can get a couple of runs for him," Zach said quietly so no one would hear.

"We'll get to him eventually," Manny replied. "I'll do it myself if I have to."

"That would be nice," Zach answered with a smile. The words were barely out of his mouth, and the Barons had a pair of runners on base. Zach and Manny joined their teammates on the top step of the dugout to cheer on the heart of the lineup. But just when it looked like they would break through the pitcher struck out the next three batters and the score remained tied at zero going into the seventh inning.

As Zach made his way out to his position, he couldn't help but think about the no-hitter. He had played baseball for a few years as a pro, but he had not been part of a no-hitter since high school. The closest he had come was in his first year of rookie ball when their pitcher lost his no-hit bid in the eighth inning. It would be a really cool thing to be part of, and the fact that it was Doug pitching made it even better.

The first batter flied out to left field on the first pitch, and the second batter hit the ball to almost the exact same spot on an 0–1 count. These guys were making it easy for Doug by swinging at pitches early in the count. Doug was throwing really well tonight, and Zach was beginning to see the difference in how Manny and Harold called a game.

Manny and Doug seemed to be on exactly the same page, and as soon as Manny gave him the sign, Doug started his windup. Maybe the quick pace of the game was throwing off the Stars. Somebody needed to get to them and tell them to step out and try to disrupt Doug's rhythm. He was on his game today, and Zach suddenly realized that not only had he not given up a hit, he hadn't allowed a runner. This wasn't just a no-hitter. It was a perfect game!

The next batter must have finally realized he needed to do something different, so he took his time stepping into the batter's box. He took two balls that were just off the plate and then surprised everyone by laying down a bunt. The ball rolled slowly toward third base before going foul by a few inches. As he returned to home plate the crowd booed him loudly. Another unwritten rule in baseball was that you didn't try to bunt to break up a no-hitter. The crowd was aware of what was going on, and they didn't want it to end that way. When Doug followed up with two nasty curveballs to strike him, out the crowd roared its approval.

Zach was due up second in the bottom of the seventh inning, and he was determined to get Doug a run. The first batter rolled out weakly to second base and as Zach walked to the plate he had a feeling he would get the job done. The pitcher had started him off with breaking balls the first two times up so he thought he would go with a fastball this time. Sure enough, the first pitch was coming in belt high and right down the middle of the plate. It was the pitcher's first mistake of the game, and Zach jumped on it.

He felt the ball hit his bat, and his arms tingled from the impact. This one had a chance to go out. The crowd rose and cheered as the ball headed to deep right center field. Zach watched the flight of the ball as he rounded first base and tried to will it over the fence. The right fielder raced to the wall and jumped. The ball landed in his glove just as it was about to disappear over the fence, and the crowd groaned.

Zach had just reached second base when the ball was caught, and he made a U-turn and made his way back to the dugout. He shook his head in disbelief and couldn't help but feel disappointed as he sat down. He wanted that ball to go out, not for him, but for Doug. How could he pitch a perfect game and the score still be tied? He had just sat down when the roar of the crowd made him stand up and rush to the top of the dugout steps.

He got there just in time to pick up the flight of the ball that Manny had crushed toward dead center field. This ball had a chance to go out too and the center fielder saw the ball sail over his head toward the seats. It didn't quite have enough and instead of going over the wall it hit about a foot below the top railing. Manny cruised into second base with his first hit of the season, and if the Barons were going to score it would be up to Doug to drive him in.

Unfortunately, Doug wasn't much of a hitter and struck out on three straight pitches. They had played seven innings, the score was still tied at zero, and Doug was only six batters away from a perfect game. The sad part was that if the Barons didn't score it wouldn't mean anything. Zach couldn't believe how close they had come and he was determined that if he got another chance he would come through for Doug.

The eighth inning was uneventful as both teams went down in order without hitting the ball hard. This had turned into a real pitcher's duel with Doug throwing a perfect game and the Stars's pitcher throwing a four hit shutout. It was a big change from the previous night when the Barons seemed to score at will. Well, that was baseball, feast one day and famine the next.

As Zach stood at his position at the start of the ninth inning he tried to savor the moment. It would be really cool to be part of a no-hitter. Check that, a perfect game. Manny was right, something special was happening and he was excited to be part of it. He took a long look around the stadium and tried to soak it all in. His eyes found their way above the Barons's dugout and he saw Sarah standing there next to her sister.

He had been so wrapped up in the game he had forgotten she was there. He had gotten her a hit, but he had not found a way to get her a ball. What was he thinking about that for? He tried to put the thought out of his head; he needed to concentrate on these last three outs. He didn't want to be the one to ruin a perfect game.

The crowd was on its feet, and he could feel their energy as they tried to help Doug finish off the last three batters. He must have felt it because he quickly struck out the first batter on three straight fastballs. He was really on his game tonight; the Stars never had a chance. The second batter didn't fare much better and struck out on four pitches. Only one more out to go!

When a pitcher was as dominant as Doug was tonight it was easy for the rest of the team to relax because they knew the ball wasn't going to be hit hard. Zach tried to stay alert; he needed to assume the ball was coming his way. If it did, he would do anything to make the play.

Doug got two quick strikes on the batter, and the crowd was going crazy. Only one more strike, and he'd have his perfect game! As Doug went into his windup for the last time, it seemed to Zach like the play was unfolding in slow motion. The batter lifted a soft pop fly toward short right field. This could be trouble! Zach ran to his left and picked up the flight of the ball. It was going to no-man's land, and he ran toward the ball along with the first baseman and right fielder.

Zach could tell he was going to have the best chance to make the catch as he raced toward the foul line. The ball was dropping quickly, and he was going to have to dive. He ran as long as he could and at the last possible minute flung his body forward. He was fully extended and watched as the ball came down toward his glove.

He felt the impact of the ground and the ball in his glove at the same time. He slid on the ground for a few feet and stopped right on the foul line. He had the wind knocked out of him, but he caught the ball! His teammates picked him up, and as they ran back to the dugout the crowd was on its feet cheering. As he approached the dugout, he saw Sarah and with a big smile on his face he tossed her the ball.

The perfect game was saved, but the game wasn't over yet. The Barons still needed to score a run, or the game would continue. His teammates crowded around Zach, congratulating him on his spectacular catch. As they huddled around him, suddenly a voice called out.

"Okay, I did my part. It's not a perfect game yet. You guys need to get me a run!" Doug was standing by the bat rack. "That's right. I said it. Perfect game. I can't do any more than that. Somebody please end this!"

The players in the dugout immediately stopped talking and looked at Doug. Pitchers never talked about no-hitters and here he was saying it out loud. *Well,* Zach thought, *you could say that his part of the game was over so it didn't matter.* Doug was right, it was time for them to score a run and finish the game. "Let's do this for Doug!" Zach yelled.

Joe was due to lead off the inning and he lined the first pitch he saw down the left field line for a double. He stood on second base and pointed into the dugout, he didn't say anything but the message was clear, someone needed to drive him in. The next batter laid down a perfect sacrifice bunt, moving Joe over to third base. All they needed was a long fly ball and the game would be over.

Zach made his way to the on-deck circle and was filled with mixed emotions. It didn't really matter who drove in the winning run but he really wanted to. That would mean the batter before him would have to strike out or pop up. He didn't like rooting against someone on the team but Doug was his friend and he wanted to end the game for him.

It looked like he was going to get his chance because Jessie Daniels, their third baseman, popped out to the shortstop. It would be up to him to win the game or force Doug to try and go one more inning. As he stepped up to the plate he looked out at the pitcher, he wasn't coming out of the game, it was his to win or lose. The last time up he started him with a fastball and he almost hit it out, so he was due to go back to the breaking ball again. If he did, Zach would be ready for it.

The crowd was on their feet, and he could feel the weight of their expectations on his shoulders. The perfect game was great, but what did it really mean if they didn't score and had to go extra innings? He stepped up the plate, determined to end it on the first pitch. The pitcher went into his windup, and just as he expected it was a breaking ball. This time Zach was ready; he waited until the last possible minute and stroked the ball over the second baseman's head into right field!

He felt like he was flying as he made his way to first base. He tossed his helmet into the air as he rounded the bag and as he turned to the dugout he saw the entire team running toward him. Doug was leading the way, and they jumped into each other's arms and screamed at the top of their lungs. The rest of the team soon joined them and they ended up in a pile on the ground in the middle of the infield. A walk-off hit to win a perfect game, how could it get any better than that!

CHAPTER 10

Doug and Zach were in high demand after the game. Apparently once the perfect game got to the eighth inning the local news had begun to give updates and had even shown the ninth inning live. Doug and Zach were interviewed by the local sports guy, Chip Sanders, right after the game ended. Zach had seen him around the stadium before, but he had never given him the time of day. Now, it was like he had a new best friend.

It was funny how things could change so quickly. Usually Chip focused on the up and coming stars and left the mid-level prospects like Zach alone. He had already done a feature story on Doug, and now that he had a perfect game under his belt he was sure to get even more attention.

The interview started off as it should with the attention on Doug. "When did you know you had a perfect game?" Chip asked.

"Only after Zach drove in the winning run. Up until that point we were still tied at zero. I'm just happy we scored so I didn't have to go back out there again."

"Did you feel like you had your best stuff tonight?"

"I felt pretty good from the very start of the game. Manny and I were on the same page. I never had to shake him off once during the entire game. He deserves as much credit for the game as I do."

"Did you know this was the first perfect game in Barons' history?" Chip asked, still focusing on Doug.

"No. I hadn't thought about it much. You know the guy you should be talking to is Zach. If it weren't for him that pop fly in the ninth would have dropped in for a hit, and if he didn't drive in the winning run we would still be playing." Doug reached over and put his arm around Zach. He was really trying to spread the credit around, but Chip was having no part of it.

"I have to tell you," Chip said. "This was the most exciting game I have ever seen. Do you think it will help you get a call-up from the White Sox?"

"I'm not thinking about that right now. I just want to get back to the locker room and celebrate with my teammates." Doug then turned to Zach and gave him a big hug and then started to walk away.

Before Doug had the chance to get too far, Zach caught a glimpse of movement from behind him. Manny had a bucket of Gatorade and was coming up fast. As he raised the bucket up over his head, Doug grabbed Zach and pulled him to the ground. Manny was unable to stop his forward motion, and instead of pouring the contents of the bucket on Doug and Zach he hit Chip square in the face.

Getting hit with a bucket of icy cold Gatorade was bad enough, but to have it happen on live TV was too much for Chip. He could have laughed it off but instead he turned toward Manny and started yelling at him. Manny turned to Doug and Zach and started laughing. Soon the three of them were standing together laughing hysterically as Chip tried to regain his composure.

He stammered for a few seconds but was able to sign off and send the broadcast back to the studio. When he finished, he turned to the three of them and tried to say something, but he was so mad it just came out as a stream of gibberish. He then turned to his cameraman for comfort, but once he had signed off he had started to laugh as well. Soaked to the skin and embarrassed, Chip stormed off.

"Fantastic game, guys," the cameraman said to them as he packed away his gear. "I'm going to save a copy of the game and that interview. Honestly, I don't know which was better. I've wanted to dump a bucket on Chip's head for years."

"Can you get us a copy too?" Doug asked.

"You bet," he replied and left them to follow Chip.

"Too bad you missed us," Zach said to Manny.

"Who said I was aiming for you?" he replied. "Didn't you see Doug make eye contact with me?"

"You were trying to hit Chip?"

"Of course not. I would never try to embarrass someone on live TV," Manny said with a wink.

"Look. If he had just been fair and talked to both of us, it never would have happened. You were as big a story as I was tonight. He was being a jerk and got what he deserved." Doug looked like he was starting to tear up. "This was a team effort. You guys were a bigger part of this game than me."

"Please. You were the one on mound," Zach said.

"Yes. But Manny called all the right pitches, and you saved the game with that catch and then won the game with that hit."

"I guess there's enough credit to go around," Zach said. "Let's get back inside and go celebrate. Dinner's on me!"

"Don't forget. You already have plans tonight," Manny reminded Zach. "Or did you forget that pretty young lady you flipped that ball to earlier?"

"Oh my God. I totally forgot. She's probably waiting for us."

"Don't worry about it. Take a look over by the dugout."

Zach turned and looked back toward the Barons' dugout, and sure enough, Sarah was standing there with her sister. She had big smile on her face and looked as cute as she had earlier in the day when he met her at the laundromat. She waved at him, and he smiled and made his way over to where she was standing.

"You sure know how to impress a girl, don't you?" she said.

"I didn't do too much. Doug pitched the game of his life." He was trying to be modest, but he knew that his plays were what people would remember. "You haven't introduced me to your friend."

"You're right. Zach, this is my sister, Amy. Amy, this is Zach."

"Hi, Amy, it's nice to meet you," Zach said, smiling at her.

"Hi," Amy said. "You played a great game today."

Zach could see that she held the ball he had tossed to Sarah in her hand. She was also wearing a Barons's jersey and had a baseball glove on her other hand. "You've got a great souvenir there. Be sure to hang on to it."

"Could I have your autograph?" she asked.

"You want my autograph?" Zach asked, a little surprised. "I think the guy you want to autograph your ball is Doug. He pitched the perfect game."

"Yeah, but you saved it."

Zach looked at Sarah, who was smiling but looked a little embarrassed. "I think we have another fan in the family, huh?"

"I told you. My parents have season tickets. She has been coming to games her whole life." Sarah shrugged. "I guess it runs in the family."

Zach turned to Amy. "Tell you what, how about I sign your ball and I get Doug to sign it too?"

"That would be awesome!" Amy said, smiling from ear to ear.

"Okay. Toss me that ball, and I'll be right back."

Zach took the ball and walked over to Doug, who was still on the field talking to a local newspaper reporter. After a brief explanation, he signed the ball, and Zach walked back over to Sarah and Amy. He signed his name as well and tossed it back to her. "There you go. You have a piece of Barons' history. Be sure to keep it in a safe place."

"I sure will."

"I think we may be a little while. Are you still okay for dinner?" he asked Sarah.

"Actually, I think I'm going to have to take a rain check. I really should be getting Amy home. I was going to take my other sister to the game tonight and she could have stayed out later, but Amy really wanted to go."

"I understand. I'll call you tomorrow and maybe we can set something up. We're going out on the road on Monday, so it may have to wait until we get back." Zach was disappointed, but he didn't want it to look like he was desperate.

"Okay. I'm really sorry." Sarah looked down at her sister, who was intently studying the signatures on the ball and shrugged mouthing, "She really wanted to come."

"It's okay." Zach mouthed back then said out loud, "I'll call you after the game tomorrow."

"You better," Sarah said, smiling.

"I will," Zach replied, then said to Amy, "It was nice meeting you."

"It was nice meeting you too."

"You better get going," Sarah said. "I'm sure there are a bunch of people that will want to talk to you tonight."

"I don't know about that," Zach said, but he could see the team's public relations director giving him the eye.

"You're a big story tonight. Go out and enjoy it. I'll talk to you tomorrow."

"Okay." He stood for a minute and watched her walk up the aisle. *Maybe there is something there,* he thought to himself. He would make it a point to call her and try to set up a time to meet. It was too bad they were going out on the road Monday. He didn't want to wait too long before they had a chance to meet up again. She was a very pretty girl and probably had guys ask her out all the time.

He didn't have much time to think about it because the PR director was tugging on his sleeve and wanted him to join Doug and talk to the newspaper reporters. This wasn't his favorite part of the job, but he knew that it helped the team and it would also get his name out there and that couldn't hurt. He sighed and gave in. It looked like his regular post game routine was going to be interrupted again.

By the time Zach finished all of the interviews, it was well past midnight, and he was ready to head home for the night. He had loaned Manny the Purple Beast so he wouldn't have to hang around, so now he had to wait for Doug to finish so he could grab a ride home. A few minutes later Doug finished up his last interview with a radio station out in Los Angeles, and he came over and sat down next to Zach.

"If I had known there would be this much involved, I would have given up a couple of hits."

"If I would have known, I would have let that ball drop," Zach said, smiling.

"That was quite a game wasn't it? Someone told me there had never been a perfect game that ended on a walk-off hit before. We are going to be linked for life."

"It will be nice to be remembered for something," Zach said, leaning back in his chair. "I'm really happy for you. This should catch the eyes of the Sox and help you get a call-up."

"That would be nice. I think it will help you too. All the highlights are of you. That catch would have been enough, but to get the final hit was the icing on the cake."

"We'll see," Zach said.

"I'm sure it made a good impression on your date too. That was who the ball was for right?"

"Oh my God. I should have kept that ball for you. That was the last out of your perfect game." He felt really bad. Maybe he could get the ball back from Sarah. They could probably swap it out for another ball and her sister would never know.

"No it wasn't," Doug said pulling a ball out of his pocket. "This is."

"No. I tossed the ball into the stands on my way into the dugout."

"This is the ball that won the game. It's the ball you hit to drive in Joe with the winning run. I want you to have it. This is the one that counts." He tossed the ball to Zach. "Read it."

Zach caught the ball and turned it over. Under Doug's signature it said, "Perfect Game 5/12/12. Saved and won by Zach Fredrickson." He had to admit, he was a little touched by the gesture. After all, there weren't many no-hitters much less perfect games and this must have meant a lot to Doug. "Thanks, Doug," Zach said. "I don't know what to say."

"You don't have to say anything. I just want to let you know that I really appreciate your effort out there. Not just today, but all the time. I think the game needs more guys like you around. I'm sure you'll make it to the big leagues some day."

"I hope so. I know that you will, and I'm glad that I had the chance to make a little history with you tonight, even if it is double A." Zach stood up and yawned. "What do you say we get out of here? We've got an early game tomorrow."

"Sounds good. It's a little late to make something to eat at home. Want to hit a drive through?" Doug picked up his bag and started walking toward the door.

"How about Taco Bell? The drive-thru is open until two a.m." Zach knew Doug was not a fan but there wasn't much else open so late.

"Okay. Just this one time. I don't want to make this a habit."

"That's what Manny said the first time he had it and look what happened to him."

"That's what I'm afraid of," Doug said as they walked through the empty parking lot.

They got into Doug's car and made the short drive to Taco Bell and then home. On the way, Zach checked his phone and saw that he had forty-two text messages. Obviously, the perfect game had made news, and everyone he knew was texting their congratulations. He scanned a few of the texts and promised himself that he would respond to all of them tomorrow.

He also noticed a number of missed calls including one from his mother and his agent. He wasn't surprised about his mom. She called all the time, but he didn't hear from his agent very often.

He usually checked in about once a month unless something was going on. He must have heard about the game and wanted to congratulate him too. He would call him in the morning. It was too late now.

Manny and Joe had already gone to bed by the time that they got home. The game had taken a lot out of everyone, and Zach actually felt like he would get some sleep for a change. Usually he was too pumped up to sleep and he thought today would have been worse because of all the excitement but he felt drained. Doug must have felt the same way because he said he was going to take his food to his room and go straight to bed.

Zach had eaten his food on the drive home, so he made his way into his room and quickly got changed and crawled into bed. As soon as his head hit the pillow he could feel himself relaxing and he started to drift off to sleep. This was the point where he would start to relive the game and think about all the things he had done wrong and what he could do to correct them. Tonight, none of those thoughts were running around in his head. Instead, they were replaced by something new. All he could think about was Sarah and the next time he would see her. For the first time in a long time, he fell into a deep restful sleep.

He awoke feeling refreshed and ready to start a new day. As usual, Manny was already up and about, and he could hear the guys talking in the next room. He got up, got dressed, and made his way out to the living room.

"Hey, look who's up early today!" Manny said as he walked into the room. "And dressed already too. Is everything okay?"

"Everything is great," Zach replied as he sat down on the couch. "Have you guys had breakfast already?"

"Today is a special day," said Joe. "Thanks to the perfect game you all played a role in yesterday, breakfast was delivered earlier this morning, compliments of the Waffle House."

"What?" Zach asked.

"Complimentary breakfast, that's what, and not just doughnuts and coffee. We have a full spread in the kitchen."

"I'm not complaining, but why would they do that?" Zach asked.

"You guys are famous. That's why," Manny said with a mouthful of waffles. "You have been all over ESPN today."

Zach turned to Doug. "Is he serious?"

"Yup," Doug said. "I guess a walk-off perfect game is really rare. They haven't been able to find a record of one before. They have been running your catch and hit all morning. You were the Play of the Day"

"No way!" If they were telling the truth, that would be awesome. Zach had always dreamed of being on ESPN. As a big leaguer of course, but this was good too.

"Way," Joe said.

"In fact, we need to get to the field early today because they want to do an interview for Sports Center," Doug said with a frown. "I really hate interviews, so I'm going make you do most of the talking."

"Why would they want to talk to me?"

"Come on, man, your plays made that game. When have you ever seen a minor league game spotlighted on ESPN?" Doug said. "You're a star."

"I wouldn't go that far. Guys make good plays and get walk-off hits every day."

"Not in a perfect game," Manny said. "You should see that catch, it was spectacular. Here, take a look. We recorded it."

Manny set up the TV, and they weren't kidding. There he was on ESPN. First, they showed the catch and then the walk-off hit. Zach had to admit, it looked pretty good on TV. They even showed their interview after the game with Chip Sanders including Manny hitting Chip with the Gatorade shower. Even though they had all seen it live, they all laughed again when they saw it on TV.

"That was awesome!" Zach said when the clip was over.

"Yes it was," Joe said. "You guys are stars, and in Birmingham apparently that means free waffles."

"And more interviews," Doug chipped in. "So you better hurry up and eat. They want us at the park by ten a.m."

"What time is it?" Zach asked. Normally, he didn't wake up until well after 10:00, but it was a day game today.

"Quarter after nine, so you better get going."

"Okay," Zach said and made his way into the kitchen. They weren't kidding. There was a ton of food. He made himself a plate of eggs, bacon, and waffles and polished off the entire plate in just a few minutes. Once he was done, he made a quick stop in his room to pick up his stuff and left with Doug to go to the field.

When they got to the field, they were immediately attacked by the team PR director, who wanted to know where they had been and why they were late. Apparently they had spent the early morning setting up the live feed for the interview, and they were going to do another series of "live" interviews starting at 10:30 that would take them right up to noon, when they needed to get ready for the game.

All of the interviews were remote, some on camera with the Barons' field as a backdrop while others were with radio outlets. The questions were generally the same, and even though it was Doug that pitched the game, most of the questions were addressed to Zach. It was quite a difference from the night before, and Doug didn't seem to mind not being the center of attention.

Zach described his key contributions to the game, now referred to as "the catch" and "the hit". He had a chance to see both again on a TV monitor, and he had to admit the catch he made to save the perfect game was pretty spectacular. They had a great camera angle that showed him racing at full speed toward the foul line and at the last minute throwing his body forward. He was completely horizontal when he caught the ball right off the top of the grass. The first baseman and right fielder almost collided, and it looked like some type of strange dance as their bodies flew everywhere.

The hit was just a good piece of hitting. He waited for the ball and just reached out and stroked it over the second baseman's head. Joe raced home with the winning run. He was a forgotten part of the storyline, and the team ended up in a pile in the middle of the infield. It was an unbelievable game and apparently the first time that a perfect game had ended in a walk-off hit.

The interviews ran right until noon, and Zach had to rush to grab a quick bite to eat before he had to get out to the field. He missed batting practice and was only able to spend a short amount of time warming up before the Barons had to give the field back to the Huntsville Stars. This was going to be the first time he hadn't followed his traditional pre-game ritual, and he was a little nervous about how he would do in the game.

"How did your interviews go?" Manny asked as they sat in the dugout waiting for the game to start.

"Pretty good I think. I mean, I hope I sounded okay. They all asked the same questions, so I felt like I was repeating myself."

"I'm sure you were fine. It's been crazy around here since last night. I've never seen so many people walking around asking questions. A few even wanted to talk to me."

"Well, you were the catcher last night. You had the best view of the game. You know you basically 'called your shot', you said something special was going to happen," Zach said with a smile.

"I was actually thinking about your new girlfriend when I said that," Manny replied. "I know you cancelled dinner, but did you ever talk to her last night?"

"Just for a few minutes. I had Doug sign her sister's ball. We were going to try and get together later tonight." Zach made a mental note to call or text her after the game.

"Don't wait too long. You made a good first impression with the game last night, but that will only last for so long." Manny made his way to the top step of the dugout. "Women don't like to be left waiting."

Zach joined him at the railing. "I won't. We're lucky it's an early game today so I can pack for the road trip and give her a call."

It was game time, and the PA announcer was calling them out to the field. "Have a good game," Zach called to Manny as they ran out of the dugout.

"You too. Be sure to wait for me today. I don't like driving that car of yours. It makes me nervous."

"I find that hard to believe," Zach replied as he ran out to second base. "That car is a classic!"

Manny just shook his head. "It's a death trap!"

Zach had to laugh. It was true. The Purple Beast had seen better days. Someday he could get a better car when he made it to the big leagues. Maybe the game last night would be a turning point for him. He had received a lot of publicity, even appeared on Sports Center. The White Sox had to know who he was now. Maybe he could even get a September call-up this year. If that was going to happen, he would have to continue to produce, so he would have to work even harder.

Just like the night before, this game was very different from the previous game. With baseball you never knew what was going to happen. The Stars scored three runs in the first inning and apparently were going to be a tougher opponent tonight. The Barons scored two runs early, and the game went back and forth with the lead changing several times.

Zach followed up his heroics from the previous night by going three for four with two more RBIs. He was standing on second base with the Barons down by a run in the bottom of the ninth inning when Manny came to the plate. He was hitless again, and Zach really hoped he could break out now and tie up the game with a hit.

As he watched the pitcher, he realized he could see the grip on the ball when he went into the stretch position. He watched the first two pitches and thought he could tell when he was going to throw a breaking ball. As he took his lead, he tried to get Manny's attention. The team had a set series of signs in case they felt they could pick up the pitch type or location, and Zach crossed his hands over chest to try to tell Manny a breaking pitch was coming.

Sure enough, the pitcher tried to throw a breaking pitch in the dirt, but it hung right over the plate. Manny waited and pulled his hands through the hitting zone. Zach could tell the minute Manny hit the ball that it was going out for a home run. He jumped and clapped his hands as he rounded the bases finally jumping on home plate amidst a circle of screaming teammates.

Manny made his way around the bases, trying not to smile to show up the pitcher, but he broke into a wide grin as he came around third base. He tossed his helmet into the air and disappeared into the circle where the team proceeded to surround him and they jumped up and down in joy, playfully beating him up. Two days, two walk-offs, what a great way to end the homestand!

CHAPTER 11

Since Manny had won the game with a walk-off home run, it was only natural that he would be the guest on the post game show. As chance would have it, Chip Sanders would be conducting the interview. It was sure to be an awkward moment since Manny had dumped Gatorade on Chip the night before.

Say what you want about Chip, but the man was a professional and he knew that it was his job to conduct the interview. As he stood on the third base line talking to Manny, Doug and Zach made their way to the dugout to grab the large jug of Gatorade from the bench. They knew that it was wrong, but they just couldn't help themselves.

So, just as Chip was finishing up the interview, Doug quietly walked into Manny's line of sight and gave him a wink. Manny smiled and nodded his head in acknowledgement.

Zach stood off to the side behind Manny, and once Doug gave him a wave he made his move. He ran toward Manny with the jug, and just as he was ready to toss it on him, Manny ducked. Chip had seen Zach coming, but he was not able to react in time and the Gatorade hit him square in the chest.

Just like the night before, he was able to finish up the interview and send it back to the guys upstairs, but he was furious. He had been humiliated on live TV the night before and now the same thing happened on the radio show. He ripped into both Zach and Manny and then stormed off the field. The tech guy was left laughing just like the cameraman the night before, and he high fived all three players as he packed up his equipment and followed Chip.

The locker-room was buzzing with excitement when they finally got in from the field. Tom had gathered the team together and was waiting for Zach, Manny, and Doug to return before he addressed them. He didn't have many meetings, but when he did they usually carried a message so the players stopped what they were doing when he cleared his throat to get their attention.

"Gentlemen," he said, "first, I want to congratulate you on a successful homestand. I've been around this game a long time and I have to say these past two games have been among the most exciting I have ever been involved in."

Coming from Tom, who had been a big leaguer for a long time and had played in countless important games, Zach knew that was a big compliment. The rest of the team knew it too, and they let out a cheer that rocked the room. Tom waited for them to settle down and continued without missing a beat.

"But you need to remember that these are only two games and this is a long season. Part of being a big leaguer is understanding that this game has ups and downs. While we are on a high right now we could easily go on a losing streak. The thing to remember is that each game is unique and we start them all at zero, zero."

Zach could feel a lesson coming on, and Tom didn't disappoint. He spent the next ten minutes talking about how they needed to be consistent and how it was easy to get wrapped up in a moment and lose sight of the big picture. His goal was to prepare them for the big leagues and while it was great to win games they needed to focus on developing their skills. He pointed out three or four mental errors from that night's game, including one for Zach.

Zach hated to admit it, but in the excitement of the moment he had forgotten the play. He was sure that he would have remembered it later that evening when he replayed the game in his head, but he was embarrassed that it had happened. It wasn't much. He had failed to get in the correct position on a throw from the outfield. It was a slow runner, and he didn't end up advancing but the point was that he was out of position and it could have cost them a run.

Tom was still going, and Zach had to bring himself back and pay attention or he would miss something. He looked over at Joe and Doug and could see that they didn't look too happy. As he scanned the rest of the room he could see the other new players didn't look happy either. Manny was sitting next to him and gave him a poke. *Oh*, Zach thought, *he must be talking about the upcoming road trip.*

Before the first road trip of the season, Tom always laid out the rules. To Zach, they were no big deal, but for some guys they seemed very restrictive. Basically, it boiled down to three things. First, be on time. That meant you could not be late for the team bus to and from the field each day or on get-a-way day.

Second, everyone had to be in his room by midnight. This was a problem for some guys as they were night owls and liked to stay out late after games. They didn't know it then but Tom would loosen this rule up as the season went on, but for now it was midnight or you were fined.

Third, don't do anything to embarrass yourself or the team. This usually went right along with rule number two. Several times over the past two years guys had gone out after games and gotten into trouble at a local bar or club. The last thing Tom wanted to do was to go pick up some player in the middle of the night and he made it clear that he would not bail anyone out if they got into trouble.

Tom finished up his talk and let them know that the bus was leaving at 8:00 a.m. the next morning for Chattanooga. The early time was not popular with the team. They would rather have made the four-hour bus ride that night so they could have the morning free to get settled in, but leaving in the morning saved the team a night's hotel expense. As it was, they would play the next five games against the Lookouts, a long series for a big league team, but standard for a double A club.

Tom had one last comment before he let the team go. "I want to see Zach, Manny, and Doug in my office. The rest of you can head out. I'll see you at 8:00 a.m. sharp tomorrow."

Uh oh, Zach thought, *this can't be good*. He looked at Manny and could see that he was thinking the same thing. Tom probably wasn't happy about Chip's Gatorade shower, and he was going to let them have it. Well, it was best to get it over with now rather than let it linger.

It was a tight fit, and they had to literally sit shoulder to shoulder on three chairs in front of Tom's desk. Tom looked at them for a minute before he finally spoke. "I assume that you know why you are here."

Zach considered saying something to lighten the mood but thought better of it and just nodded his head. Doug and Manny did the same and they sat in silence until Tom spoke again.

"You do realize that if you are going to make it in this game you will have to deal with the media, and not everyone is going to be nice. You can't go around dumping Gatorade on every reporter you don't like."

"It was an accident," Manny said.

"Really?" Tom replied. "Which one, yesterday or today."

"Both," Doug said.

"Is that what you expect me to tell Chip? He's really mad and has been making a stink about it with management. The club depends on positive coverage from the media. If they don't like us, they won't talk about us on the radio or in the paper. Playing ball is only half the battle. This club needs revenue to stay afloat, and the media is a necessary evil."

"We didn't mean to cause any problems, Tom. We just thought it was funny."

"I know Chip can be a jerk, but he is a professional. You just can't embarrass him like that."

"To be honest, he had it coming," Doug said. "I haven't been around long, but I can see the way he treats the players. He ignores you until he needs something then expects you to make time for a quote."

"That may be true, but you need to learn how to deal with it. Maybe somewhere down the road when you make it to the big leagues you can do things differently, but a friend in the media when you are starting out is a good thing to have."

"Understood," Doug said. "It won't happen again."

"What about you two?" Tom asked Zach and Manny.

"I get it," Zach said.

"Me too," Manny added.

"Good. Remember, keep your noses clean, especially now. You three are on a short leash. Next time, it will be a fine, and you'll sit a few games. Now get out of here and get ready for the trip." Tom turned to the stack of papers on his desk.

"That wasn't so bad," Doug said when they got back to their lockers.

"It could have been much worse," Zach said. "He means it when he says he will fine you or sit you for breaking team rules. He has even released a couple of guys the last few years over things less than this."

"Really? It was just a joke. I'm sure he did things like this before."

"Probably, but he's not a player anymore. He has to deal with the media all the time, and I'm sure he heard an earful." Tom had let them off easy, but Zach didn't like being put in that position. He would be much more careful from now on.

"Zach's right," Manny said. "We probably could have gotten away with it once, but the second time was too much. I'm not going to lose my career for a joke."

"I think you guys are making way too much out of this," Doug said. "If he was really upset he wouldn't have let us off with a warning. Management told him he had to do something and now he can tell them he talked to us. No big deal."

"I hope you're right," Zach said.

"Trust me. I am." Doug stood up and started to walk away. "I'm going to hit the showers; then I'm outta here. See you guys at home."

"Do you think he's right?" Manny asked Zach when Doug was gone.

"I hope so," Zach said. "But there is nothing we can do about it now. Let's take a look at today's video and get out of here."

They spent the next thirty minutes reviewing their at-bats. Manny had to replay his game winning home run at least ten times before he let Zach put the iPad away. After they were done, they hit the showers, packed up their things and got ready to head home. They both needed to finish packing and it would be 8:00 a.m. before they knew it. After today's talk, they could not afford to be late for the bus.

"Taco Bell?" Manny asked with a hopeful smile.

"Why not?" Zach answered. "It's not every day you have a walk-off hit."

"That's a walk-off home run, thank you very much. You had a walk-off hit yesterday. I like to end games in style, not with some bloop single."

"Really? You think your hit was better than mine? Mine won a perfect game."

"Whatever. I had style. You know everybody loves the long ball." Manny got into his batting stance and took a swing, admiring the flight of an imaginary ball as it cleared the fence. "Style. That's what it's all about. That hit is going to get me started on a hot streak. I can feel it."

"I hope you're right," Zach said. He decided to let Manny enjoy his big night. "Let's get going. I need to pack, and I want to try to call Sarah."

"Look at you," Manny said with a smile as they walked out the door. "I didn't think you had it in you."

"That makes two of us. I didn't think you had that home run in you. Usually your hits land on the warning track."

"Not anymore. I'm going to harness the power of the Chalupa and hit a few more on this trip."

"Okay, big guy. We'll see," Zach said. They made their way across the parking lot to the Purple Beast, hit Taco Bell and made their way home.

Zach spent the rest of the evening finishing up packing for the trip. When he first started out, traveling was one of his favorite parts of being a ballplayer. He had never gone anywhere as a kid, so it was exciting to see different parts of the country. Most guys hated the four- or five-hour bus trips, but Zach loved it. He would stare out the window and imagine what it would be like to live in the places he was visiting.

Now a couple of years into his career his opinion had changed a little, and the trips were more of an inconvenience than anything. He had to make sure he had enough clothes for the trip and even had to find places to do laundry if it was a particularly long one. Most were four or five days, but they usually had a couple that lasted for more than a week and those were tough.

It was one thing to share a room with someone in a house. You always had someplace to go to get a little privacy. When you were with someone on the road you were stuck in the same room with them for most of the trip. That is why most of the guys were upset about a curfew. They just needed time alone. Sure you could go sit in the hotel lobby or a restaurant, but it wasn't the same as sitting in your living room at home.

Zach and Manny had been roommates on and off the road for two years now, so they had settled into a routine. Joe and Doug had already commented on how they acted like an old married couple, and it was true. They knew each other very well. Zach had never had a brother and was pretty closed off most of his life, but Manny and life as a ballplayer in general had made him come out of his shell.

He could joke around with Manny and talk to him about anything. He had turned into a very good friend, and Zach knew that he could count on him if he needed something. Zach had travelled to visit Manny in the Dominican Republic over the winter and met his wife and kids. They made a great couple, and he could see how much they loved each other. It had to be really hard to be separated for six months of the year,but they made it work somehow. Manny always said that once he made it to the big leagues all the time apart would be worth it.

Manny was always organized and ready to go days before a trip. Zach tended to procrastinate, so he had to finish up packing in the near darkness of their room because Manny had already turned in for the night. It didn't help that he was on the phone with Sarah earlier for a couple of hours. That had really set him back. It was worth it though. He really enjoyed talking to her and was looking forward to coming back home and seeing her in person.

He finished packing and put his things by the door in the living room and went to bed. As usual, Manny was already asleep, and Zach tossed and turned for a while. He replayed the night's game in his head, and other than the missed cutoff he tried to stay focused on the positive. Funny thing was, he wasn't obsessing about every little thing tonight. In fact, he found his mind drifting back to his conversation with Sarah. If he was thinking about her this much already imagine how it would be when he really got to know her.

It had been an exciting couple of days, and he knew that he had to get up early in the morning so he tried to will himself to sleep. It was turning out to be a good year after all, now that he was hitting he couldn't wait to see how the road trip went. He was also excited about his potential new relationship with Sarah. It was too soon to make much of it, but he had a good feeling. Just thinking about it made him relax, and he quickly fell asleep.

The buzzing of the alarm clock woke Zach from a dead sleep and it took him a minute to realize where he was. The only time he used an alarm clock was on travel days so it always startled him. Manny was already up and about so he quickly made his way to the shower got dressed and headed to the living room.

"Ready to go?" Manny asked.

"Sure. Let me grab something to eat real quick. Where are Joe and Doug?"

"Gone already. They were worried about missing the bus," Manny said with a smile. "Rookies."

"Well, we better not be late either. I'll grab some toast, and we can go," Zach said as he dropped some bread into the toaster.

"Don't worry. I've got the snack bag packed in case you get hungry." Manny held up a small cooler. "You know we won't stop until we get to Chattanooga."

"I can always count on you to have stockpile of food," Zach said with a smile.

"I've been stuck on buses too many times to not be prepared. I remember a bus breaking down once and sitting around with nothing to eat for eight hours. That won't happen to me again."

"Hopefully it will be an uneventful trip today." Zach grabbed his toast and headed toward the door.

"Right behind you," Many said as he followed him out the door.

It was only 7:45 a.m. when they got to the stadium, but they were the last ones to arrive. Apparently Tom's message got through to everyone, and they were afraid to miss the bus and be left behind. Zach and Manny always sat in the back row, and when they found a couple of new guys in their seats, they pulled rank and made them move. Even in the minor leagues there was a pecking order, and Zach and Manny were considered the top of the food chain since they had been around for a while.

Even though Tom had said they needed to be there by 8:00 a.m. the bus didn't leave until after 9:00 a.m. since it took a while for the equipment managers to load all of their gear on the bus. This didn't sit well with a few of the players as they weren't happy to get up early for no reason. Zach and Manny knew the drill, so they weren't surprised. Tom just wanted to make sure everyone was on time and he had to tell them to be there early to eliminate any stragglers. Soon enough, the bus was packed and they started on the four-hour drive to Chattanooga.

Zach had seen bus trips depicted on a bunch of different movies over the years including *Bull Durham* and *A League of Their Own*. Those movies made is seem like the bus ride was a party where the players talked, sang, and played cards. In fact, once the bus got going most of the guys plugged in their iPads, iPods, or other games and just zoned out. It was actually a pretty quiet trip, and Zach spent the time catching up on e-mails.

About an hour or so into the drive, there was a loud bang and the bus slowed and made its way to the shoulder of the highway. They had a flat tire, and it ended up taking over an hour to get it changed. This made the players even grumpier, and since many hadn't taken the time to eat a big breakfast they were now hungry. Fortunately for them, Zach and Manny had the snack bag, and pretty soon they had a line of guys looking for a handout.

They shared what they had, which wasn't much, and that helped to lighten the mood a little bit. After a short time they were on their way and made it to the field without any further incidents. They had time to grab a quick bite to eat and drop off their things at the hotel, and then it was time to go to the field for that night's game.

The routine on the road was pretty much the same as when they were home except as the road team they took the field after the Lookouts completed their warm-ups. That meant there was a shorter amount of time before the game started, and Zach always felt a little bit rushed. It usually took him a day or two to get adjusted, and he usually struggled the first game of a trip. Since he was riding a hot streak, he hoped today would be different.

Maybe it was the long drive and the change in scenery or just the natural letdown from back-to-back exciting games, but the Barons came out flat and were never in contention. Both Zach and Manny went hitless, and the team could only manage five hits and a single run. The final score was 7–1 in favor of the Lookouts. The only good news was that they could go back to the hotel, get some rest, and try to make the most out of the next four games.

The next few days felt basically the same, get up in the morning and try to find something to eat. Zach tried to stay busy by going to the movies or hanging out around the hotel during the day. Then he tried to find something to eat for lunch and then would make his way over to the field for the game. Play the game and then find something to eat and back to the hotel. Some days it seemed like all they did was think about their next meal. It was easy to get bored and the games were the only thing that kept Zach sane.

Well, usually it was the games that kept him sane, but now he had something else to keep him occupied in his down time. He spent most of it either texting or talking to Sarah on the phone. It was a little awkward at first. He wasn't familiar with her schedule, so he didn't know the best time to get in contact with her. After a few days of trial and error, they had established a regular routine. She would text him in the morning before she went to school, and he would call her before every game.

He would have loved to see her in person but that would have to wait until he got back home. Their time on the phone together helped Zach get to know her and he probably shared more with her than he would have if he had been sitting with her face to face. She had a way of making him feel safe and comfortable, and he even found that he could sleep better at night.

While things with Sarah were going well, the trip turned out to be a disaster as the Barons lost four of the five games. The only bright spots were another shutout by Doug and Manny's hot hitting. He had two home runs in the three games that he started, including a massive three-run shot in Doug's win. Zach played in four of the five games but only managed three hits and a walk. It was not a terrible performance, but he was hoping for something a little more. He would have to take a look at the video from the trip when they got home and see if he had fallen back into his old habits again.

Rather than spend the night in the hotel after the last game, they had to take the bus home right when it ended. It made for a very long day, especially after they lost, but that was business as usual for a minor league team. By the time they got back to the stadium and made their way home, it was after 4:00 a.m.

The people who made the schedule must have had a sick sense of humor because they had a game scheduled for that night. Zach was so tired when he got home that he didn't even bother to change and spent the night sleeping in his clothes. He was happy the trip was over and was looking forward to a week at home, getting back to his routine, and seeing Sarah.

CHAPTER 12

For one of the first times that Zach could remember, he woke up before Manny. In fact, he woke up before Joe and Doug too. It had been a long day, make that night, for all of them, and it was hard to believe that they had another game later that night. That was the thing about baseball. There was always another game. They didn't have to wait a week to play again like in football. If a football player had a bad game, he had to wait and think about it for days before he had a chance to redeem himself.

As it was, this was going to be a very quick turnaround today. It was already past noon, and the guys didn't seem like they would be up any time soon. He made his way to the kitchen to look for something to eat only to realize that since they had been gone for the past five days, there wasn't much around. Along with laundry, shopping for food fell to the bottom of the list of things to do. He was lucky to find a couple of eggs and bread and made himself a late breakfast.

Maybe it was the smell of food cooking, but it wasn't long before first Manny, then Joe and Doug made their way into the kitchen. They all were able to find something to eat, but the pickings were getting pretty slim and it was obvious that someone was going to have to go to the store. Either that or it was a couple of days of fast food or whatever happened to be served after the game.

"So who feels like going shopping today?" Zach asked.

"I can do it," Doug volunteered. "I don't have to pitch for a couple of days, so I have a little more time than you guys."

"Pitchers," Joe scoffed. "You guys have it so easy, only having to play every five days."

"I spend a lot of time prepping for my starts. Just because I don't play every day it doesn't mean I don't work every day."

"I'm just saying, it would be nice to come back from a road trip and be able to sit in the dugout all night and rest."

"You have no clue. I'm just as tired as you are. It was a long night for all of us."

"Exactly. And you don't have to play today." Joe just wouldn't let go. "In the majors they'll send the starting pitcher ahead sometimes so that they can rest."

"Look. I offered to help out by shopping for all of us. You can starve for all I care." Doug was trying not to get mad, but Joe had a way of pushing all of their buttons.

"No," Manny interjected. "We would all appreciate it if you would pick up some stuff for the week. Don't you think, Zach?"

"Absolutely. I think it was a very generous offer." He turned to Joe and gave him a look. "Isn't that right, Joe?"

"Okay. Okay. Maybe I'm a little grumpy." He put on his best fake smile. "Thank you for the offer, Doug."

"Not the most sincere response I've ever heard, but I guess that will have to be enough." He pulled out a piece of paper and a pen. "What do you guys want?"

They spent the next twenty minutes talking about how they wanted to restock the pantry. Joe and Doug tended to want healthier things like fresh fruits and vegetables while Zach and Manny opted for prepackaged things that were quick and easy to make. They each chipped in some money, and Doug excused himself to go get dressed so he could head to the store before the game.

Once he left the room, Zach turned to Joe. "Why did you have to start up about pitchers not working hard?"

"What? Oh, you know you feel the same way. Most pitchers are primadonnas. They think the world revolves around them.

You know they don't work as hard as we do, but they get paid the same, or better. Doug's a nice guy, but he's still a pitcher."

Manny was quick to come to Doug's defense. "Come on. I work with the pitchers every day. They may not play, but they are always preparing. It's more of a mental game for them sometimes."

"Exactly my point. For a position player it's a mental and a physical game. I'm dead tired today, and I've still got to play. Except for the guy starting tonight, they all have the day off."

"What about relief pitchers?" Zach asked. "They can play every day."

"They are just as bad." Joe laughed. "They pitch an inning or two, and they are done. I wish I could go back in time and make myself a left-handed pitcher. Those guys can play forever and only come in to face one batter most of the time."

Zach and Manny looked at each other. It was obvious that this was going nowhere. One thing they had learned about Joe in the short time they had played and lived together was that he could get a little grumpy. Rather than argue it was best to concede the point and move on.

"You're right about that. There are many days I wish I was left handed," Zach said. "But I'm not and I've got to get myself ready to play today, so I'm out." He put his dishes in the sink and excused himself before Joe could get going again. Manny gave him a "why are you leaving me look," but Zach left before he could say anything.

By the time Zach got out of the shower and was dressed he found Manny sitting on the edge of his bed waiting for him. "That was not right," Manny said with a frown. "Why did you leave me in there with him?"

"Sorry. I just didn't want to get into it with him. He seems to get in these moods, and I can't deal with it."

"I don't want to either, but you just can't walk away. I was stuck for the next fifteen minutes listening to him ramble on about nothing. I think he's just tired or something."

"Maybe, but we're all tired. I'm just looking forward to the game tonight so things can get back to normal. I'm going to head over to the field. Do you want me to wait for you?" Zach was hoping Manny would say no so he could leave.

"I'll ride over with Joe. Hopefully he'll be back to normal in a little bit. Remember, you owe me now for leaving."

"Okay. Next dinner is on me." Zach always knew he could get back in Manny's good graces through food.

"Deal, but my choice."

"You're on. See you at the field." Zach gathered his things and made his way out the door and over to the stadium. He didn't want to say anything to Manny, but he wanted to talk to Sarah before the game. The locker room would be quiet for a while, so he could have some privacy. He was hoping to set up some time later that week for them to get together. Dinner after the game didn't work the last time, so he was going to ask her to lunch.

The locker room was empty when he arrived. Most of the guys were probably going to get in right before their warm-up time since they had gotten in so late the night before. Zach shot off a quick text to Sarah and spent the next few minutes waiting for her response. It was funny how things changed. Normally he would be obsessing over the game, but here he was waiting for a text from a girl. Maybe it was good to have a distraction after all.

It took about fifteen minutes for her to respond. It turned out she had a class that night and couldn't come to the game, but she was free the next day. Zach was disappointed but didn't want to sound desperate so he agreed to meet her at the Waffle House to make up for their lost date from the night of the perfect game. He was excited to have something scheduled with her but bummed he had to wait to see her again.

Oh well, he thought, he had plenty to keep him busy until they got together. There was a new team in town, the Jackson Generals, who were affiliated with the Seattle Mariners, and they were there for the next five games. After that, they had four games with the Montgomery Biscuits. It was going to be a nice long homestand, and Zach was hoping he could find a way to spend some time with Sarah before they headed out on the road again.

Zach went about his usual routine, checked his new video and spent some time in the batting cages below the stadium before the rest of the guys showed up. He could tell everyone was a little tired from the late night, and that could either be a good or a bad thing. Sometimes they had their best games when tired, maybe because they didn't try so hard and let the game come to them. It had been a rough couple of games, so hopefully they could get a good start today and make it a successful homestand.

The Barons did get off to a good start, scoring four runs in the first inning. Zach did his part, lining a single to left to knock in a run. The game was never in much doubt as they shook off their weariness and pounded the Generals 12–2. Zach ended up the game 2–4 with a run scored and an RBI. He also made an acrobatic play at second base in the fourth inning, taking a throw from third base and turning a double play. He had to leap over the oncoming runner and landed hard on his right shoulder, but he quickly got up. It would take more than that to knock him out of a game.

With the game in the books and a lunch date with Sarah on tap for the next day, Zach was looking forward to an early evening and maybe even trying to get some sleep. Manny, however, called in his IOU for dinner, and they ended up in the drive-thru at Taco Bell again. It seemed like they were there every other day, but their options were limited since their games ended so late. Zach was actually looking forward to seeing what Doug had bought at the store that afternoon, but a deal was a deal.

"Do you want to hit the laundry mat tomorrow?" Manny asked between bites of chalupa.

"Maybe another day. I'm meeting Sarah for lunch tomorrow," Zach replied, not wanting to make a big deal out of it.

"Really? You actually made the move to ask her out? I'm impressed."

"I told you I was texting and talking to her while we were out on the road." In fact, Manny had been teasing Zach about it for a week.

"I know. But this is a big step. You are moving out of the virtual world and into the real world." Manny eyed his burrito but made the decision to wait until they got home to finish eating.

"It's no big deal. We are just having lunch."

"Where are you meeting her?"

"At the Waffle House."

"Really?" Manny rolled his eyes. "You couldn't do better than that? This is your first date you know."

"Well that's the kind of guy I am. I'm not into fancy dinners. If that's what she's looking for, then she's got the wrong guy. I figure we should get that straight early on."

"Well I hope it goes well. I have to say, you've seemed like you have a little more balance in your life lately. I think that is a good thing."

"I guess. Truth is, it's kind of nice to have someone to talk to," Zach said.

"Thanks a lot. What am I, chopped liver?" Manny pretended to be hurt. "Not good enough for you anymore?'

"You know what I mean. It's different to talk to a girl. I mean, she just makes me feel good. I can't explain it." Zach felt a little embarrassed and wanted to drop the subject. Fortunately, they were pulling up to the driveway, and he could change the topic when they saw Joe and Doug.

"Oh, I get it," Manny laughed. "I'm just glad that you do now too."

"Please don't say anything to the guys. I don't want to hear it from them too. At least not yet, okay?"

"Okay. It will be our secret. But I want to hear all the details when you get back."

"Fine. I'll tell you everything. Just let me bring it up from now on. I don't want to jinx it." Zach knew he would tell Manny everything, but he wanted to do it on his own schedule. Manny agreed, and they walked into the house to find Joe and Doug in their usual spots on the couch playing the Xbox. They finished their dinner, and after some small talk around the recent road trip and upcoming homestand they all turned in for the night.

The morning couldn't come soon enough for Zach. As usual, he spent the night tossing and turning and didn't end up sleeping much. Unlike most nights though, he wasn't thinking about his batting stance or something that may have gone wrong during that night's game. He was thinking about how he could fill a couple of hours alone with Sarah. Manny was right. It was one thing to talk in cyberspace. It was another thing to sit across from her and engage her in a conversation. He ran through some potential topics in his mind and eventually drifted off to sleep.

The morning passed without event, and Zach was able to sneak out without having to share where he was going with Joe and Doug. He made his way over to the Waffle House and sat down at a table to wait for Sarah. He didn't have to wait too long as she arrived about five minutes later. He hadn't seen her in over a week and had already forgotten how pretty she was. She was wearing a denim skirt and an open blouse over a tank top. Her hair was pulled back into a ponytail, and when she saw Zach she broke into a big grin.

"I was afraid you wouldn't show up," she said as she sat down in the booth across from Zach.

"Why would think that?" he asked.

"Oh, you never know. It's one thing to text or talk on the phone but it's another to actually meet someone face to face. I mean, you're a professional baseball player. You probably don't have much free time."

"I have lots of free time. Unfortunately it's in the day when most people are working, so it's hard to do things. You have to be creative to find ways to kill time before you go to the park at night."

"So that's what this is for you? Killing time?"

Sarah gave Zach a look that made his heart drop and he tried to recover. "No, no, not at all. I didn't mean today, or you. I meant in general. We have so much free time it's nice to have someone new to spend it with for a change. You get tired of being with the guys all the time." Zach tried to be cool, but inside he was panicking.

"I was just kidding," she said, breaking into a smile. "I'll give you that one, but next time, think before you speak. A girl wants to think you've been counting the minutes until you see her."

Zach felt instantly relieved. "Actually, I have. This date today has been what's keeping me going for the last week or so."

"Now that's much better." She reached out across the table and took his hand.

Zach felt all the blood rush to his head, and he felt a little dizzy. Her hand felt so soft, and her eyes seemed to look right through him and he sat there and stared at her, unable to say anything.

After a minute, she moved her hand and picked up a menu. "So, will it be breakfast or lunch?

"What?" Zach said, lost in the moment.

"I said, breakfast or lunch. What did you have in mind?"

Zach shook his head and tried to concentrate. "Oh, I was thinking breakfast. I had a craving for pecan waffles today. They are my favorite."

"Really? Mine too."

The waiter came over, and they placed their order. Pecan waffles, eggs, and bacon for both of them. Zach had a hard time believing that she would be able to finish the whole thing. She was a petite girl and the waffles here tended to be big. He was feeling so nervous he didn't know if he could eat. He had a long night ahead, so he'd have to get over that or else he'd be starving later.

"So tell me about the road trip. Pretty tough, huh?"

"Yeah, we didn't do very well. I mean, Doug had one good start, but the rest of the games were terrible." Zach loved the fact that she followed the team and that he could talk baseball with her.

"It must be hard going out on the road all the time. Do you get tired of it?"

"Sometimes. I mean, at first it was fun, travelling all over the place, staying in hotels. We didn't travel much when I was a kid so it was all new to me. After a while though, it gets tough. You spend too much time on buses and in hotel rooms. It seems like some days all you do is try to find something to eat."

"Still, it must be exciting to get paid to do what you love." She smiled. "I mean, a professional baseball player, how cool is that?"

"It's what I've wanted to do for as long as I can remember."

"Living the dream."

"Almost. Living the double A dream. I want to make it to the show. Hopefully this is my last year here." As soon as Zach said it, he wished he could take it back. Here he was with her on their first date, and he was talking about leaving.

"Well, I hope you make it someday, but I'll be sad to see you go."

"It probably won't happen soon. The White Sox are pretty stocked at second base."

"You never know," she said, "funny things can happen. The Barons have sent a lot of players to the majors. Why not you? If it's meant to be, it's meant to be."

"So do you believe in destiny?"

"I think so. I mean, I think we have some say in how things turn out, but I also believe there is a master plan for everyone. We just don't know what it is and it's hard to see it sometimes."

"So we were destined to meet at that laundromat? And you were destined to forget your detergent?"

"Maybe. I mean, it was destiny that you were there, but I played a little role." Her faced turned red, and she looked down at her lap.

"What do you mean?" Zach asked.

"I didn't really forget my detergent. I just needed a reason to talk to you." She looked up at him and smiled. "I couldn't just walk up to you for no reason."

"Are you serious?" Zach found it hard to believe that she had wanted to meet him.

"You are a famous baseball player you know."

"Hardly," Zach said, laughing. "I am not famous."

"You are around here. You know you are one of the most popular players on the team, right?"

"I am?"

"Absolutely. The people in the stands that know baseball think you're great. You must hear them cheering for you."

"I really don't hear the crowd. I mean, when I first started playing I did, but now, I just focus on the game." Obviously, Zach knew there were people watching the games, but he didn't think about it too much.

"Well, Zach, you are loved in Birmingham." Sarah reached out and took his hand again.

Zach had a strange feeling that she wasn't talking about Birmingham and felt himself getting dizzy again. Who was this girl? What did he do to deserve this? "That's nice to know," he said as he reached out and took her other hand and looked into her eyes.

Of course, this was the exact moment the waiter brought the food to their table. They paused for a minute and then each pulled back their hands to make way for their food. Zach had forgotten how hungry he was but the sight and smell of the fresh pecan waffles made him realize he was starving. He looked at Sarah, and he could tell she was thinking the same thing. The moment passed, and they hungrily attacked their food.

They spent the rest of their time together talking about how they ended up in Birmingham. Zach told her about all of the other teams he had played for and, if things went right, where he would go next. She really was a fan and knew most the teams he had played for. It was nice to be able to talk to someone who seemed to understand how his career would make him move around.

She was studying to be a nurse at the University of Alabama-Birmingham and only had one more year to go to become an RN.

She was born and raised in Birmingham and other than a few short trips had never really left the state. She seemed fascinated by Zach's stories about bus trips and minor league stadiums and actually seemed a little jealous of his vagabond life. She was close to her parents and had two sisters: Amy and Louise, who was twenty and also attending UAB. Unlike Zach, whose parents were divorced, her parents had been married for almost thirty years.

They talked and talked, and it was past 3:00 p.m. before they knew it. Zach didn't want to go, but he needed to get ready for that night's game. She had class the next two days, so she wouldn't be able to get together, but they promised to text and call until they could find another time to meet. As they stood in the parking lot saying good-bye, Zach felt the urge to pull her into his arms and kiss her. He felt like he was getting a good vibe from her, but he didn't want to rush things so he held back as he stood next to her by her car.

There was an awkward moment or two while they stood there trying to say good-bye. Zach was about to give up and walk away when she reached out and took his hand. "You know you can kiss me if you want?"

Zach smiled. "You were reading my mind."

After another brief moment, Zach took her in his arms and gave her a kiss. It wasn't a long lingering kiss, but just enough to let her know that he cared. He pulled back and looked at her, moving a piece of hair from her eyes. "I'm glad you lied about your detergent."

"Me too."

He kissed her again, this time with a little bit more behind it and then reluctantly let her go. He watched as she got in her car and drove away and felt as happy as he had been in a long time. After a few minutes, he got in his car, ran back to the house and then headed over to the field for the night's game.

CHAPTER 13

During the game Zach was still on cloud nine from his afternoon with Sarah. For the first time he could remember, he had wandered into the locker room just before the team headed out to the field. More than one person had commented on his tardiness, and he just brushed them off when they asked why he was late. He didn't prepare at all, and he wasn't worried about it. All he could think about was Sarah and how it felt when he held her in his arms.

Oddly enough, he had one of his best games ever that night. He went four for four with two doubles, two home runs, and six runs batted in as the Barons rolled over the Biscuits for the second straight night 14–4. His performance was the talk of the team that night, and several people suggested he should come to the park late every day. He didn't think that was going to happen, but if he had a chance to see Sarah before a game, he wouldn't think twice about being late again.

Zach started on a hitting streak. Over the next few weeks, it was like he could do no wrong. It seemed like every ball he hit was hard and the few that weren't would find a gap in the defense and fall in for a hit. He had a hit in sixteen straight games, and the Barons charged out to a six-game lead in their division.

After his first afternoon with Sarah, they had made plans to meet before games as often as her schedule would allow. It was never enough for Zach. He wished he could see her every day, but she had to keep up with her classes. When he was with her, he just felt at peace, and nothing else seemed to matter. He still did his game prep. That would never change, but he stopped worrying about things so much. He was sleeping better and just felt like a changed man. Manny said that a good woman would bring calmness and order to his life, and maybe it was true. Whatever it was, he was playing well and was happier than he had ever been before.

After some hesitation, he had even invited her over to the house and introduced her to Joe and Doug. He was afraid that they would either tease him or embarrass him in some way, but they were always on their best behavior. Among her other endearing qualities, it also turned out that she was an expert at Halo. Zach and the guys laughed their heads off when she took on Joe and consistently beat him at his own game. It seemed like she could do anything she set her mind to, and Zach loved that about her.

The only bad part about his new relationship was when they had to go out on the road. He would still talk and text with her every day, but it wasn't the same. He missed being in the same room with her. The days passed more slowly than usual, and Zach tried to use the time to work out and catch up on his e-mails and to stay in touch with his friends. He had spent a lot of time building up his professional network, and although he loved being with Sarah, he couldn't let that go.

It was during one of these interactions that he first found out about the upcoming round of drug testing. They were usually tested several times a year. Though they never knew when it was coming, once one player was tested they started to spread the word. The first round had occurred during spring training and had generated a couple of fifty-game suspensions. Zach had not been selected then but that didn't guarantee he would be selected this time. In fact, he better not get picked because if he was he could be in real danger. He wasn't sure what it took to generate a positive test but since he made the decision to go back to his little black box for help he was definitely at risk.

So much had happened since that night he had almost forgotten about it. Everything had been going so well: the excitement of the perfect game, meeting Sarah and his recent hitting streak. He had only done it once, and it was pretty clear from his recent play that he didn't need it. Maybe he wouldn't get picked, or maybe the stuff had already cycled out of his system. He tried to put in out of his mind, but it was sitting there and he was going to have to live with it until he found out.

It was a pretty simple process. The tester would make arrangements with the clubs to come on a certain day to collect samples from selected players. They would head off one by one to take care of their business and give the sample to the tester. Everything was documented, and you had to sign off that you had done your part. Other than one famous example with Ryan Braun, the process was so tight if you tested positive it meant that you were going to get suspended.

Over dinner one night while they were on the road, Zach decided to bring it up with Manny. "Have you heard testing started again?"

"Yeah, I heard it might be coming," he said, not looking up from his dinner. "If you're clean you have nothing to worry about."

"Do you really think so?" Zach asked. "I mean look at Ryan Braun. He tested positive and was going to be suspended but had to appeal."

Braun was a player on the Milwaukee Brewers who had tested positive right around time he was named National League MVP. His testosterone levels were the highest ever measured and he was suspended for fifty games. His people had argued the testing process was flawed and as a result the test was ruled invalid. He had won the appeal, but most people looked at him differently now.

Manny looked at Zach, "Do you really think he was clean?"

"I don't know. Something happened. I mean if he was dirty, they would never have overturned it, right?"

"Overturned what?" Joe asked as he sat down and joined them.

"Ryan Braun's positive test," Manny said with a look that said he didn't believe it.

"You're kidding right? Everyone knows he got off on a technicality." Joe wasn't one to hold back. He had made it clear once before that he had no sympathy for people who tried to cheat the system.

"How can you say that?" Zach asked. "You weren't there. You don't know what happened."

"His results were off the charts. What else do you have to know?" Joe was about to get worked up again.

"Really Zach, how else can you explain it?" Manny asked.

"I can't, but I don't have to. The burden of proof is on Major League Baseball, I mean you are innocent until proven guilty, right? His numbers haven't changed since the test."

"Whatever," Joe said. "I know what I think, and that is not going to change. I don't care how well he does. He is guilty in my mind."

"I'm with Joe on this one," Manny added, "I mean, I hope it's not true, but how else can you explain it?"

"He doesn't have to. That's the point." Zach really thought they would be on the player's side and he was surprised by their lack of support. How would they feel about him if they knew what he had done. "If I were accused of something I would hope you guys would stand by me."

"Look. I consider you a friend, but some things are non-negotiable. Fail a test and you're dead to me. I don't care about the reason. It's not right," said Joe.

"That's pretty harsh," Zach said, a little taken aback by Joe's response.

"Like I said, some things are non-negotiable. If you are going to lie about something like that, how can I trust you about anything?"

"I would probably still talk to you. But you would have a lot of explaining to do," Manny said. "But it doesn't really matter because we are all clean, right?"

"I know I am," Joe said. "They could test me every day."

"Of course," Zach added. "But aren't you a little afraid you may have done something and not realized it?"

"No," Joe said. "I'm not worried about that at all."

"I guess I just trust the system," Manny said. "I mean it seems pretty secure to me."

"Tell that to Ryan Braun," Zach replied.

They fell into an uncomfortable silence for a few minutes. Doug joined them, and the conversation switched to a less controversial subject, and the rest of the evening passed without any additional comments on the subject. Zach was glad it passed. He didn't want to think about the test. He was afraid that he could end up in the same boat as Ryan Braun and he didn't have the resources available to fight it.

The road trip came to an end, and they returned home to find that sure enough, testing was here. Zach, Manny, and Joe were among eight players selected for this round. Zach headed off to the restroom to provide his sample and cursed the fact he had not drunk more water. Maybe it was that, or the fact that he felt like he was signing his own death warrant but it took a while for him to fill up the cup, and when he did he handed it over to the tester where it was verified and then sent off for processing. They said they would know the results in about two weeks. Zach had a feeling that those days would pass by very slowly.

Now that they were home, the good news was that he got the chance to spend time with Sarah again and they made the most of their time together. Zach continued to hit, and approaching the fifty-game mark of the season he was among the league leaders with a .347 average, eight home runs, and thirty-five RBIs. He was on pace for his best season ever, and it was beginning to look like he was finally reaching his potential and a late season call up might be on the table.

Zach was sitting in the living room when he received the call from his agent, Steve Tailsmen. After a few pleasantries, Steve dropped the bomb. "Zach, is there anything you need to tell me?"

"What do you mean?" Zach asked.

"Do you remember the test you took a few weeks ago?"

"Sure. What about it?" Zach felt his stomach drop. What did this mean?

"It came up positive for Boldenone. As a first-time offender, you are looking at a fifty-game suspension."

"You can't be serious. I couldn't have failed the test." Zach had to sit down, or he felt like he would pass out. All of his hard work, everything he had wanted for so long was slipping away right in front of him.

"Look. I don't want to know if you did or didn't do it. I'm with you either way. I just need to know what you want me to do." Steve then laid out his options, admit it and accept the penalty, admit nothing and accept the penalty, or fight it.

"Of course I'm going to fight it," Zach said.

"Are you sure? Sometimes it's better just to move on."

"Don't you believe me?" Zach needed some reassurance, and he wasn't getting it from his agent.

"It doesn't matter if I do or don't. I will support you either way," Steve said.

"That's comforting." Zach made a note to look for a new agent when this was all over. He needed someone who would fight for him, and it felt like Steve was just going through the motions. He obviously didn't believe him.

"I'm just doing my job, Zach. I can't help you if I'm too attached."

"I understand. What's our next step?" Zach didn't really understand, but there was no point in discussing it now.

Steve spent the next fifteen minutes describing what would happen next. First, he was not to tell anyone about the test. That was easier said than done. Zach felt the need to tell someone. Maybe Sarah or Manny, he'd have to think about that. Second, the suspension would start immediately unless they filed a dispute, which could take a few weeks. If all went well with the dispute it would all go away and no one would ever know. Worst case, if the results were upheld the dispute and ensuing suspension would take a couple of months, and Zach would miss the remainder of the season. There would be a few games left on the schedule but why bother? It would be better to get a clean start the next year.

It was a lot for Zach to absorb, and he felt the need to get out of the house and find someplace quiet to think. Steve had said that the team had been informed, but he didn't think they would tell the coaching staff, so he would still be able to play that night. The guys were all in the middle of doing their own thing, so he decided to head out for a while. He made his way over to a local park, where he would go sometimes when he felt the need to get away. He really needed to think about his next move. What should he do?

He could call his mom. She was always there for him and would probably give him good advice, but he felt like it would be such a disappointment for her that he didn't want to deal with that right now. Maybe he could talk to Sarah? No, it was way too soon to approach such a serious topic with her. Maybe someday, but again, he felt like she would be really disappointed in him too and he couldn't deal with that right now. That left Manny. Maybe he would understand. Even though he didn't do it, he said once that he felt the pressure to take steroids. Maybe he would understand how he had panicked and made a mistake.

Round and round it went for the next couple of hours. Zach would consider and reconsider the people that he could talk to. His agent was obviously not going to help. It really was just a choice between his mom, Sarah, and Manny. All three had good sides and bad sides. He would have thought it would have been his mom first, and he would have to talk to her, but not now. It would be too hard. Same for Sarah. It would have to be Manny.

But when? It was too late today. It was almost time to head over to the field. Maybe after the game? It would be late, but they could go someplace and talk over dinner. He really didn't want this day to end without getting it off his chest. He needed some guidance, and Manny was his best bet. He would hit him up before the game, maybe say it was about Sarah. He would buy that. It sounded like a plan. Now he just had to make it through the game tonight.

Once again, Zach made it to field just when the Barons were scheduled to start warm-ups. Manny wasn't starting, so he would have a chance to talk to him while they were shagging balls in the outfield. He waited until he had taken his turn hitting, took a few balls at second base and then found Manny standing near the left field foul line.

"Hey, I was wondering what happened to you. Another hot date?" Manny smiled at Zach and made a kissing sound.

"Not today. I had to take care of something."

"Well, I know it wasn't your laundry. That's still not done yet. Is everything okay?" Manny knew Zach had a routine, and if it was different two days in a row then something was up.

"Just a lot on my mind," Zach said. "How about we skip Taco Bell tonight and I buy you dinner at the Waffle House?"

"Okay. I'll never turn down a free meal. Are you sure you're okay?" Manny said with concern in his voice.

"I'll be fine. Just need some advice."

"Oh. Things getting too serious with Sarah for you?"

"You could say that. I just need to decide which direction I'm going to go." It was not really a lie, Zach thought. He did have a decision to make.

"Well, when it comes to women, you need to follow your heart. It will never let you down."

"I hope not." Zach didn't want to turn this into a whole discussion, so he changed the subject to the game. They had beaten up the Biscuits pretty good the last few nights, so if things worked the way they usually did, it would be a tough game tonight. Baseball had a way of evening out over time. It was hard to dominate a team three nights in a row.

Zach had a hard time concentrating during the game, and it showed. He finished the night 0–4 with three strikeouts, just missing a golden sombrero, or four strikeouts without a hit, when he popped out in his last at-bat. The team however, continued on a roll with an easy 6–1 win. Zach never liked it when he had a bad game, but at least his poor night didn't cost the team a victory.

After the game Zach made it a point to find Manny and remind him that they needed to talk and would have to skip their post-game video routine. Never one to miss a meal, Manny quickly showered and dressed and was ready to go by the time Zach got out of the shower.

"So what is this all about?" Manny asked as they drove out of the parking lot.

"I'd really rather wait until we got to the restaurant," Zach answered. He wasn't exactly looking forward to this conversation, so he preferred to put it off as long as possible.

Manny could tell by the serious look on his face that Zach didn't want to talk, so he just said, "Okay," and they continued driving in silence until they reached the Waffle House.

After they had sat down and placed their order, they sat in silence for a few minutes before Manny finally spoke. "So, what's the matter? You didn't bring me here to just sit and stare at each other did you?"

"No. I guess there is no easy way to do this, so I should probably just spit it out." Zach closed his eyes and took a deep breath. He exhaled slowly and looked at Manny. "I failed a drug test."

Now it was Manny's turn to sigh. "When?"

"This last round, I tested positive for Boldenone."

"I don't understand. How could this happen?" Manny asked in disbelief.

"It's a long story and I'd rather not get into it right now. Let's just say I made a bad decision and leave it at that. I regretted it the minute I did it, and I've been stressed out about it ever since it happened." Zach felt himself tearing up, and he wiped his eyes with a napkin. It sounded worse when he said it out loud.

"Have you told anyone yet?" Manny asked.

"No. You're the first."

"What are you going to do?"

"Well, I was thinking about disputing it. Maybe there was something wrong with the test, like Ryan Braun." Zach looked down at the table. He couldn't bear to look Manny in the eye. "But the more I think about it, I should just accept the suspension and try to move on."

"That may be the best thing for you to do. You can still get past this. There have been other guys that tested positive and came back and played. You're a good player; you can make it on your own talent. I told you I felt the pressure to do it once. I wish you would have said something to me about it. Maybe I could have stopped you." Now it was Manny's turn to stare at the table.

"It's nobody's fault but mine," Zach said. "I made the decision to do it. I knew it was wrong, but I did it anyway and now I have to face the consequences."

"That may be the best thing, just face it and try to move on."

"Honestly, I don't have any other choice because it's going to come out. I just hope it doesn't ruin my chances to make it to the majors or cost me my relationship with Sarah." Zach was afraid he would lose both and he didn't know what he would do if that happened.

"Try not to get too far ahead of yourself. Take one thing at a time. It will all work out in the end. There is always a reason for everything; sometimes we just don't see it right away. What's your next step?"

Leave it to Manny to keep me focused on the task at hand and not think too far ahead, Zach thought. He was right of course. There was only so much he could do at this point. His bed was made. He had to lie in it.

They spent the next hour or so discussing who he should talk to next. They both agreed he needed to tell his mother, Sarah, Tom, Joe, and Doug in that order. It wouldn't be easy, but if he was going to accept responsibility for his actions and try to move on he would have to talk to the people he was closest to before the news came out.

By the time they were finished, Zach felt a little bit better and actually believed that he might be able to make it through the next few days. Manny had been great. He didn't judge or even ask for details about what happened. He only offered to be there if Zach needed him with no strings attached. Zach didn't know if he would be able to take him up on that offer, but it was nice to know it was there.

As they made their way home, Zach couldn't help but wonder if he would have been as understanding if the shoe had been on the other foot. He liked to think that he would have been there for Manny if he had been the one with the failed test, but he wasn't sure. As it was, he felt lucky to have such a good friend and some day he hoped he could return the favor. For now, the offer of help was nice, but he would need to take care of this on his own.

CHAPTER 14

Whatever good feelings Zach had after talking to Manny quickly disappeared as soon as he lay down in his bed and tried to go to sleep. His mind always ran wild at night anyway, thinking about the last game, the plays he made, the hits he did or didn't have. His thoughts had drifted back to his secret the past few months, but he was usually able to push them away and focus on the games. He always knew that he could get caught, but he never really thought it would happen.

Now that his secret was out in the open, he knew he would have to pay the price. The questions were sure to come, who gave him the stuff, when and where did he get it, how often did he use it, did he know of other players that did it? The truth was he didn't know much about the guy that hooked him up. He met him one night at bar in the Dominican Republic when he visited Manny over the winter.

Zach had spent most of his time with Manny and his family, but there was one night when he couldn't sleep and wandered over to a bar in town. He wasn't much of a drinker, but every now and then he would have a beer or two to take the edge off a tough day. On this particular evening he was feeling a little bit down because it was his first exposure to the quality of players in the Dominican Republic and they were really good.

Manny and his brothers ran a baseball academy, and they had invited Zach to help out for a few weeks. Although he didn't speak Spanish, baseball is a universal language, and he was able to share tips and pointers with the kids in camp. It didn't take him long to realize there were a number of players that could easily take his place if given the chance. He was feeling down and doubting his ability to compete and pursue his dream of playing in the major leagues.

While sitting at the bar, a man came over and sat next to him. It was obvious that Zach wasn't from the area and the man had struck up a conversation. Since this was the first new person he met that spoke English in a few days Zach welcomed the opportunity to talk. The man knew Manny and his brothers, everyone in the town did, and they talked about baseball, the academy and Zach's career to date.

Zach didn't usually open up to people right away. Maybe it was the beer or the fact he was far from home and doubting his future, but he found himself opening up to this man. He would nod his head often and seemed to really understand how Zach felt. He had been a player when he was younger, but an arm injury had sidelined him before he had made a name for himself and got off the island.

He now acted as a freelance scout and would go from town to town recruiting players for the local teams and academies. If he was lucky, one of his players would get signed by a major league team, and he would get a piece of their bonus. He had a little success but noted that many of the players were using performance enhancing drugs and it was hard to compete if you didn't. He said he personally had never tried them but if he was still playing he would be tempted to try, just in order to keep pace.

Zach had felt a little uncomfortable with where the conversation was heading, but he didn't stop it or get up to leave. He was obviously aware of performance enhancing drugs, or PEDs as they were known, but he had never considered using them. Players were warned from the day they were signed that the penalties were severe if you were caught. Anyway, he wanted to make it on his own and not because of some drug. But he was in a vulnerable state, and he found himself asking questions.

The man was hesitant to talk about it at first, but after another beer or two he started to open up. He gave Zach an overview of the drug market in the Dominican and estimated that a high percentage of players were on something. The key he said was knowing what to use and when to cycle on and off the drug to avoid getting caught. He seemed to know quite a bit, and despite some reservations Zach found himself asking more and more questions. Eventually, they agreed to meet the next day to talk some more about it.

Over the next week or so, they met and talked more about what to use. He recommended Boldenone because it was easy to obtain and could slip through the cracks of the test if used properly. Still, Zach had doubts and let him know that he didn't think he could go through with it. The man said he understood but gave him the name of a person in the states if he changed his mind. That was the end of it until Zach was getting ready for Spring Training.

The doubts started to come back as he got ready to report. He thought about the players he had seen in the Dominican, and he knew that there was another group of players entering the White Sox system he would have to compete with. It was going to be his third season in Birmingham and he was certain it would be a make or break year for him. Before he realized what he was doing, he found the number and made arrangements for a shipment.

Once he received the package he read the instruction note that was included and injected himself multiple times over the next few weeks. It didn't take long before he started to feel the effects. Maybe it was all in his mind, but he felt like he could lift more and the general soreness he had after a workout didn't seem as bad. He reported to camp and physically felt great, but mentally he was a wreck.

He was sure someone would find out. He knew that there was a chance he could be tested and even though he was told if he limited his usage he would pass, he was scared. He had even more trouble sleeping than usual and the positive effects he initially felt seemed to disappear as quickly as they arrived.

Once the initial round of testing came and went he started to feel a little bit better, but when the season started all the doubts returned. He had brought the stuff with him to camp and on more than one occasion he looked at it and wondered what if? When he started the season poorly, he decided to try it one more time. He immediately regretted it, especially after Manny's confession that he had thought about it and decided not to and Joe's reaction to Joey Woodword's suspension. Zach knew there would be more testing later in the year, and he was afraid he would get selected.

Now, here he was awake in the middle of the night regretting his decision. He couldn't believe he had been so reckless. He had worked so hard to get where he was, and now he was going to throw it all away. He didn't even think the stuff worked, Manny was probably right, it was mostly in your mind. He had been playing great recently, and he hadn't even used it after the last time. He felt like he had finally turned a corner and was going to get his chance, but now everyone would doubt his recent results and think they were because of the PEDs.

He went over and over it in his mind and didn't sleep at all. When he woke up the next morning, he knew the first person he had to call was his mom. He decided that he needed to be someplace quiet so he could talk and went back to the park, where he knew he wouldn't be disturbed. He sat for a while and then finally dialed the number. She picked up the phone on the second ring, and Zach took a deep breath and told her his story. It took about twenty minutes for him to get through everything, and she listened patiently before she finally spoke.

"We all make mistakes, Zach. Part of being a man is admitting when you are wrong and making amends. I don't agree with what you did. You didn't need it. You have the talent and attitude to do it on your own. We always talked about how there are no shortcuts to success. It's all about hard work and dedication. I'm not going to lie to you. I am very disappointed, but I am still your mother and I love you and will support you."

There really wasn't much that Zach could say in response to that. "I am so sorry, Mom. It was a mistake, and I should have been stronger. I just want this so bad. I would do anything to make it."

"You still can, Zach, and it will mean so much more when you do it the right way." He could hear the disappointment in her voice even though she was trying to hide it.

"I know, but I don't know if I will have the chance. I have no idea how the team will handle this. At the very least, I am probably done for the season."

"You need to admit what you did and accept whatever punishment they give you. If you try to be one of those players who deny it and end up serving a suspension anyway it will always hang over your head."

"You're right. That's what I'm going to do. I just hope I get another chance." Zach was really unsure what the White Sox policy was around PED suspensions. He would have to serve the suspension no matter what, but the team could easily release him and then he would have to try to hook on with another team.

"I'm sure you will. You may have to start out back at another level or with another team, but you are talented so someone will give you a chance. You will just have to work twice as hard now."

"I plan to. I am going to work harder now than ever before." Zach felt he had turned a corner recently, and he was confident he could make it now.

They talked for a few more minutes. He gave her an update on Sarah and how well they had been getting along. He confessed he was unsure of how she would react, but she tried to reassure him that it would all work out. He also let her know that he planned to come home right after he met with the club officials, and they agreed to try and find a way to take a few days to go somewhere and get away.

When he hung up the phone, he felt a little bit better. It was such a relief to talk about it and get it out in the open. It had been so hard keeping it to himself, and sharing it made it easier and harder at the same time. He knew he had more people that he would have to deal with, but at least now he had Manny and his mom on his side. He just needed to figure out who to tell next.

He knew he should call his agent and let him know that he wasn't going to fight the suspension anymore, but he was afraid the news would leak out before he had a chance to tell Sarah, so he decided to wait a little bit longer to make that call. He couldn't remember if Sarah had class that day, so he sent her a text to see if she was free. She replied a few minutes later that she had a project to complete but could meet him for lunch. They agreed to meet at the Waffle House at noon.

Zach felt very nervous about. It had only been a few weeks with Sarah, and although he felt they had a very strong connection, he really wasn't sure about how she felt. She came from a pretty conservative background, and since her family was really into baseball he was sure they had strong opinions on the subject. Most people did.

He got to the restaurant a few minutes early and found a table facing the door so he would able to see her when she arrived. Once he saw her walk in the door his stomach felt like it was holding a butterfly colony and he found himself getting more nervous. Even though she was dressed casually, she just looked so good. Zach felt like he had to force himself to stop from running across the room and take her in his arms. He waved to her, and she smiled and made her way to his table. He stood up and gave her a hug and a kiss.

He must have held on a little more than usual because she sat down and said "Wow, I guess you missed me, huh?"

"I always miss you," Zach said, blushing a little.

"That's nice to hear. I miss you too." She reached her hand out across the table and took his hand in hers.

The touch of her hand made Zach melt. How was he going to do this? The last thing he wanted to do was to bring up something that would ruin this moment. He closed his eyes and tried to burn an image of this moment, this feeling in his mind. He knew he would need to draw on it when times got tough later on.

"Are you okay?"

"Not really. I need to talk to you about something," he said, letting her hand go.

"Nothing bad I hope. Did you get called up?" she asked with a mixture of hope and sadness.

"No. I wish that was it, but it's something else. It's a long story and I wish I didn't have to get into it, but it's going to come out and it's best that you hear it from me." He took a deep sigh and looked up at the ceiling trying to gather the courage to tell her. He was about to say something when the waitress approached.

They quickly decided on what to order and sent the waitress on her way. It really didn't matter what they ordered. Zach was sure they wouldn't be eating anyway after he told her. He sighed again and looked at her, but once again he didn't think he could look her in the eye and tell her. This was going to be harder than he thought.

"Hey," she said, "it's okay, you can tell me anything. What's wrong?" She looked very concerned, and that made Zach feel even worse.

"I guess I'm just going to have to say it." He looked up at up at her and hoped this would not end up being the last time he saw her. "I made a mistake and it's going to come out very soon and I wanted you to hear it from me first."

"Okay," she said, reaching out and taking his hand again. "Just tell me."

He let go of her hand and covered his face with his hands. He sighed again and decided just to say it. "I was selected for this round of drug testing, and I failed the test."

"What do you mean you failed the test? Failed it for what?" She looked concerned, not angry, maybe it was going to be okay.

"I tested positive for a steroid called Boldenone."

"Did you do it?" She didn't mince words, which was of the things Zach liked about her. She got right to the point and didn't look too happy.

"Yes." There wasn't much else he could say.

"Why? You are a good player. You don't need that."

"It's a long story. I was struggling, and I felt like I was going to be stuck in double A for another year. I met someone and they said that it would help and I wouldn't get caught. I only did it a couple of times, and I don't even think it did anything."

"But you knew you would be tested. Did you really think you could get away with it? Even if you did, would it really have meant anything to you if you made it because of the drugs?" She looked confused and disappointed, and Zach felt terrible.

"I don't know. I wasn't thinking about that. I just felt like my dream was slipping away, and I needed to do something, anything to keep it alive."

Of course, this was the moment the waitress returned with their food. When she asked if there was anything else that they needed, Zach wished he could ask her for a time machine. He would give anything to go back in time and make this all go away. They picked at their food for a few minutes in silence while he thought of something to say.

She broke the silence and asked, "So what are you going to do now?"

"I told my agent to dispute it, but I changed my mind and decided to admit it, accept my punishment and try to move on. I wanted to tell you first, before you heard it somewhere else."

"I appreciate that. You needed to tell me. I wouldn't want to hear something like this on the news."

"So what do you think about it? I mean, does this change anything between us?" He hated to ask the question, but he needed to know.

"I have to be honest, Zach. I don't think I can say right now. I mean, this is wrong, and you knew it was wrong and you lied about it."

"I never lied," Zach said. "I called you and told you what happened."

"Yes you did. You've been lying for months. To your family, your friends, your teammates, everyone. I've only know you for a short time, but you have been lying to me from the moment I met you." She was starting to get worked up, and she stopped for a moment and tried to compose herself. "I thought I knew you, Zach, who you were and what you believed in. I thought we had something, but now I feel like I don't know you at all."

"I'm the same person. I just made a mistake. I've told you things that I have never told anyone before."

"You didn't tell me about this. If you hadn't been caught, would you have told me?"

Ouch. She didn't pull any punches did she? Zach didn't know how to respond. He would like to think he would have told her eventually, but he couldn't be sure. It was a dirty little secret and he had hoped it would have been his secret and that no one would ever have found out. He couldn't lie to her again, so he decided to tell her the truth.

"I don't know," he said. "I would like to think that I would have told you, but I knew it was wrong and I just wanted it to go away."

"Having secrets is not the best way to start a relationship."

"I know." He didn't want to ask this, but he had to, "so, where do you think this leaves us?"

"I can't tell you right now. I need some time to process this."

She looked sad, and Zach wanted to reach out to her, hold her and tell her it was going to be okay, but he couldn't. It was bad enough that this mistake could cost him his career, but now it could cost him something more. He wished he could take it all back, but it was too late now.

"I hope you can forgive me," he said. "This is not who I am. You've gotten to know me a little bit, and I think you can believe me when I tell you that. I made a mistake and now I am going to pay for it. It will never happen again, and I am not going to let this define who I am. I am going to prove to everyone that I'm better than this."

"I hope that's true. You need to prove that to yourself first and then worry about everyone else. The sad part is, you didn't need it. Everyone has doubts and is tempted to take the easy way out, but it is the hard times and how we react to them that define us. You failed this time, but it is how you respond to this failure that will really define who you are and what you become."

Zach knew right then that this was the woman for him. He would have to prove himself to her and that would take some time, but he would do whatever it took to win her back. He just wished he could take her in his arms or just reach out across the table and at least hold her hand, but this was not the time.

"I'll do whatever it takes," he said. "I'm going to meet with the team and then decide after that what I'm going to do. I'm pretty sure that I'm done for the year, but I'm going to take some time and think about it and then move on. If it's not with the White Sox, I'll find whatever team that will take me."

"I hope it all works out for you," she said.

"I still want to talk to you, see you, if I can."

"We'll see. I can't commit to anything right now." She placed her napkin on her plate, which she had barely touched. "I'm really disappointed in you. Not so much about what you did, but the fact that you didn't tell me. I mean, I guess I can understand it because we just met, but I felt like there was something more between us. To think this was going on while we were together and you didn't tell me, that just feels wrong."

"I know. I should have said something, but I was lying to myself so how could I tell anyone? It was wrong, and I just wanted it to go away."

"Do what you need to do to take care of this, and when some time has passed, give me a call. I'm not promising anything, but we'll see."

They stayed and talked for a little while, Zach felt like he needed to give her more of an explanation of what happened so there would be no surprises later on. As he told her the story, he realized how bad it sounded. It made no sense, why would he risk everything he had worked so hard for on the advice of some man he met in a bar one night. He would never make a mistake like that again. He would make it on his own, or he wouldn't make it at all.

They stood by her car in the parking lot and he felt the need to reach out to her and hold her one more time. He really needed that to make him feel like they could get through this, but he could tell by her body language he shouldn't even try. He kicked himself again for this mistake and had to let the moment pass. After a few minutes of idle chat she simply got into her car and drove away.

The afternoon was quickly passing, and Zach had one more phone call to make before heading over to the stadium for what would be his last game for a while. He called his agent and told him that he wanted to drop his challenge of the results and admit what he did, accept his punishment, and move on. Just like during their initial conversation, his agent had no comment either way and agreed to set up time with the team the next day.

Well, it was done now, Zach thought as he got into his car and made his way over to the stadium. Technically, he wasn't suspended yet, so there was no reason to take him out of the lineup. He didn't know if Tom was aware of what was going on. He was the team's manager after all, so it was possible, but he hoped he still got the chance to play. If he did, he would be sure to make the most of it and savor every last moment.

CHAPTER 15

As he walked into the locker room, Zach couldn't help but feel like this could be the last time he would be there. He had spent the better part of two years in Birmingham, and although his goal from day one was to leave, he didn't want to go out this way. He walked in late again, but this time nobody seemed to notice and make a big deal about it.

It was funny how routines could change so quickly. He had always been the first person there, and all it took was a couple of days of coming in later and the guys had already adjusted and it was no big deal. The same thing would probably happen after the news broke and he left the team. He would be missed for a few days, and then he would just become another memory of someone they used to know.

That was the nature of the game really, especially in the minor leagues where the goal was to not stay around for years at a time. Sure, when he made it to the majors he would love to spend his career with the same team, but that was very rare these days. The game turned players into migrants, and they would travel from town to town and never set up roots. It was hard enough when alone. Zach could only imagine the strain it would put on a family or a relationship.

He was determined not to dwell on the negative today. He wanted to try to enjoy this night as much as possible because his whole world was about to change. He sat at his locker and looked around the room. When he had first started to play, he felt uncomfortable in the locker room around the other players. In high school he kept mostly to himself at first, but over time he began to think of the team as a second family. He didn't have any siblings and his dad was not around, so the players became his brothers and the coaches like a father or uncle.

Once he moved to the minor leagues, he slowly came out of his shell and became more social. He always held a little bit back, but he was usually able to create a bond with a handful of players each year. Slowly but surely, his network grew and he felt more comfortable around people in general. Baseball really had a positive impact on his life, and even if he never played a game again he was thankful he had the opportunity because it had changed his life for the better.

"You doing okay?" Manny asked as he sat down at his locker.

"It's been a rough day," Zach replied.

"Talk to your mom?"

"Yes. She was disappointed, but she'll be there for me." Zach sighed. He got so wrapped up in his conversation with his Sarah, he had almost forgotten he had spoken to his mom today too.

"Not surprising. She is your mom. That's her job. How about Sarah?"

"Met her for lunch. That didn't go so well. I think it will take some time to get her back. I really like her. I hope she can get past this someday."

"Give it time. I see the two of you together. I think there is something there if you give it the chance." Manny was trying to be positive, and Zach appreciated the effort.

"Well, I hope I get the chance. Right now, I'm not so sure." Zach leaned back in his chair and stared at the ceiling. "I wish I could just take it all back."

"I know. But you can't. All you can do at this point is just keep moving forward. Did you talk to your agent?"

"Yes. He is dropping the appeal. I don't know when I'll end up talking to the team about what is going to happen." Zach assumed it would be sooner rather than later but didn't know how the process worked.

"Well, at least you're in the lineup tonight. Try to make the most of it. You can't fix tomorrow today, so just try to do the best you can." Manny picked up his glove and got up to leave. "I've got to hit the field. I'll see you out there."

"Okay." Zach watched Manny as he walked away and realized he would really miss him. He was the best friend he had, and he was really sad that they would probably not get the chance to play on the same team again.

He finished getting ready and made his way out to the field. He quickly picked up his routine and completed all his warm-ups. He made idle talk with the other players and tried to take in all the sights and sounds of the ballpark. He was going to miss it, the smell of the grass, the fans in the stands. He tried to memorize all of it as the stadium filled up and the anticipation of the game started to build.

After warm-ups and a brief break in the locker room, it was time for the game to start. As he stood on the dugout steps and listened to the national anthem, he felt a little teary-eyed and tried his best to hide it. When he ran to his position in the bottom of the first inning he looked around the stands. After two years, he actually recognized a few faces. He wondered what they would think when the news came out. He hoped they would remember the good times, like the perfect game, and not think of him as just another guy that got caught breaking the rules.

He didn't have much time to get caught up in the moment since he had to make plays on the first two batters in the game. Both were routine outs, but Zach could remember a time when he would have had difficulty making either play. He had come a long way from the early days of playing by himself in his backyard. Most guys never even got as far as double A, so getting this far could be considered quite an accomplishment. Zach wasn't satisfied though; he had his eyes set on a bigger prize.

The game moved quickly, too quickly for his liking. Before he realized it, he was coming up to bat in the bottom of the seventh inning. It was possible that this could be his last at-bat of the game. The Barons were ahead by a run and might not need to bat in the ninth inning if the lead held up. He already had two clean singles, a run scored and a run batted in tonight, but it would be nice to finish up with another hit.

He settled into the batter's box and tried not to be impatient. He made the sign of the cross and tapped the plate, again with the sign of the cross. The pitcher went into his windup, and even though he didn't want to swing, he couldn't help himself. He tried to pull up and check his swing, but it was too late. The ball hit his bat and popped straight up. The catcher took two steps into fair territory and caught his weak, check swing, pop out. Unless the Barons found a way to lose the lead and had to bat in the ninth inning, that could be it for him. It was not the way he wanted to go out.

Normally, Zach would be unhappy if the visiting team had a big inning and took the lead from the Barons, but not tonight. When the Memphis Braves scored five runs in the top of the eighth, it meant he might get one more at-bat. When the Barons sent a few men to bat and scored a run in the bottom of the eighth it meant that he would be up second in the bottom of the ninth.

As he stood in the on deck circle waiting to hit, he took one last look around the stadium. He was really going to miss this. He made himself a promise right then, just as he had that day in his backyard when he would try to hit the ball into his neighbor's yard. He was going to make it to the big leagues. It was going to be hard for a while, but he would find a way and this time there would be no attempts at a shortcut.

After the batter ahead of him popped out to short, it was his turn to hit. He was determined to make this moment last and decided that he would not swing at the first pitch. This time he kept his word and looked at a called first strike. The next two pitches were balls, low and away. Stepping out of the batter's box, he knew what was coming next, something inside. He gathered himself, stepped back in and got ready.

Sometimes it looked like a golf ball was coming at and he knew he had no chance. Other times, it looked like a balloon floating up to the plate and all he had to do was be patient and wait for it. This pitch just seemed to hang there, and Zach held back for as long as he could then unleashed his swing. He felt the ball connect solidly and take off on a line into right center field.

He could see the ball in front of him as he ran to first base and knew if he hustled that he could make it to second base. He rounded first, hit the bag hard and tore toward second. He saw the right fielder cut the ball off before it made it to the wall, and he could see it was going to be a close play.

He could feel the tag on his shoulder but not before his foot hit the bag. The umpire called him safe and he stood up and dusted himself off. He stood on the bag and smiled. He would remember that hit for a long time. Unfortunately, he was stranded on second based as the next two batters struck out. Just like that, the game, and maybe his career, were over.

Back in the locker room he tried to fall back into his regular post game routine, but it just didn't feel the same. Manny felt it too and didn't press him too hard to stay and look at video. They ended up leaving much earlier than usual but not before Tom came out and called Zach into his office. Zach knew what was coming and preferred to talk about it later, but there was no way he could refuse.

"Please close the door," Tom said once they were inside.

Uh oh. Zach thought. *This can't be good.*

"I got a call from the general manager today. He and a representative from the White Sox would like to meet with you at 10:00 a.m. tomorrow. They didn't tell me what it was about. Is there something you need to tell me?"

He didn't raise his voice or look upset. If anything he seemed genuinely concerned. This was yet another conversation that Zach did not want to have, but it didn't look like he would have a choice.

Zach sighed. "You are going to find out, so I might as well tell you." Zach looked down at his feet. He at least owed it to him to look him in the eyes. He sighed again and looked up. "I failed a drug test."

Now it was Tom's turn to sigh. He started to say something and then stopped himself. He stood up and turned his back to Zach and ran his hands through his hair. After a minute he turned around and sat down. "Yes or no. Did you do it?"

"Yes."

"You know, I have never had a player I managed suspended for steroids before and I never thought I would. That is not what I have taught you the past two years. You may think that this only impacts you but it also impacts the entire organization."

"I know and I'm sorry. I shouldn't have done it. I don't know what I was thinking."

"The first thing you need to do is be honest with yourself. This was not a random event. You made a conscious decision to go down this path."

"I don't know what to say, Tom."

"There is not much you can say, Zach. At this point you just need to accept the suspension and try to move on."

"Do you think I can ever make it back?" Zach didn't want to ask the question, but he needed to know what Tom thought.

"It's going to be hard. People will have a hard time trusting you again. I know I will."

That really hurt, and Zach dropped his head into his hands. He had played for Tom for over two years. If he didn't know if he could be trusted again, how could anyone else?

"There is no point in beating this to death," Tom continued. "I'll make the announcement to the team tomorrow. Do you want to be here?"

"I don't think I can face the team," Zach said, avoiding eye contact.

"I think you should, but it's your decision. I'll tell them tomorrow."

"I appreciate that."

"You know that you will never be able to let this go. It will always be with you. Even if you make it, there will always be doubters."

"I know."

"My advice to you is to always tell the truth. Everyone makes mistakes. It's what you do after that counts. Good luck."

"Thank you, Tom." Zach shook his hand and headed out the door.

He found Manny waiting by the car and filled him in on his conversation with Tom. As they got in the car to start home, he turned to Manny and said, "I guess I should tell Joe and Doug tonight."

"It would probably be a good idea. Word will get out fast tomorrow."

"I'm afraid of how Joe is going to react. He is going to go off on me." Zach was sure Doug wouldn't be happy either, but Joe had been very vocal on the subject.

"Nothing you can do about it now. Better to at least tell him face to face instead of letting him hear it from someone else."

"You're right, but it is not going to be easy."

"Nobody said it would. It is what it is. You can't change it now. Just keep moving forward."

"He's going to want me to leave the house, you know that, right?"

"You are going home anyway," Manny said.

"I mean tonight; he won't want me there." Zach was afraid that Joe would want him to leave then and there, and he had nowhere to go.

"No he won't. And if he does, I'll say something." Manny was trying to be reassuring, but Zach still felt nervous.

"Okay. Either way, by the time you get back from the next road trip. I'll be gone." Fortunately, they were scheduled to go out on the road in two more days, so his time around the house would be limited. He planned to pack and take off as soon as he finished with his meeting. This time tomorrow, he would be on the road home.

"You don't have to run off like that. I mean, we're still friends right? You do plan to keep in touch?"

"Of course. I may lay low for a while, but I'll still be watching you, waiting for you to get your chance." It was only a little lie. Zach wanted to keep in touch, and maybe he would eventually, but he couldn't bear the thought of leaving. Regular contact with Manny would just be a reminder of what he lost.

"You better. I mean that, or else I will come and hunt you down." Manny was serious, and he stared at Zach long and hard.

"Okay, okay. I will stay in touch. In fact, if you make it with the White Sox this year I will even come to see you play."

"I don't know if that will happen, but I'll make you a deal. You come and see me and I will be there for you too. Don't assume you won't stay with the White Sox, and if you do, we can still make it together."

"We'll see. One step at a time. Let me get through tonight first, and then I'll worry about tomorrow." With that, he started the car, and they headed home. He only had two more times to go through this, and the sooner he made it home he could get one more out of the way. He was tired of talking about it.

When they got home, they found Joe and Doug in their usual spot on the couch playing video games. Zach knew that it was best if he just got this out of the way,so after he dropped off his things in his room he made his way to the living room and sat down. Manny followed a minute later and found a seat on a chair across from Zach.

"Hey guys," Zach said, "I need to talk to you about something."

"Can it wait?" Joe asked. "We need to finish his daily beating."

"Actually, I'd like to get it out of the way," Zach replied.

"I'm okay to stop," Doug said, putting down his controller. "I've had enough for today anyway."

"This better be good," Joe said, putting down his controller and turning toward Zach. "What's up?"

There was no way around it, so Zach just said it. "I have a meeting with the White Sox tomorrow morning. They are coming down to talk to me about the last round of drug testing." He sighed, this was it. "I failed a drug test a few weeks ago. I tested positive for Boldenone."

As expected, Joe was the first one to speak. "Did you do it?"

"Yes."

"That's the same thing that Joey Woodward got popped for, right?" Joe looked at Zach straight in the eye, and he could see the look of disgust. "Were you in on it together?"

"No. I got it from someone in the Dominican Republic over the winter. I tried it before Spring Training and didn't think it did anything for me. When I started the season off slow this year, I panicked and did it one more time. That is what caused the positive test."

Joe turned to Manny. "So he got it in the Dominican. Are you in on this too?"

"No," Manny replied, "he only told me yesterday."

"This has nothing to do with Manny. It's all on me. I made a mistake, and now I'm going to face the consequences." Zach resented the fact the Joe thought Manny was involved and couldn't believe he'd said that.

"So how are we supposed to react? Do you want us to feel sorry for you or what?" Joe was starting to get worked up. "We've talked about this before. I couldn't believe you sat there and tried to defend people that were cheating. Then again, maybe it makes sense now that we know you were doing it too."

"I don't want you to feel sorry for me. I just thought I should be the one to tell you before you heard it somewhere else. I know it was wrong, and I shouldn't have done it and now I'll have to pay for it."

"Fifty games isn't enough if you ask me. There is no place in this game for cheaters. I told you before I want nothing to do with someone that can't follow the rules. As far as I'm concerned, we're done. When are you leaving?" Joe stood up and started to make his way to his room.

"I have to meet with the team and I plan to pack up my stuff and head out. I'll be gone by the time you get back from the road trip."

"Good. The sooner the better." With that, Joe walked to his room and closed the door.

They sat in silence for a few minutes, and then Zach turned to Doug. "So, what about you?"

"I don't know Zach," Doug said "I mean, part of me feels the same way the Joe does. We all go through the same meetings around PEDs at the beginning of every season. I can't believe you thought you could get away with it."

"I wish I could tell you what I was thinking. Even though I knew it was wrong, it made sense at the time and it just happened."

"It didn't just happen. You made a conscious decision to do it. It took thought and planning. It's that kind of talk that gets Joe upset." Zach could see that Doug was upset too, but he seemed like he was trying to understand.

"You're right. I've been lying to myself for a long time. I tried to take the easy way out."

"We all feel the pressure. This game is supposed to be fun, but when you get to this level it turns into a job and everyone is on you to succeed." Doug stood up and walked around to the back of the couch and leaned over, resting his head in his hands. "You're a good guy, Zach, and a good player. You didn't need to do this. It's such a waste."

"I know, and I'm going to do everything I can do to show myself and everyone else that I can still make it."

Doug stood up and looked past Zach to the wall behind him. "I'm not like Joe. I'd like to think I could get past this. It is just going to take some time. I hope you do make it. Just do it the right way this time." He looked down at Zach, shook his head in disbelief, and walked to his room without saying another word.

They sat in silence for a few minutes before Manny spoke. "That went well, don't you think?"

"I'm still in one piece. I guess you could call that success." Zach closed his eyes and sank deeper into his chair. "I'm tired of talking about it. I wish it were six months ago or six months in future. Any time but now."

"Only one more to go."

"Yup, and then the hammer comes down. I'm sure I'm done for the year. I just wonder if they release me on the spot." Zach fully expected to be released by the team; it was just a matter of when it would happen.

"You don't know that for sure. It could just be a suspension. Just tell them the truth. It was a mistake. They have invested time and money in your career; they won't just throw that away."

"I'm not so sure. This will be the second suspension for the team in just a couple of months. Remember, Joey Woodward was caught for the same thing. It could look like a pattern in the organization. They are not going to want that."

"Maybe you're right. But you can still hook up with another team. I've been released before. Someone will always give you a second chance." Manny was trying to be helpful, but it didn't make Zach feel any better.

"We'll see. Right now, I'm just exhausted, and I'm going to try to get some sleep." Zach got up and started toward his room. He took a few steps and then stopped and turned toward Manny. "Thanks for everything."

"No problem," Manny said as he got up from his chair, "that's what friends are for."

"I don't just mean for the last few days. I mean for the last couple of years." Zach was trying not to get emotional, but he couldn't help it. "You're been a great friend, and I'm going to miss you."

"I told you before, we'll keep in touch." Manny smiled at Zach. "I'm looking forward to the day we're both in the big leagues. I hoped it would be on the same team, but if not, I'll be looking forward to finding a way to strike you out. I know your swing better than you do."

"We'll see about that." Zach wasn't feeling confident right now and wasn't ready to debate how he would fare in the future, so he decided to let it go. There would be time to think about that later. Now he just wanted to go to bed and get the next day over with. He gave Manny a wave and headed off to bed.

Fortunately, sleep came quickly that night, and the alarm woke him up early the next morning. He didn't want to run into Joe or Doug, so he got dressed and got out of the house. He had time to kill before his meeting, so he went to the park and sat on a bench to ponder his future. He didn't know what to expect from his meeting. Would it be a long discussion about his future or just a review of his case and then out the door? The last few days had been very tiring, and he just wanted to get it over with. He walked around for about an hour thinking about everything over and over again and then headed over to the stadium.

He arrived at the stadium and made his way to the club offices. There were three representatives from the team waiting for him, and they waved him in and he took a seat across from them at a large table. After a few introductions they got right to the point and showed him a copy of the test results. They then read from a copy of the official drug policy and informed his that he would be suspended for the next fifty games effective immediately.

Zach listened carefully and nodded at the correct times, all the while thinking to himself "How did I get here?" At one point he acknowledged that he had taken the banned substance, and he was surprised that they did not ask for any additional details. When they were finished talking, they asked if he had any questions. The only thing he wanted to know was if he would be able to play again this year and the status of his future with the club.

They told him it would be best if he just sat out the remainder of the season and that his future with the club would be determined later that winter at the team's annual meeting. They also informed him that the contents of his locker were already packed and waiting for him in the hallway. With nothing else to review, they stood up, wished him well, and the meeting was over. In about thirty minutes it was done, and his five years with the White Sox organization placed into limbo.

CHAPTER 16

Manny wasn't surprised when Zach didn't come home after his meeting with the club to discuss his upcoming suspension. It had been a little tense at the house the night before when he told Joe and Doug that he had failed the drug test and expected to be out the rest of the year. He was sure that Zach just wanted to give them a little bit of space and they would all sit down and talk about it today. He wasn't prepared to see the empty locker next to him at the ballpark. That was sure quick.

Manny had known that the team would remove Zach's things, but the speed of the change was interesting. At this point only Manny, Joe, and Doug knew what had happened, the rest of the team was in the dark. A couple of guys had made comments to Manny and asked what had happened to Zach. Manny really didn't have any answers for them. He didn't feel it was his place to say anything, so when asked he simply said he didn't know.

In some ways that answer was true. Manny had no clue where Zach was or his plans for the future. He mentioned that he was going to go home, but he didn't say when. He wanted to stay with the White Sox, if they still wanted him, or he would hook on with another team if they didn't. Beyond that, Manny had no clue where Zach was or what he was doing.

He had tried to call and even sent him a few text messages, but he had received no response. He must have been really upset to not even talk to Manny, and he decided that it would be best if he just gave Zach the space he so obviously needed. Tom had called a meeting for the team before the game, and Manny figured that he was planning to discuss the situation at that time.

After batting practice, the team gathered in the locker room and waited for Tom. There were several theories floating around about Zach, from he was called up to he had to leave to take care of some type of family emergency. No one suspected that he could have failed a drug test. Manny never would have expected it either, but then again, he had been tempted once so anything was possible.

Tom entered the room, and everyone immediately stopped what they were doing and waited for him to address the team. He wasn't one to show his emotions, but Manny could tell that he was upset. Whether it was anger or sadness, he couldn't tell, but it was more emotion than he had shown in the two-plus years Manny had been with the team.

"I'm sure that you noticed that Zach's locker is empty," he started, "and you're wondering what happened. Today, Zach was notified that he was in breach of the Minor League Baseball drug testing policy, and he has been suspended immediately for the next fifty games. Zach and the team also decided that it would be in his best interest that he not return to the club this season."

Manny took a look around the room to see the team's reaction. Most of the players looked surprised. They would not have expected this from Zach. There were a few, like Joe, that just shook their heads and looked disgusted. No matter what they felt, everyone was shocked by the speed in which Zach had been removed from the team. It was one thing to see someone promoted or even released, but you usually got the chance to say good luck, or good-bye. Zach was just gone, with a very limited explanation.

"It's important that you all know that the Barons, the White Sox, Minor League and Major League Baseball all take drug testing very seriously," Tom continued. "It is very easy to be tempted to cut corners to succeed. You are all grown men, and you have a choice in how you act and what you put into your body. People come and go in this game, and it will continue on, with us or without us. No one is above the game, remember that."

He went on for a few more minutes, talking about the temptations the game presented to players. Much of the conversation was around trying to cut corners and bypass the hard work and dedication needed to succeed at the major league level. He made it clear to all of them that he expected more from his players and that he took Zach's suspension personally and that any time one of his players made an error in judgment it reflected on the entire organization. He looked at each person when he finished his remarks and abruptly left the room.

Usually, the locker room was full of conversation and music, but not today. Most players kept to themselves, but a few gathered in small groups. As Manny looked around the room, he couldn't help but think it had the feeling of a wake or a funeral. He could hear a few snippets of conversation, and the general consensus was that if this could happen to Zach, it could happen to anyone.

The team was definitely in shock, and they were in no mood to play a game that night but they had no choice. One thing about baseball, the games would go on. Tom was right, no one was bigger than the game, and they all still had jobs to do, with or without Zach.

They couldn't do much at the plate that night and could only muster six hits and a single run. On defense they made three errors and a few other plays that would not be considered errors in the box score but were damaging. The visiting Memphis Braves took advantage of everything the Barons gave them and cruised to an 8–1 victory.

The locker room was very quiet after the loss, and everyone was eager to pack up for the night and get ready for the next road trip. Hopefully the change of scenery would be good for them, and they could return to their winning ways.

Manny was going to miss Zach, personally as much as professionally, He had really become a good friend over the past two years, and he had come to lean on him quite a bit. It was tough to be away from his family for long stretches of time, but Zach had helped him cope with the loneliness. On the field, Zach was a solid performer, and he made everyone around him better. He always put the team first, whether it was on the field or off, and you didn't realize the impact of those types of players until they were gone.

Manny caught a ride home with Doug and was looking forward to seeing Zach and hearing about his meeting with the team. Maybe he had been given some type of indication on his future. Tom had mentioned he would not be back this year but he didn't say if he had been released. Maybe the decision hadn't been made yet or if it had, Tom didn't want to share with them. Either way, Manny was sure Zach would tell him, and no matter what happened, he would be there for him and try to help his friend deal with the situation.

When they pulled up to the house, they saw Zach's car parked in its usual spot, so at least he had made it home. When they opened the door, the living room was dark, and it appeared that no one was home. "That's odd," Manny said as they entered the room, "Zach's car is outside, but it looks like no one is here."

"Maybe he's out with Sarah," Doug suggested as he made his way to his room to drop off his things. "I'm sure that he would want to see her if he's leaving."

"Maybe. But he made it sound like she didn't want to talk to him." Manny decided he would try to give Zach a call and walked to his room.

He was shocked with what he saw when he turned on the light. All of Zach's things were gone, and on his bed was an envelope with the word "Manny" on the outside. It was heavier than he expected, and when he opened it he knew why, Zach's car keys were inside. He set them on the bed and read the note.

Manny,

During my meeting with the team today about the drug test they also informed me that they were shutting me down for the season. My future with the organization will be decided at the team's annual winter meeting.

I didn't want to face the guys again, so I decided to head home this afternoon. When I was packing up the car, I realized that I was leaving you without transportation, so I left you the keys to the Purple Beast. Even though you say you can't drive, I know you can, and this way you don't have to depend on Joe or Doug for rides. We'll figure out what to do with the car when the season ends.

I am sorry that I disappointed so many people by my recent actions. I should have known better, and I will regret those decisions for the rest of my life. You have been a great friend to me for the past two years, and I wish you success in reaching your dream. You have all the talent in the world, and I know it is just a matter of time until you make it to the big leagues.

I am going to try and put all of this behind me and get back on the path to reach my own dream. This time around though, no shortcuts, I will put in all the work necessary and prove to everyone that I can do it on my own. Hopefully, we'll both make it, and we'll either compete on the field or end up as teammates again.

I need some time to myself now, so don't expect to hear from me for a while, but remember, I will be watching you and I'll be there for you when you make it.

Your friend,
Zach

Manny had to read the note twice before it sunk in that Zach was really gone. He had always assumed that they would get the chance to say good-bye, but Zach must have felt really bad after the meeting today to leave so suddenly. Even though Manny knew Zach wouldn't answer, he tried to call his cell phone. Not only didn't he answer, but the call didn't even go to voicemail. He tried to text him a message, but it came back as undeliverable. It looked like he wasn't kidding about not hearing from him for a while, and Manny wondered when, or if, they would ever speak again.

Maybe he just needed time to absorb all that had happened the last few days. It had to come as a shock the way it all went down. He would never really understand what Zach was going through, but if he had to stoop so low as to try steroids, he must have been desperate. It really was too bad. It looked like it was all coming together for him and he had even started a relationship with Sarah, and then this. Zach was a creature of habit, and this was going to shake his whole world to the core. Manny actually felt worried about his well-being.

His thoughts were interrupted by a knock on the door, and Doug peaked his head inside the room. "Whoa, where did all of Zach's stuff go?" he asked.

"He took off earlier today, while we were at the game." Manny held up the note. "He left me a note and the keys to his car."

"What does it say?"

"Not much, just that he is sorry for the way things went down and he won't be in touch for a while." Manny looked at the note and the keys in his hand. "I tried to call him and text him but got no response. It's like he dropped off the grid and doesn't want to talk."

"I'm not surprised; it's been a rough few days. I would probably do the same thing."

"I guess, but it seems a little odd. I'm kind of worried about him."

"I'm sure he'll be okay. Maybe give his mom a call in a few days if you don't hear from him."

"Maybe I will." Manny knew he had Zach's mom's phone number around somewhere. He would take it with him on the road and try her in a few days.

"Joe just got home. Why don't you come out, and we'll fill him in on what happened with Zach," Doug said.

"Okay. Give me a minute and I'll be right there." Manny put the keys back in the envelope and put it on his nightstand. He didn't want to talk to Joe, because he knew that he wasn't happy with Zach, but he was their roommate and filling him in on the day's events was the right thing to do.

When Manny walked into the living room Joe and Doug were already talking. He made his way to a chair across from the couch where they were sitting. Once he sat down, they stopped and looked at him like he was going to say something important.

"Why are you guys looking at me like that?" Manny asked.

They looked at each other first and then Joe turned to Manny. "We were hoping you could give us the real story about what happened to Zach."

"What do you mean the real story? You guys know as much as I do."

"Come on," Joe said, "you're Zach's best friend. You have been living with him the past two seasons. You must know more than you are letting on."

Manny could feel where this was going. "What are you talking about? Zach never told me what he was doing. I found out when you did."

"Really? Didn't he say he got the stuff in the Dominican? When he went down to visit you this winter? Also, didn't Joey Woodward go to your camp this year too?" Joe put his hands up in the air. "When two guys get popped for the same thing and were at the same place, it makes you wonder."

Now Manny was starting to get angry. "Wonder what, Joe? Why don't you just come out and say it. You think I hooked them up with something?"

"You're the one who said you thought about doing it before."

"And I told you I didn't," Manny said, his voice rising. "I can't believe you think I would do anything like that."

"I'm just saying, it doesn't look too good for you," Joe said.

"I passed my test. This year and every other year. I'm clean. Just because I thought about doing something once doesn't mean I'm a suspect every time something goes down." Manny was angry with Joe, but at the same time he could see how he could jump to that conclusion.

Doug had been listening but had not spoken yet. He looked at Joe and said, "I told you already, I don't think Manny was involved. You heard Tom today. Zach made his own decision, and now he is paying for it."

"I never said Manny did anything," Joe started before Manny interrupted him.

"You pretty much did."

"No, I just said it makes you wonder. You have to admit, both guys got popped for the same thing after visiting your camp in the Dominican."

"Our camp is clean! We teach the kids to play ball the right way. We don't allow drugs or anything else there. Don't assume something is going on because a couple of people did something stupid. That's not right." Manny was getting mad at Joe now, and he wasn't going to hide it. They had worked hard to build that camp, and he wasn't going to let anyone question it.

Joe wouldn't back down. "I'm just saying, you should probably take a look at the people that are around there. If I'm thinking it, I'm sure other people are too."

"I don't care what people think. I know it's clean," Manny said.

"It's not always what you think. Perception is reality. And the perception is that something is going on there, and you're going to get lumped in with Zach and Joey whether you like it or not."

"I'm not going to sit here and take this from you. You have no idea what you are talking about." Manny got up from his chair. "I'm clean, and our camp is clean, whether you believe it or not."

Joe got up from his seat. "I hope you're right because I would hate to think I was living with two cheaters the past few months."

Manny took a step toward Doug and thought better of it. "You better be careful, Joe. Zach is my friend, and even though he made a mistake he's still my friend. Don't be so quick to judge other people."

Doug stood up and moved between them, "Hey, let's try to stay cool here. Everyone is a little upset right now. Don't let it get out of hand."

"I'm fine as long as he keeps his mouth shut," Manny said.

"I'll say whatever I want," Joe replied.

"I don't care what you say. Just don't say it around me." Manny was not about to get in a fight with Joe, but if he stayed much longer he wasn't sure what he would do. "What's done is done, just let it go."

"They got what they deserved. I'm glad they're gone, and I don't care if they come back. When someone gets popped for drugs it makes us all look bad."

Doug tried to be a peacemaker. "Come on, guys. We're all upset. Let's just try to drop it before somebody says something they regret."

"I'm not going to regret anything I say. I'm right, and if you guys want to stand beside some cheater that's fine for you. I'm not going to, now or later. Zach is as good as dead to me. I don't care what happens to him."

"That's just wrong. He's still a person. He was your friend," Manny said.

"I didn't know him that long, and apparently I didn't know him that well. So it's no loss on my part. Once a cheater, always a cheater in my book. I'm not going to waste any more time thinking about him." With that, Joe turned and walked to his room.

Manny and Doug stood in silence for a minute before Manny spoke. "Why is he so angry?"

"I don't know," Doug replied. "Some people see things as black or white, and Joe is one of them."

"I don't agree with what Zach did," Manny said, "but I've lived with the guy for two years. This was not in his character. He panicked and made a mistake, and now he is going to pay for it. Maybe with his career. What more does Joe want?"

"He's like a lot of people. He wants to make an example of Zach so that nobody else will do it."

"It has gotten better," Manny said. "I mean, when I first started out, drugs were everywhere, and now you hardly hear about it."

"You've been around longer than I have," Doug said. "This is the first time I've been around anyone that was doing it."

"Believe me. It was worse. Testing has made a big difference. The game is basically clean now."

"Do you think Zach will try to come back?" Doug asked.

"Definitely. The guy lives and breathes baseball. That is all he has ever wanted to do. He'll make it back, and when he does, he will be clean and guys like Joe won't be able to do anything to stop him."

"There will always be doubters. You know he'll have this hanging over his head forever now."

"I know and he knows it too. I think that will be his motivation. To prove everyone wrong." Manny smiled. "And you know what, he'll make it."

"What makes you so sure?" Doug asked.

"I think he was finally getting it."

"What do you mean?"

"He was finally realizing that his whole life couldn't be just baseball. He needed something else to fill the void."

"So what was going to fill the void?"

"You're going to think this is corny," Manny said.

"I won't say anything."

"Love. I think Zach found love, and it helped to provide some balance in his life. He stopped thinking about the game all the time and let it come to him. It's really too bad. He was just getting it, and people will think it was the drugs, but it was really because he found someone to fill the void in his life."

Doug shook his head. "You've been watching too many movies."

"No. It's true. It made a big difference in my life when I met Maria. I haven't made it all the way yet, but I never would have made it this far without her." Manny couldn't help but smile thinking about her. She was his rock and had supported him from day one. If it wasn't for her, he would have given up the game years ago.

"I don't know if I believe you or not, but for Zach's sake, I hope you are right."

"I know I'm right," Manny said. "I just hope Sarah will give him another chance. He would never admit it, but he really fell for her."

"I guess time will tell," Doug said. "If it was meant to be, it will happen for them."

"Yup. We'll see."

"Well, this has been a roller coaster of a day, and I'm beat. I'm going to head off to bed. I'll see you in the morning." Doug patted Manny on the shoulder as he passed by on the way to his room.

Manny turned off the lights in the living room and made his way in the dark to his room. For the first time in two years he would spend the night alone without Zach. He couldn't help but feel a little bit lonely, and he wondered where Zach was spending the night. He wished he could at least talk to him.

He packed his things for the trip and lay down in his bed. Usually sleep came very easy for Manny, but tonight he found it hard to calm his mind. He was still upset with Joe about the things he had said. He didn't like the implication that his camp was dirty. He and his brothers had built it from nothing, and it was a source of pride for his family. The more he thought about it he realized his anger was not directed toward Joe but toward Zach. He told him that he would be there for him and he was a man of his word, but it was going to be harder than he thought. He felt betrayed.

Manny tossed and turned for a while, but eventually his mind drifted to Maria and he felt himself calm down. Even though she wasn't with him, just thinking about her helped him to relax and gain perspective. He really wished she could be with him but it was too hard during the season. Maybe someday, when he made it to the big leagues she could join him, and he would finally feel complete. For now, he would just have to be satisfied with thinking about her until he drifted off to sleep.

CHAPTER 17

The next few weeks passed quickly. It felt strange not to have Zach around but Manny found himself falling back into a routine again, just this time he was alone. He had spent so much time around Zach the past few years it was almost like losing a brother. They were together every day during the baseball season, at the field, at home and rooming together on the road. With Zach gone Manny found himself dealing with a whole new set of emotions.

He knew better than to even bring up Zach's name when Joe was around, but he did talk from time to time with Doug. The hardest thing was that he had not heard from Zach at all. It was almost as if he dropped off the face of the earth. He did get in contact with his mom, who confirmed that he had made it home, but she said he didn't want to talk and Manny decided not to push things.

Doug had lost a friend in a car accident a few years before, and he mentioned to Manny that his reaction to Zach's leaving sounded like he was working his way through the seven stages of grief. Manny had never heard of it before, but after he looked it up online he had to agree with him.

The first stage was shock and denial. That pretty much summed up what Manny first felt when Zach had told him that he had failed the drug test. His initial reaction had been there must have been a mix up in the tests. He felt that he knew Zach pretty well and would have never believed that he would try to take some drug to increase his chances of making it to the big leagues. Even after Zach had been gone for a few days, Manny still expected him to show up one day and say it was all just a mistake.

After a while though, Manny realized that the test must have been correct and that Zach wasn't coming back. Maybe it was when they got back from the road trip and he saw that Zach's things were still gone. It really sunk in that day. It had been the first time in two years that Zach was not Manny's roommate on the road. It happened so fast that Manny wasn't assigned a roommate, so he ended up alone and had a lot of time to think. That's when he entered the second stage.

Pain and guilt. Stage two was tough. Manny felt a tremendous amount of guilt, mainly because Zach had first met the guy who set him up with the drugs while he was visiting him in the Dominican. It had taken a lot to get Zach even to make the trip in the first place. Manny had spent almost two years convincing Zach to come down for a couple of weeks. He really thought it would be good for Zach to get out and experience something different, see the world a little. Nice idea, but look what came out of it.

Manny knew that it wasn't his fault, but it took him a long time to reconcile the fact that he had played a role in the situation. He had spoken to both of his brothers, and they agreed that they were going to make it a point in the off-season to try to track down the guy that met with Zach. It was bad enough that he had already turned one person on to taking a short cut, but they had a camp full of young kids they needed to protect. Manny felt guilty already. Imagine if it happened so some seventeen-year-old kid who really had a chance to make a better life but got caught up with the wrong crowd?

He also felt bad that Zach didn't talk to him before he decided to take the drugs or even after he did. He had been there himself at one time, even had the needle in his hand, so he felt like he could have talked him out of it if Zach had only given him the chance. Even now, Manny felt like he could help Zach get through this difficult period. Maybe Zach felt like he needed to do it on his own, hopefully he was talking to someone. There were a few times Manny felt worried for Zach's safety. He hoped he wouldn't do something foolish.

Stage three was anger and bargaining. Manny was angry all right. At Zach for taking the easy way out and putting his career at risk. At himself, for not being a good enough friend that Zach could talk to him before he made such a stupid decision. At the guy who told Zach about the drugs. He hoped they could find him, Manny wanted to have a little talk with him to set him straight.

He wished he could go to the team and talk to them about giving Zach a second chance. He had no idea if Zach would be back the next year or if the White Sox would release him. Maybe he could go to the club and offer to be his "life coach" and keep an eye on him. It worked for Josh Hamilton, an All-Star outfielder with the Texas Rangers. He had a drug and alcohol problem and the team paid for someone to basically keep an eye on him and keep him out of trouble. Maybe he could make a deal with the team to keep an eye on Zach.

If he was going through the seven stages of grief, Manny felt he was probably in stage four now: depression, reflection, and loneliness. Now that they were back home, it had really begun to sink in. Zach's locker was still empty at the stadium, and his side of the room empty at home. Manny drove to and from the games by himself most nights and spent time after games reviewing video by himself. He still had the rest of the guys on the team to talk to, but he found himself more reserved than usual.

Even at home, he would make small talk with Joe and Doug, but the truth was he had only known them for a few months, and it took time for him to open up around people. Plus, Joe still had a lot of anger toward Zach. He must be stuck in that stage, and it was hard for Manny to talk to him much. Doug was a little better to deal with. They could always talk about pitching, and Manny found himself spending more time with him. Doug's star was rising quickly. Maybe if he was lucky, Manny could become his personal catcher and ride his coattails all the way to the White Sox.

Getting to the majors kept pushing Manny forward. That and his weekly conversations with Maria. They had a standing date to talk on Sunday evenings, which was Manny's favorite day of the week. Thank God for Skype. It was so nice to see her face. The guys always asked him why he played better on Mondays. The answer was obvious to Manny. His tank was empty by the end of the week, and Maria filled it up for him on Sundays.

She had really helped him work through his emotions, and he was confident he could get through the next few stages: stage five, the upward turn; stage six, reconstruction and working through; and stage seven, acceptance and hope. He read online that it could take some people years to go through all seven stages. Manny was confident that it wouldn't take him that long. Zach was still alive after all, but he still needed to get through them all. As he packed up his things for the last road trip before the All-Star break, at least he felt like he could see the light at the end of the tunnel.

A knock at his door interrupted his thoughts. When he opened it, he found Doug there with an exasperated look on his face. "What's up?" Manny asked.

"Did you get anyone assigned to room with you on this trip?" Doug asked.

"No. I'm by myself. I'll probably get someone the next trip. Why?"

"Can I stay with you? Joe is driving me crazy, and I can't stand the thought of sharing a room with him for a week."

"Sure, what's wrong with him? Still hung up on Zach?" Manny knew Joe had a hard time letting things go, and he still made a random comment from time to time.

"No. He's been Googling himself lately and found that his name has popped up in a few trade rumors. He is freaking out."

"Really?" Manny was surprised. One thing Zach had taught him was to keep an eye on what was going on around baseball. He had a few sites that he visited regularly, but he had not seen anything on himself or his teammates.

"Yeah. Popped up on the Internet today. The White Sox are looking for some power at first or third and supposedly have been talking to the Oakland A's. Joe's name was mentioned as a prospect who could go in the trade."

"That's not a bad thing. It means that you are being noticed." Manny had been around for a while, and he knew that any time your name was brought up it was a good thing. He only wished he was a high enough level prospect that he could show up on someone's radar.

"I know, but he thinks that the White Sox are giving up on him."

"No. He's thinking that the glass is half empty. It's actually half full; the A's want him."

"Try telling him that. I'm done talking to him about it. Let me room with you this trip, and it will probably all blow over by the time we get back in town."

"Sure. No problem." Manny would actually welcome the company. He was used to having a roommate, and it would be nice to have someone around.

"Great. Let me know when you're ready and we can head over to catch the bus." Doug looked like he had a huge weight lifted off his shoulders, and he even seemed to skip a little as he made his way back to his room.

Manny grabbed the rest of his things and tried to fit everything into his suitcase so they wouldn't end up wrinkled. There was nothing worse than getting to the hotel and realizing that you had to iron all your clothes. One thing he had learned over the years was how to pack efficiently. In fact, during the season he had learned to live with very few things. In this business they never knew when they were going to get a phone call and have to pack up and go.

Unfortunately for him, Manny had never received a call that he had been promoted to the big leagues, or even to a high level in the minors. He was usually assigned to a team during spring training and that is where he stayed for the year. The only phone calls and conversations he had were around the terms of his release. That had happened too many times for his liking.

The team representatives were usually very nice about it and always said it was either a numbers game or that they just had too many players at his position. Manny was a very nice guy and well liked in the clubhouse, so management was always sensitive to how they treated him. He also knew that he had a pretty good reputation because he always landed with a new team.

Joe would figure that out at some point too. Even though he was drafted by the White Sox it wasn't a guarantee that he would end up in the majors with them. This game really was a business, and as a player he had to look at it that way. Guys in the Dominican didn't care who they played for as long as they got to the states. Guys in the U.S. usually had a favorite team while they were growing up and always wanted to play for them. More often than not, they got drafted by a rival and they were disappointed but eventually came around and were just happy to get the chance to play.

It was always hard this time of year as the trade deadline in the majors approached. There was always some rumor about this player or that player changing teams. You had to figure out whether you were a buyer or a seller. The White Sox looked like buyers this year. They had been playing well and currently had a five game lead over the Detroit Tigers in the American League Central Division. If anything, they needed a corner infielder and maybe a pitcher.

Everyone thought that Doug was going to be the pitcher. He was very well thought of, and the White Sox kept a close eye on his starts. They felt he had a bright future but didn't want to rush him too much. They were pretty well stacked in the outfield, so it kind of made sense that they could offer Joe in a trade. Oakland's third baseman had power and was a free agent at the end of the year. They probably weren't going to sign him so it made sense to try and get something for him.

Even though he had been a jerk lately, Joe had been playing very well and was third in the Southern League with a .342 batting average. He was considered a solid prospect and could provide some outfield depth for the A's. In fact, they were a little thin in the outfield compared to the White Sox so Joe could end up making it to the majors faster if the trade went down. It would be easy to get distracted by the talk, but the reality was no one controlled their own destiny when they were in the minor leagues.

Manny finished up packing and dropped his things by the front door. A few minutes later he was riding with Doug to the stadium to catch the bus. They had left Joe at home on purpose, he would probably be upset but they didn't care. Once on the bus, Manny took his familiar spot in the back and placed his ice chest on the seat where Zach used to sit. It wasn't long until everyone was on board and they started off to Nashville.

As trips went, this was a pretty short one, a five-game series and then it would be time for the Southern League All-Star game. Manny didn't expect to make the team, so it would end up being a three-day break from the rigors of minor league life. He had been thinking about the break for a while and he had thought about going home for a few days, but logistically it just wouldn't work out. It was too far to go and he would basically spend two days traveling to spend one day at home.

Maria had offered to come up to visit, but Manny had turned her down. It would have felt strange to have her stay in the house with Joe and Doug, and he couldn't really afford to get a hotel room for her to stay in. He would make it a point to spend some extra time on Skype with her, and that would have to do for now.

About an hour into the ride Tom stood up at the front of the bus and picked up the microphone. "Gentlemen, may I have your attention for a minute please?" he asked.

"I just wanted to share some information I just received from the club. I am pleased to share that the Southern League All-Star team has just been announced and the Barons have two representatives. Joe and Doug, you have been selected to the team, and when we get to Nashville Jerry will work with you to make arrangements to get to Jacksonville for the game. Congratulations."

The players broke into a cheer and one by one congratulated Joe and Doug on their achievement. Just like in the majors it was a pretty big deal to be selected to the All-Star team. It was great exposure, and most of the players that made it on to the team ended up in the majors in a few years. Joe and Doug were definitely worthy of going, but Manny couldn't help but think that Zach might have made it too this year if things had turned out differently.

"Hey Manny," Doug said as he came down the aisle and took a seat next to him, "I guess you are going to be on your own for a few days. Joe and I are going straight from Nashville to Jacksonville."

"Really? I hadn't thought about that. What am I going to do without you guys around?"

"Maybe you can have Maria come up after all. You'll have the whole place to yourself. Even have her bring the kids."

"Nah, that's too much for her to deal with for such a short amount of time." Manny didn't want to think of her trying to wrangle a five- and three-year-old by herself on the plane.

"Well, why don't you see if someone can watch the kids and she can come alone?" Doug suggested.

"That's a thought," Manny said. "Maybe that would work out."

"Sure, why not? I bet it would be nice to see her for a few days."

"I would love it. I'll send her a text and see if her mom can watch the kids, and I'll check for flights." Manny was starting to get excited. He had not see Maria since he left for Spring Training. It would be a real treat to see her in the middle of the season. He sent her a text and pulled out his iPad to search for flights.

"You know the team's traveling secretary could probably help you make arrangements instead of doing it yourself," Doug offered when he saw Manny pull out his iPad.

"You think so?" Manny had not thought about that.

"Sure. He's done it for a few guys this year."

"Maybe I'll ask him. Where is he sitting?" Manny asked.

"Third row, driver's side." Doug pointed to a young man in a Barons's hat. "He's already set Joe and I up for our trip to the All-Star game. The guy is a wiz."

Manny made his way to the front of the bus and sat down on the empty seat next to Jerry Morris, the team's traveling secretary. It took him a few minutes to explain what he was thinking about and Jerry took a few notes, asked what he was willing to spend and told him he would have some options for him by the time they got to Nashville. Manny thanked him and headed back to his seat.

"All taken care of?" Doug asked when he got back.

"He said he'd have a few options for me later today."

"Cool. I hope it works out for you." Doug then got up and made his way back to his original seat leaving Manny alone.

Technology was an amazing thing. By the time they got to Nashville, Manny had confirmed with Maria that her mother could watch the kids and Jerry had found a very affordable flight for her. Jerry promised to take care of everything and even made arrangements for a car to pick her up at the airport and their landlord to let her in the house. In just a few days she would be in Birmingham waiting for him when he got back from the road trip.

The next five days flew by. The Barons finished the first half of the season winning four of the five games, and Manny's bat was the main reason. He started all four games they won, hitting three home runs and driving in eight. He was playing like a man possessed, and everyone on the team was teasing him about his newfound power. He didn't care. He just wanted to get back to Birmingham and see Maria. The bus ride home seemed to drag on and on, but they finally made it back home late on Sunday night.

He had ridden to the stadium with Doug, so he had to bum a ride from another guy on the team. He was so excited he couldn't sit still, and he felt like a kid on Christmas morning. Once he got to the house he could see that the lights were on and someone was inside. He opened the door and immediately the smell of Maria's tamales hit him and brought a smile to his face. "Maria! I'm home," he called out and walked toward the kitchen.

It was just like they were back at their house in the Dominican. She was standing over the stove with a big steaming pot of tamales. He was biased of course, but he thought his wife was the most beautiful woman he had ever seen. She was barely five feet tall and had long dark hair and dark brown eyes. She turned toward the door when Manny walked in, and her smile warmed his heart. He engulfed her in his arms and gave her a lingering kiss.

"It is so good to see you," Manny said. "I can't believe you are actually here."

"Me either. I've missed you so much," Maria replied. "For some reason, this year has seemed much harder."

"I know. So much has happened and there is only so much I can share on the phone. To have you here is the best thing in the world." Manny never felt truly whole when he was away from home. It always felt like there was a piece of him missing and back home with Maria.

"We're lucky your roommates made the All-Star team. It gave us the place to ourselves," she said with a mischievous smile.

He returned her smile and pulled her close. "I love you so much."

"I love you too. I'm sure it's been a long trip. Let's sit down and have some tamales."

"I was waiting for you to say that."

They stayed up the rest of the night eating and talking. Manny filled her in on Zach's story in much greater detail than he had before. She listened patiently, which was what she did best, and reassured him that he had done all that he could to help Zach. Manny still thought he could have done more, but Maria always made him feel better about things and he finally felt like he was able to let it go. Whenever something was bothering him she helped him work his way through it. She would have made an excellent psychologist or even a good bartender; she had an ear for helping people.

They spent the next three days catching up on all the comings and goings of their hometown. Manny missed it, but he wanted to pursue his dream. He knew that he was asking a lot of his wife and their kids, but she was so unselfish and giving she let him do what he needed to do. He could not have picked a better woman to marry, and he was determined that he would make it so that he could repay her for all the time they had lost.

Just as quickly as she got there, it was time for her to go. Manny really wished she could stay with him, but with the kids, it just wouldn't work right now. He was on the road so much they wouldn't see him anyway. At least back at home they had their families around to support them. Manny knew she was in good hands, and he counted the days until they could be together again.

He wanted to take her to the airport but she wanted to say good-by in private. It was hard to see her go but he knew that she had given him the strength to make it through the rest of the season. With any luck, he could take the next step and make it to the major leagues. He just needed to hit a little bit more, and he could make a great back up or personal catcher for some team. She had left him a freezer full of food, which would help sustain him and provide him fuel for the next month or so. Maybe a September call-up could be in his future; only time would tell.

CHAPTER 18

Manny already knew that he preferred living with Maria as opposed to Joe and Doug, but if he had any doubts they evaporated the minute they returned from the All-Star game. The house, which had been quiet and relaxed while they were gone, took on a new vibe the minute they returned.

Joe was immediately back on the Xbox making up for all of the time he missed while he was on the road. Doug was quieter, but he was more of a slob. He tended to leave things here and there throughout the house, a dirty dish here, a pair of shoes there. He eventually got around to picking things up, but he was not in a hurry.

Their trip to the All-Star game had been a success. Joe had two hits and an RBI, while Doug pitched two scoreless innings with three strikeouts. Manny tried not to be jealous. In his heart he knew they were both better players than he was, but he still felt a little left out. They were gracious and filled him in on everything they had seen and done, but there was definitely a distance between them that wasn't there before they had left. Maybe it was just in his own mind, but something seemed a little off.

He didn't have too much time to bring it up because as quickly as the break had come it was gone and the daily grind of the season resumed. The Barons were going to be home for the next nine days before they headed out on the road so it was easy to get back into a routine. Manny's days consisted of getting up in the morning, finding something to eat, hanging out during the day, playing a game at night, home and then bed. They only thing that changed was the name of the team they were playing.

Baseball really was a game of attrition. You did your best to stay sharp, but the days seemed to drag at times, and you had to work hard to stay focused. All it took was a few extra base hits to increase your average and improve your chances of making it to the big leagues. Zach had figured it out once. Over a 162 game season the difference between hitting .300 and .250 was only 26 hits.

That seemed like a lot, but it really was only one extra hit about every six games. You could lose that many hits on good plays by the defense or hitting the ball hard right at someone. You could gain that many hits by beating out a grounder to short or have a pop fly drop untouched in the outfield. Those 26 hits didn't seem like much but a guy hitting .300 had a much better chance of making it than someone hitting .250.

The team was playing pretty well, and Manny in particular had seemed to find his groove right around the time that Maria visited. He had three home runs right before the break and turned around with three more in the first five games of the homestand. He knew he had the ability to hit for power, but his hits seemed to always die on the warning track. Lately, they carried a bit more, and although they weren't clearing the fence by much, they were going out.

Maybe it was a coincidence, but his newfound power also started at the same time the notes appeared. He hadn't told anyone on the team about it, but just before the road trip he had found a note in his locker before a game. It wasn't signed. All it said was "Don't forget to use your legs." He didn't understand it at first, but then one night while he was looking at video he noticed he was hitting with his arms and wasn't generating power from his legs. He spent a day or two working on it in the cages, and sure enough his power surge started soon after.

His first thought was the Zach had sent him the note. It was the kind of thing they would have picked up in their nightly video sessions, but Manny had not heard from Zach since he left and how could he have gotten a copy of his at-bats? Even if it was Zach, he surely wasn't in Birmingham, or was he? It was possible that he could attend the games and see Manny hit. That didn't seem likely, and even if it was true, how could he have gotten into the clubhouse to leave the notes?

The only other options were the players or the coaches, and why would they leave him a note? It would be much easier to just talk to him about it. Why all the mystery? It just didn't make any sense. The mystery only got deeper when the next note appeared in his locker. "Don't tip your pitches." He had to think about that one for a while. He couldn't tip pitches when he was hitting. Was he giving away signs while he was catching?

Manny took pride in his ability to call a game, so when something he was doing was questioned, even by an anonymous source, he took it seriously. If he was tipping the pitches he called, it could put his pitcher at a serious disadvantage. He spent two days reviewing video, and sure enough there it was.

He was not tipping the type of pitch that was coming. It was the location. Catchers always set a target for a pitcher, trying to frame with their glove where they wanted the pitch. It wasn't always the type of pitch that got the hitter out but where it was located. If the hitter had an idea that Manny was setting up outside for example, they knew they could extend their arms over the plate and drive the ball to the opposite field. If it was an inside pitch they could shift their weight and pull the ball.

Again, the change was very subtle, but it was there. Manny would shift his shoulders depending on where he wanted the ball. If it was outside, he was turning his body away from the hitter. For inside pitches he was turning toward the batter. Maybe that explained why Doug had struggled in his last few starts. He still pitched better than most guys, but for him, he had given up more hard hit balls than usual. Manny made a mental note to reverse what he had been doing in the next game and see what happened.

He still had no clue who was sending the notes, but now he really thought it could be Zach. That was the kind of thing he would notice from his position at second base. He could easily have seen the same thing from behind home plate or even from the outfield. Zach had played in Birmingham for over two years. Surely someone would recognize him, but then again maybe not. All players looked different when they weren't on the field.

Manny decide to give Zach's mom a call and see if he was around and maybe wanted to talk. Before he headed out to the next game, he called her. She picked up on the third ring and seemed happy to hear from him. Yes, Zach was still staying at the house. He had been there ever since the suspension. He didn't want to talk to anyone and was spending most of his time alone watching TV. She sounded a little worried, and Manny tried to make her feel better by telling her he was sure Zach would snap of it soon.

She promised to give him the message and try to convince him to at least give Manny a call. Manny wished Zach felt better. He must be working his way through the seven stages too, but if he was home, who was leaving the notes? He felt kind of silly asking Joe or Doug. They wouldn't get it, maybe some of the clubhouse guys? They would know if someone was sneaking around the clubhouse. He would make it a point to ask them tomorrow.

Manny made a few inquires around the clubhouse before the next game asking the attendants if they had seen anyone around that didn't look like they belonged. They all looked at him strangely, except for one guy named Fred, who had a guilty look on his face that he just couldn't hide. Manny pulled him aside in a corner of the clubhouse.

"So Fred, I couldn't help but notice that you looked like you might have something to share when I asked if there was anyone hanging around the clubhouse earlier."

"No, I haven't seen anything," Fred replied nervously.

It's no big deal. I don't want to get anyone in trouble. I've just noticed some strange things going on," Manny said.

"Like what?"

Manny hesitated; he didn't want to give too much away in case Fred really didn't know anything. "Just some things around my locker."

Fred shifted from one foot to another. "If I tell you will you promise not to tell anyone?"

"Sure. It will just be between you and me."

"Well, I think some of the guys have been taking equipment and things from the player's lockers."

That was not what Manny was looking for, but he had asked so he had to follow up. "Why do you think that?"

"I've heard them talking and seen them come in during the games and wander around. When I come in, they just turn around and walk out quickly."

"Hmm. That's what I thought. Tell you what, I'll say something to Tom and we'll let him take care of it." Manny hadn't noticed anything missing from his locker. Things we showing up, not disappearing, but now that he heard something he would have to pass it on to Tom. Unfortunately, it didn't look like he would get any answers to his real questions.

"Just keep my name out of it okay? This is my first year here, and I want to keep my job."

"No problem. I won't say where I heard it."

"Thanks, Manny." Fred looked around one last time and left the room.

Manny made his way back to his locker and sat down. Well, he was no closer to an answer than he was before, and now he had to tell Tom there might be a thief in the clubhouse. That was not what he expected to come out of that conversation.

Manny had another good night at the plate with two solid doubles and three RBIs. He also tried out the changes to his catching position, and maybe it was just a coincidence but the Barons won the game easily 6–1 with no hard hit balls. It seemed like his game was really coming together. He was on a hot streak at the plate, and his catching skills were solid. If he could keep this up, maybe he would get a September call up.

He stayed late as usual, and by the time he got home Joe and Doug were deep into a game of MLB12 on the Xbox. They were in the middle of a conversation when Manny walked in but stopped abruptly when he came into the room.

"What's going on, guys?" Manny asked as he sat down.

"Nothing much," Joe said.

"What were you talking about when I came in?"

"Nothing," Joe said again without making eye contact.

"Why don't you just tell him?" Doug asked Joe.

"Tell me what?" Manny asked.

"We were just talking about your recent hot hitting," Joe said. "It's nice to see things coming around for you."

"Thanks. Why was that so hard to say?" Manny asked. They were acting strangely and not telling him everything.

"Tell him," Doug said to Joe.

"You heard the same things. Why don't you tell him?" Joe replied.

"Somebody better tell me something soon," Manny said, "or else I'm going to get upset."

Joe and Doug looked at each other for a minute or so. Doug sighed and said, "There was some talk at the All-Star game around the White Sox and the players that failed the drug tests."

"So, what does that have to do with me?" Manny asked.

Joe and Doug just looked at each other and then down at the floor.

Manny was starting to get frustrated. "What does that have to do with me?"

Joe looked Manny straight in the eye. "We were just talking about your recent power surge, and we're wondering where it came from."

"Hang on a minute. Do you guys think I am on something?" Manny couldn't believe what he was hearing. "Why would I do that?"

"You did say you thought about it once and you've got all this new power all of the sudden," Joe said.

"So you assume I'm on something? Maybe I'm just on a hot streak. I mean I'm not the player you guys are, but I have been playing for a few years you know."

"And you've never hit like this before," Joe said.

"So immediately I'm a suspect?" Manny was getting angry now.

"Well, you and Zach were close, and he got his stuff from the Dominican."

"Guilt by association." Manny turned to Doug. "Is that what you think?'

"No. I've seen guys get hot before," Doug said. "Some guys did talk about the Sox being a dirty organization, but Joe brought this up about you."

"I can't believe this. So because I come from the Dominican and my friend got caught doing something, every time I get a few hits I'm going to be suspected of doing steroids. That's not right."

"I'm just saying what other people are thinking," Joe said.

"You want to know what I think the difference is?" Manny asked.

"Sure," Doug said.

"I got a mid season visit from my wife that meant a lot to me. She was a reminder as to why I'm here. I feel more inspired to succeed than I was before." He hesitated for a minute. "And someone has been slipping notes in my locker with batting tips."

"Oh please. What kind of story is that?" Joe scoffed. "Some mystery person slips you a note that fixes your swing."

"I'm telling you. It's made a difference, that and seeing Maria."

Just then, Joe's cell phone rang. He looked at the caller ID, and a puzzled look came over his face. He got up and walked to his room without saying a word.

"I wonder what that is all about?" Doug said once he had left.

"Who knows? You don't think I'm on anything do you?" Manny asked Doug.

"No. You're too smart for that. Guys get hot. It happens."

"Yeah. But I hope other people don't feel the same way as Joe."

"You can't help what other people think. I learned that a long time ago."

"Me too. Part of being a ballplayer, but it still hurts sometimes," Manny said.

"I know, but you've been tested and come out clean. There will always be guys like Joe around to question things." Doug looked toward Joe's room. "I wonder what that call is about?"

"Maybe another anonymous tip about steroid usage among formerly light-hitting catchers," Manny said disgustedly.

They didn't have to wonder for too long because Joe walked out of his room a few minutes later with a dazed look on his face.

"What's the matter?" Doug asked.

"I've been traded to the Oakland A's," Joe replied. "They want me on the next plane tomorrow morning."

"Where to, Midland?" Doug asked, referring to Oakland's double A team in Texas.

"No."

"Sacramento?" Manny asked, thinking about Oakland's triple A team.

"No."

"Where then?" Doug asked.

"Kansas City. They are calling me up to the big leagues to join the A's. Their left fielder pulled a groin, and they want me to start tomorrow night. The Sox are getting some left-handed reliever."

"Seriously? They are calling you up?" Manny asked.

"Yeah. I guess I can thank some guy's bad groin for that."

The tension that had been in the air just a few minutes earlier quickly evaporated as the reality of Joe's news sunk in. As with many things in baseball the news was so sudden it took a minute for it to register. It was hard to say what was a bigger surprise, the trade or the fact the Joe would be playing in the big leagues the next night. Despite their recent interactions, Manny really did like Joe, and he was happy for him. It was every player's dream to make it to the big leagues, and Joe was about to get his shot.

"Congratulations," Manny said reaching his hand out to Joe. "I'm sorry to see you go, but it's great that you're going to get a shot with the A's so soon."

Joe reached out and shook Manny's hand. "Thanks. I don't know what to say. I mean, I just assumed that I would end up with the White Sox."

"It doesn't always work out that way," Manny said. "I've been with a bunch of organizations. It really doesn't matter how much you bounce around in the minors, it's that first major league team that you play for that you will remember."

"Think about it," Doug said, patting Joe on the back. "This time tomorrow you will have made your major league debut."

"You're right. I can't believe it," Joe said with a dazed look on his face.

"So are you excited?" Manny asked.

"Yeah, of course, but it kind of ticks me off that the Sox didn't think that much of me and just traded me away."

"You can look at this two ways," Manny offered, "either the White Sox didn't want you or the A's did. Remember, baseball is a business. The Oakland A's thought enough of you to make a trade to get you to be their left fielder because you are better than anyone they have in their organization."

"I guess you're right," Joe said. "They wouldn't have made the trade if they didn't think I could help the team."

"Exactly. In a good trade, both teams make out well. Who knows when the Sox would have called you up? This way you have a chance to make an immediate impact instead of waiting around for someone on the Sox to go down with an injury or something." Manny had been around long enough not to take things too personally. Being released a couple of times could do that for you.

"So how is this supposed to work?" Doug asked. "What do you do with your stuff?"

"They told me to pack up enough clothes to last me a week and make arrangements to ship the rest of my stuff later. Looks like I'll be in hotels for a while."

"Pack whatever you can tonight and we can take care of getting the rest of your stuff for you later," Manny volunteered.

"You would do that for me?" Joe asked.

"Sure. Why not?" Manny responded.

"I mean, we were just going at it a few minutes ago."

"Water under the bridge. I'm happy for you." Manny was still upset, but he knew he was clean so it didn't really matter what Joe thought.

"Well, you're a bigger man than I am. I don't think I would feel the same way."

"Everybody is entitled to their own opinion. I can't change the way you think." Manny shrugged. Things still felt uncomfortable but there was nothing he could do about it. At least now with Joe leaving, some of the tension in the house would be gone.

"Looks like you've got a long night ahead of you," Doug said.

"I've got to call my parents. They're not going to believe this! I need to see if they can make it to Kansas City tomorrow. I'll see you guys later." With that, he excused himself and left the room.

Manny and Doug watched him walk away and then sat down on the couch in the middle of the living room. "And then there were two," Doug said, smiling at Manny.

"Crazy how that works, isn't it?" Manny said. "It was just a few weeks ago that we had four guys living in this house."

"I know. It's going to be strange with both Zach and Joe gone."

"We could ask somebody else if they want to move in." Manny said.

"From the team? No way. I think I can deal with just one roommate for a while. It's a three bedroom house, we'll just have an extra room. That is unless you wanted to have Maria come up."

"For the rest of the season?" Manny was surprised Doug would make that offer.

"Sure. You two could take Joe's room and the kids could take your room."

"You would seriously consider that?"

"Why not? I haven't met Maria, but she sounds great and I know from the food she left behind she's an excellent cook."

"What about the kids. They are pretty young. We stay up pretty late, so we'd have to be quiet when we came home because they would be asleep."

"Joe is the night owl, not me. That wouldn't bother me at all."

"I'll have to think about it," Manny said. "It was hard enough getting her to come up at the All-Star break. We kind of had an understanding that she wouldn't come up to the states until I made it to the big leagues."

"You should consider it. I can see the difference in you since she came to visit. It must be hard to be apart so much. This is a golden opportunity to spend some time together," Doug smiled at Manny. "Plus, I think we are going to get tired of each other pretty quick if it is just the two of us."

"Speak for yourself. I've never lived with only one person before. Well, except Maria of course. I'm kind of looking forward to it."

"We still have a couple of months to go. We'll see how you feel then." Doug smiled.

"Honestly, I don't think you are going to be here much longer," Manny said.

"What makes you say that?" Doug asked.

"You are tearing this league up. You need tougher competition. I give it only a few more weeks until you get called up."

"Maybe if someone blows out an elbow or something."

"No way, an injury is not the only way you are getting called up. They don't realize it yet, but they need you."

"Do you really think that?"

"Absolutely. I've caught a lot of guys. Including ones that have made it to the majors. You have the best stuff I have ever caught."

"That means a lot coming from you. Sometimes you wonder if you have what it takes or not."

"Trust me. You've got it," Manny said.

"Thanks. I appreciate it." Doug smiled. "You know it's been a pretty long day. I think I'm going to turn in."

"Okay. I'll see you in the morning."

"You bet."

Manny stayed up for a while to see if Joe would come back to living room, but after about twenty minutes he gave up and turned off the lights and went to bed. Joe had been a bit of a jerk lately, but Manny did like him and was happy that he was going to the majors. He was sure that Doug was next and he had to admit he wondered if he would ever get his chance. Based on what they said the talk was at the All-Star game there seemed to be some doubts about him around the league. He hoped the rumors weren't too wide spread, he was clean and it wasn't right that people assumed he was dirty because he was friends with Zach.

As he lay down on his bed, Manny began to think about Doug's offer to have Maria and the kids come stay with them. Having her around for a few days was like a boost of energy for him. He could only imagine what it would be like if she was there every day. Maybe that would be what it took to put him over the hump.

CHAPTER 19

Manny awoke the next morning to find Doug standing at his door. "Joe's leaving. Do you want to say good-bye?"

"Sure. One second." Manny rubbed the sleep out of his eyes. What time was it? A quick look at the clock told him it was only 6:30. This had to be the earliest Joe had ever gotten up in the time Manny had known him. He must have an early flight, there was no other reason he would be up this early.

He found Joe and Doug by the front door looking at a piece of paper. They seemed deep in conversation, so Manny took his time getting across the room. They stopped talking when he approached, and Manny waited for one of them to say something.

"I'm not exactly used to getting up at this time," Joe said.

"Did you get any sleep?" Manny asked.

"Not really. I was trying to think of everything I needed to do before I left. Finally gave up and wrote it all down." He gestured to the piece of paper in Doug's hand. "Hopefully you guys can help out."

"No problem," Doug said. "We can take care of everything for you."

"I appreciate it. I don't know where my head is at right now."

"You'll be fine," Manny tried to reassure him. "At the end of the day, it's just playing ball. You've been doing that your whole life."

"I guess that's true. But this is a whole different level. I mean, it's the major leagues. I hope I can keep up with them."

Joe never lacked confidence, so his tone took Manny by surprise. "Don't doubt yourself. They are calling you up for a reason. You have been tearing it up around here. Just picture them in a Huntsville Stars's uniform."

"Or just picture them naked," Doug chimed in. "That is supposed to help with stage-fright."

Joe stared at him for a minute then burst out laughing. "I've seen enough naked ballplayers in locker rooms over the years. I don't think I want to start picturing them in other places too."

"Hey," Manny said, "whatever works." With that he opened his robe and flashed Joe. That got him laughing even more, and the doubt seemed to disappear.

"I think that image will haunt me for a while."

"How about this one then? Doug said as he turned his back to Joe and pulled down his pants. "Don't forget me."

"Okay, okay. I get it. I'm going to be fine. These guys all had to make their way through the minors too, right? I'm going to light them up."

The gleam in Joe's eye returned as quickly as it had left, and Manny knew that he would be okay. "Be sure to keep us updated on how you are doing."

"Just look for me on Sports Center."

That was it. Now he was back for sure. A few minutes later he got a call that his taxi was there to take him to the airport. Joe picked up his things and headed for the door but not before a couple of man hugs on the way out. Manny couldn't help but think that despite all they had been through the past few weeks he was going to miss Joe. Hopefully, he would do well with the A's and hold on to his starting spot. He definitely had the potential to be a star.

With Joe gone, Manny and Doug took a look at the list of things he left for them. It wasn't much really, just what to pack and where to send it and a reminder to forward his mail. The biggest issue was what to do with his car. He'd decided just to leave it parked at the house and asked them to start the engine everyone once in a while to save the battery. He would pick it up when the season ended.

With nothing much else to do until the game later that night Manny and Doug went their separate ways for the day. Manny had some laundry to catch up on, and since Doug was pitching that night he liked to keep to himself. Manny figured he would get out of the house for a while and give Doug the space he needed.

While Manny was packing up his things he thought about the time that he and Zach went to the laundromat and met Sarah. He'd looked for her each time he had gone back but she had never shown up again. He was going to call her and see if she had been in contact with Zach, but he didn't have her phone number. He knew she went to the games sometimes, but he had not seen her at the stadium.

It was too bad how that situation played out. Manny knew that Zach was very fond of Sarah and she had been a positive influence on him. It wasn't a coincidence that Zach had started hitting after he met her. Manny was a firm believer that you had to have balance in your life to succeed, and Zach had only found it after he met Sarah. If Zach had only met her sooner maybe he would not have turned to steroids to help get him over the hump.

Manny pulled into the parking lot grateful to have Zach's car to drive. Leaving him the car really meant a lot to Manny and helped reinforce to him that Zach was a nice guy who made a bad decision. It was probably a big inconvenience for Zach to not have a car, and Manny would have been really stuck without it.

The first thing Manny noticed when he walked in the door was a woman on the far side of the room. He wasn't sure, but it looked like Sarah. As he got closer he realized that is was her. What were the chances that he would run into her again after all this time? He wasn't sure how she would react, but he decided to approach her anyway.

"Hey there, stranger!" Manny called from across the room.

She looked up, startled at the interruption, but then broke into a wide grin. "Hey there yourself!"

"It's been a long time. Where have you been?" Manny asked as he dropped his things and spread his arms wide for a hug.

She didn't hesitate, and when she got closer she gave him a big hug. "I've been around. I've seen you at the games. You just don't see me in the stands."

"You still come to games?" Manny asked, a little surprised.

"Of course, I'm still a Barons fan. Always will be. Sorry, but you guys come and go. I root for the team." She shrugged and gave him an "I'm sorry" face.

"Ouch. That hurts a little, but I guess it's true. Players do come and go around here don't they?"

"Sure do. You try not to get too attached," she replied, lowering her head. "But sometimes you can't help it."

"I'm sorry about how all that stuff with Zach went down. I had no idea what he was doing. If he had ever said anything about it, I think I could have stopped him."

"Don't beat yourself up, Manny. There was nothing you could have done. Zach is a big boy. He knew the consequences of what he was doing."

"I know, but still, I wish I could have done something."

"Me too, but you can only go in as far as someone will let you." Sarah sighed.

"Have you spoken to him since he left?" Manny asked.

"He tried to call me a few times, but I didn't pick up or call him back. How about you?"

"I talked to his mom. She said he is doing okay. I know he's having a hard time though."

"Well, I'm sure he'll be fine. He'll get what he wants someday." Sarah looked up at Manny. "Did he ask about me?"

Manny wanted to tell her that Zach asked about her, but he hadn't. "I just spoke to his mom."

"So that's a no then?" she said, looking disappointed.

"That's a no. But, I know he was upset when he left. He was very embarrassed by this whole thing. He was disappointed in himself, and he felt he let people down, including you."

"Still, he didn't ask about me."

"He did try to call you. You didn't pick up."

"I know. I was upset. He really hurt me." Sarah looked like she was about to cry, and not for the first time thinking about Zach.

"I have to ask you, Sarah. Why does this bother you so much? I can see why other players and the White Sox would be upset, but this really has nothing to do with you. It doesn't change how he feels about you."

"It has everything to do with me. He lied to me." Her tears were quickly fading, and her eyes turned angry.

"With all due respect. He didn't lie to you. Taking steroids was wrong and he shouldn't have done it, but it's like some regular guy doing something wrong at work, it doesn't mean he doesn't love his wife or girlfriend." Manny knew it was a fine line, but it was true, Zach's actions had nothing to do with how he felt about Sarah.

"I don't see it that way."

"In fact, if you want to be technical about it, he took them before he met you. I think he stopped because of you. He knew he didn't need them after all."

"Why do you say that?" Sarah asked.

"I told him for years he needed a better balance between his professional and personal life. He was never going to be successful if he couldn't find that balance. Once he met you, he had it, and look at how happy he was and how well he played."

"You really think so?"

For the first time, Manny could see a glimmer of hope in her eyes. "Absolutely. He was a changed man."

"I don't know. It's still hard."

"Just take it slow. Give him a call and talk to him. At least that way you won't wonder what could have happened." Manny was sure that if given the chance they could work it out, but it would be up to Sarah to initiate something.

"I'll think about it."

"Good. That's all I can ask," Manny said.

They spent the next twenty minutes catching up on what else had been going on, including Maria's recent visit and Joe's trade to the A's. It turned out she wasn't kidding about watching the team. She was up to date on everything that had been going on, including Manny's recent hot streak.

"So what's the secret of your newfound power?"

"You wouldn't believe me if I told you," Manny replied.

"Try me."

"Okay. Well, first it was seeing Maria. Having her up during the All-Star break for a few days gave me a big lift. I told you that you need balance in your life to succeed, and she gives me that."

"That's great. Why doesn't she come up more during the season?"

"It's too hard with the kids. But, with some extra room at the house, Joe suggested they come up for the rest of the year." Manny still couldn't help but smile thinking about it.

"Is she going to come?" Sarah asked.

"We're still thinking about it. I'll know pretty soon."

"That would be great. But, you said 'first.' Is there something else?"

"Well, there is something else, but if I told you that you wouldn't believe it."

"Try me, or is it a big secret?"

"Not really a secret. It's just. I've found a couple of notes in my locker." It felt silly saying it loud.

"What did they say?" Sarah asked.

"Just batting tips and something I was doing wrong on defense."

"Hmm. Must be someone that knows baseball. Maybe attends a lot of games," Sarah said smiling.

"Yeah. I thought at first it was Zach."

"Who says it has to be a man?" Sarah said and smiled again. "Sorry, looks like my dryer is finished. Excuse me for a minute."

Manny noticed that his clothes were done in the wash and as he moved them to a dryer he thought about what Sarah had said. He had never considered that it could be a woman. Maybe. *Hey*, he thought to himself, *is Sarah saying it was her?* She did go to a lot of games. Some of the clubhouse guys could know she went out with Zach for a while so she could get the notes to him.

"Hey. My stuff is done. I'm going to take off," she said when she returned from folding her clothes.

"Okay." Manny stopped for a second and looked at her closely. "Hey, are you leaving me the notes?"

"Don't be silly Manny," she said with a smile. "I'm just a woman. I wouldn't know if you weren't say, using your legs, or if you were tipping pitches."

Manny smiled. "No. I guess you wouldn't, would you? But if you ever did, you can always call me to tell me. You wouldn't need to leave me a note."

"Understood. In fact, give me your number. You know, just in case I see something."

They exchanged numbers and promised to keep in touch. Although he couldn't get her to commit to calling Zach, she at least said she would consider it. Sarah was a perfect fit for Zach, and if she gave him a chance maybe they could get things to work out. He watched her walk out the door and thought about calling Zach to tell him he had seen her, but eventually he decided to let things happen on their own.

He finished up his laundry and headed back to the house. Doug was gone. He must have been out and about trying to keep his mind off the game. Manny decided to take a quick nap and then give Maria a call before he headed out. He would tell her about Doug's offer so she could start to think about coming out for a while.

He really wanted her to come, but she would still be stuck alone quite a bit while they were on the road so she might not want to go for it. Oh well, it couldn't hurt to ask. He set his alarm for two hours so he wouldn't miss the game and quickly fell asleep.

Manny was a little disappointed when he couldn't get Maria on the phone, but there really wasn't a rush. He could talk to her about it later. He made his way over to the stadium, and as he expected, news had leaked out about Joe's trade to the A's and everyone was talking about it. Unlike when Zach left, the players were happy for Joe although a few were jealous of his immediate call-up to the majors.

As if Joe's situation wasn't enough, there was an even bigger rumor going around. Bobby Calhoun, the Cy Young Award winning pitcher from the White Sox, was getting ready to go out on a rehab assignment, and it looked like he could come to the Barons. Calhoun was recovering from an elbow sprain and was expected to make two rehab starts before returning to the Sox. The Barons' schedule looked like it would line up with his timeline so he could join the club for a few days.

It was always exciting when a current big league player came down for a rehab assignment. For one thing, tradition dictated that the player spring for the post-game meal while he was in town, which meant a few days of good food for a change. Plus, depending on the guy, you could get some good information from him, tips and suggestions on how to improve your game.

Most guys that came down were pretty nice, but there were a few that would show up with an attitude that they were better than the rest of the team. They would usually keep to themselves, get their work in and go. You could tell with others that they remembered what it was like to struggle in the minors, and they went out of their way to offer words of encouragement.

Manny had heard that Bobby Calhoun was a great guy. Just twenty-six years old he had already won the Cy Young Award, which was given to the league's best pitcher, for going 22–6 with a 2.34 ERA two years before. He had recently signed a five-year $85MM contract that had given the Sox a significant discount on what he could have earned on the open market. That alone meant that he valued the team and just wasn't out for the money.

Manny was just about to head out to the field when one of the clubhouse guys told him that Tom wanted to see him in his office. A call to the manager's office was usually not a good thing, especially so close to game time, so Manny was a little concerned. Tom's door was partially closed so he stopped outside and knocked before he entered.

"You wanted to see me, Tom?" Manny asked as he stuck his head inside the door.

"Yes. This will just take a minute. I know you want to get out to the field."

"First, I wanted to thank you on the tip about one of the clubhouse guys getting sticky fingers and taking equipment. We took care of that today."

"No problem," Manny replied nervously. He didn't want to get into how he had found out about that, but thankfully, Tom didn't ask.

"So I'm sure you heard that Bobby Calhoun was coming down for a rehab assignment?" Tom asked.

"I heard something, but didn't know if was definite," Manny answered.

"Well, it is now. I just got off the phone with the training staff for the White Sox. He'll be here to start day after tomorrow and then the last game before we head out on the road."

"That's great," Manny answered, wondering what this meant to him.

"So I have two things for you. First, I want you to catch both his starts. He is mostly here to test out his arm, so nothing fancy. We just don't want him to get hit too hard, so you're the best one to take him through the other team's lineup. Second, since Joe is gone, I was going to ask you if he could stay with you and Doug while he was here."

"With us, why?" Manny was surprised. Visiting players usually stayed in a hotel when they came on rehab, not with other players.

"We thought it would be a good thing for Doug. Give him a chance to pick his brain for a few days. We were hoping you could bring it up to him."

"Sure. I don't think that would be a problem." Manny would also love to pick his brain. It wasn't often you got the chance to hang out with a Cy Young Award winner.

"Great. I'll let you talk to Doug. I know he's getting ready for the game and doesn't like to be disturbed."

"No problem. When will he get in?" Manny asked.

"He is flying in from Chicago tonight. He'll be at the ballpark in time for the game tomorrow. Afterwards you guys can just take him home with you."

"Okay. I'll talk to Doug later," Manny said and turned toward the door.

Tom stopped him before he could get away. "Manny, this could be good for you too. You are swinging a hot bat lately. Spend some time with Calhoun. I hear he gets attached to his catchers. If you hit it off, who knows?"

"Got it," Manny understood immediately. Bobby Calhoun was a star pitcher, and star pitchers got to pick their catchers. If they could hit it off, maybe he could end up as his personal catcher. That wouldn't be a bad job. He would be sure to be well prepared for the next few games and try to make him look good.

The game that night went about as good as it could. Doug was on his game and easily dispatched the visiting Pensacola Blue Wahoos in short order, giving up a single run on five hits. Double A was not providing Doug much of a challenge, and Manny knew it was just a matter of time before the White Sox either moved him to triple A Charlotte or straight to the big leagues.

Manny had a good game himself at the plate, no home runs tonight, but a couple of solid singles and an RBI. Sometimes this game was so simple, just see the ball and hit the ball. Players talked all the time about "slowing down" the game. It sounded strange, but it was true. Sometimes the pace of the game just seemed to slow to a crawl and everything was crystal clear. The ball looked huge when it was coming toward you and it wasn't a question of if you would hit it, but how hard.

That's the way it had been for Manny since Maria had come to visit and the notes started. He had gone through some hot streaks before but nothing like this. He was looking at his at-bats while he was waiting for Doug. He looked so balanced at the plate, his swing so smooth. Why couldn't it be like this all the time?

"Reliving another good game I see," Doug said as he came up from behind Manny. "You sure are on fire lately."

"I wish I knew why," Manny said as he closed his iPad. "I would have done it a few years ago and saved myself all this time in minors."

"Who knows? This game is hard to figure out sometimes. Just enjoy it."

"I guess you're right. You haven't been too bad yourself lately," Manny added.

"I feel really good right now. I hope it lasts." Doug shrugged, humble as ever. "Did you hear about Bobby Calhoun?"

"I heard before the game today. Figured you were too busy to hear about it."

"I was just talking to one of the clubhouse guys. He was getting his uniform ready. That will sure be strange for him, putting on a Barons jersey."

"I bet. Especially after winning the Cy Young and signing a big contract," Manny said.

"I hope I get a chance to talk to him a bit. I bet he could give me some good insight on pitching."

"You know what? I think you're going to get your wish," Manny said, realizing he had already told Tom that it was okay for Calhoun to stay with them before he talked to Doug.

"Why do you say that?"

"Well, Tom called me in before the game and asked me if he could stay with us, since Joe just left. He kind of put me on the spot, so I said yes. I hope you don't mind."

"Are you kidding? That's awesome! Now he'll have no choice but to hang out and talk to us." Manny immediately felt better.

"He's coming in before the game tomorrow, and Tom said he'll just come home with us after and stay for a few days. The Sox really wanted you to spend some time with him, so I think that's a good sign for you."

"Hey, and you too. I'm sure that you are going to catch him, right?" Doug asked.

"Yes. Both games."

"Cool, you can make an impression too, you know," Doug said.

"We'll see. For now, I'm just looking forward to catching a guy that has won the Cy Young. What were the odds of that happening around here?"

"Not very good I would have to say."

"And hang out with him too." Manny was getting excited. It was going to be a fun week.

"True. Tell you what. Let's clean up the house a little bit and pick up some food. I think things are a little bare right now."

"Sure thing. I'm going to finish up here, and I'll meet up with you tomorrow morning and we'll take care of it." Manny started to pack his things up to head home.

"Sounds good. Don't stay up too late. We've got a lot to do," Doug said as he picked up his things and headed toward the door.

"Okay." Manny didn't have much left to do tonight, so he quickly wrapped up and started home. Calhoun staying with them would delay anything happening with Maria coming to stay, so he would have to update her tomorrow. He was a little disappointed, but since he had been on the fence about it anyway, a week wouldn't make much of a difference. It would probably take that long for her to make arrangements anyway.

Once he got home he quickly put his things away and headed to bed. They had tons of work to do in the morning to get the house ready for their visitor. Joe wasn't the cleanest guy in the world, and Manny hadn't been in his room for a while so he was nervous about what they would find. Well, whatever it was, cleaning it would be worth it to get the chance to hang out with a guy like Calhoun.

CHAPTER 20

When Manny made his way to the kitchen the next morning, he found Doug already there making breakfast. The smell of coffee, bacon, and eggs quickly cleared his head from the previous night's sleep, and he thought to himself the next day at this time Bobby Calhoun would be here.

"Up early for the day after a start, aren't you?" Manny asked Doug as he poured himself a cup of coffee.

"Well, I took a peek into Joe's room last night when I got home and when I saw what was waiting for us today, I knew we would need a good breakfast and an early start."

"Please don't tell me that," Manny pleaded as he looked over his shoulder to Joe's room. "How bad is it?"

"Pretty bad. I mean, I wouldn't want my family staying there without a deep cleaning."

"Great. I knew he was a bit of a slob, but I never gave much thought to what his room looked like," Manny said.

"I know. I'm bad, but nothing like this. But now we have to deal with it. I thought we could pack up his stuff and kill two birds with one stone." Doug filled up a plate with bacon and eggs and placed it on the table for Manny.

"Thanks. You didn't have to make breakfast," Manny said, but he was happy he did because he was starving.

"You're going to need your energy," Doug said as he sat down at the table.

"Did you see how Joe did last night?" Manny asked.

"Yeah. Two for four. Got a hit in his first at-bat," Doug said with a smile.

"Good for him. I hope he can keep it up."

"I think he is going to be okay. Unfortunately, we're stuck here with his mess," Doug said with a sigh.

They spent the next few minutes talking about the previous night's game. It was a good one for both of them, but they were a little concerned about the prospects for the team for the rest of the year. Losing Zach and now Joe was going to put a serious dent in their offense, and their hopes of making the playoffs were going to take a hit as a result.

While getting to the big leagues was every player's dream, they still wanted to win while they were in the minors and looked forward to the playoffs and maybe a championship. Not only was it more fun to win, that also meant the season lasted longer and you got to play more. The big league teams didn't always feel the same way. They were interested in player development and the success of the major league team. Many times a high flying minor league team that looked like a lock for the playoffs early on crashed and burned at the end of the year when they lost some of their key players to call-ups.

Hopefully the Barons would keep things going. Manny was sure Doug would be the next to go, so he wasn't counting on a trip to the playoffs this year. It looked like the highlight of the year was going to be rooming with Bobby Calhoun for a few days, and that would only happen if they could give him a clean room to stay in.

Manny found out soon enough how bad it was a few minutes later. Joe's room was a mess. There was stuff all over the floor: clothes, papers, old food wrappers. The closet consisted of various piles of clothes, some clean, some dirty, but nothing on a hanger. The bed wasn't made, and there was a layer of dust on all the furniture so whenever they moved anything a hazy cloud circled the room.

Doug had brought some trash bags and boxes from the stadium, and they spent the next two hours sorting out the trash from Joe's things. By the time they were finished, they were both ready for a nap, but they had four bags of trash and three boxes packed and ready to ship to Joe.

They decided to split up to finish the rest of their chores. Doug would take care of shipping out Joe's things and run to the store and finish grocery shopping while Manny cleaned the rest of the house. By about 2:00 p.m. they were finally finished and the house deemed fit for their new houseguest. They spent the rest of the afternoon just hanging around the house waiting for the game and their chance to meet Bobby Calhoun.

When they got to the stadium later that afternoon, they were immediately called into Tom's office. There sitting in one of the chairs in the corner of the office was Bobby Calhoun. It was kind of odd to see Tom laughing and joking around since he had always seemed pretty straight-laced around the team, but here he was chatting away with Bobby like he was a long lost friend.

"Come on in and have a seat, guys," Tom said when he saw them standing by the door. "I'd like you to meet Bobby Calhoun."

Manny and Doug both shook Bobby's hand and then squeezed into the two remaining chairs in the office. They exchanged a little small talk, and then Tom got right down to business. "Bobby and I go way back. I was his first manager in rookie ball, so you can imagine how proud I am of all his success. I was the one who asked him if he would like to stay with you guys while he was here. I thought it would be a great opportunity for you to get a taste of the big leagues without going there yet."

"I was happy to help out," Bobby chimed in. "Tom has told me about both of you, and I'm looking forward to the next few days."

Manny and Doug both sat perfectly still, and neither knew quite what to say. Manny finally broke the silence. "It's our pleasure."

"Yeah," said Doug, "we've got everything set up for you back at our place."

"I appreciate it. It's rough going out on the road again. I've been dealing with the elbow for weeks. Hopefully, everything is straightened out now."

"Bobby will be starting tomorrow night on a strict fifty-pitch limit. He has a few things he would like to focus on. Manny, I'm going to sit you down tonight so you can spend the game going over the hitters so he knows what to expect," Tom said.

"Sure. I would love that," Manny said, and he meant it. Not only would he get to catch Bobby, he was going to spend the game talking to him.

"I told Tom it wasn't necessary."

"That's okay. I was probably due for a night off anyway."

"Okay," Bobby replied, not making eye contact with Manny. The room seemed to get cooler.

"We'll bring in some good food after the game tonight." Bobby didn't seem to mind that he was on the hook for meals.

"Great. Well guys, Bobby and I have a little more catching up to do, so why don't you go ahead and head out and you can meet up later," said Tom as he gestured to the door.

Manny and Doug took the hint and got up to leave, making sure to shake Bobby's hand before they left. "Did I say something wrong?" Manny asked as they left the room.

"I don't think so," Doug replied. "Maybe he's just a little nervous about rehabbing his injury. I wouldn't worry about it. I'm glad we cleaned up. I would have been embarrassed if he found Joe's room the way it was."

"Me too. I wouldn't have wished that room on anyone. Still, he seemed kind of cool towards me."

"Hey, have you had a chance to talk to Maria yet?" Doug asked, trying to change the subject.

"Not yet, we can't seem to connect. It happens sometimes, but I'm going to try again tomorrow. I did bring it up in a text, but we haven't spoken yet."

"Okay. Maybe once Bobby's gone, you can set it up."

"We'll see. It would be nice, but she would still end up alone quite a bit when we go out on the road."

"Okay. Just know that I'm good with it," Doug said.

"Thanks. I appreciate that," Manny said as they got back to their lockers. He would talk to Maria about it tomorrow, but tonight, he was going to really focus on his time with David and pick his brain. It was always fun to talk to someone that knew how to pitch, and as a former Cy Young winner, Bobby definitely knew what he was doing.

Manny was sitting with Doug in the dugout when Bobby came out a few minutes before the game started. He was in his Barons uniform, which must have felt strange. It took him about ten minutes to get from the end of the dugout to where Manny and Doug were sitting since everyone wanted to introduce themselves to him.

"How do you feel putting on a different uniform?" Manny asked when he sat down.

"No big deal," he replied.

"How does the elbow feel?" Doug asked.

"As good as can be expected. We'll find out tomorrow night. To be honest, I would rather not talk about it. Just treat me like one of the guys."

"Are you sure about that?' Manny asked. "We can be a pretty nasty bunch."

"I'm sure," he said, then turned to Doug, "so tell me about this team."

"Manny's the guy you should talk to. I just follow his lead."

"Okay," Bobby said, finally looking at Manny, "you're up."

The game started, and Manny would go over each of the hitters, and Doug would chime in with how he pitched them the night before. Bobby would ask questions and even took notes on his iPad. Manny was shocked at the level of detail they went into. Obviously, Bobby took all of his starts seriously, including rehab starts that didn't really mean anything.

The game went quickly, and with Manny and his hot bat out of the lineup, the Barons had a rough time stringing hits together and lost by a score of 5–1. The mood in the clubhouse was a little bit lighter than usual after a loss since the team found a full spread of southern BBQ waiting for them in the clubhouse. Bobby had done his homework and picked one the better restaurants in town to bring in food. If this was what they could expect for the next week, they were all going to put on a few pounds.

After the game they quickly showered and changed so they could take their guest back to the house to settle in. After they helped Bobby bring his things in, they hung out for a little bit in the living room watching Sports Center and the MLB Network. Bobby was due to make his first rehab start the next day, and he let them know that his pregame routine was pretty specific and he didn't like to talk much before a game. Both Manny and Doug told him that they understood and agreed to meet up with him at the stadium the next afternoon.

Bobby excused himself after a while leaving Manny and Doug sitting together. "Is it just my imagination, or does he not like me?" Manny asked as soon as he was out of earshot.

"He definitely seemed pretty cool toward you," Doug answered.

"Did I say something wrong?"

"Not that I heard, we were just talking about the game."

Manny shook his head. "This is going to be a long couple of days if he's going to have an attitude towards me. I guess all I can do if focus on prepping him for the game."

"I can't believe how much he paid attention during the game tonight. He really takes this seriously, even though he'll probably dominate these guys tomorrow night," Doug said with admiration.

"I guess that's what you have to do to make it to the top. Prepare every day like it is the seventh game of the World Series."

"Well, I don't know about you, but I'm taking mental notes of everything he says," Doug said, standing up and stretching. "He is a real pro, and he's already given me some things to think about."

"Me too. I can't wait to catch him tomorrow." Manny got up off the couch. "But now I'm beat. I think I'm going to turn in. See you later." With that they went their separate ways for the night.

By the time Manny got up the next day, Doug was already dressed and in the kitchen, and Bobby was long gone.

"What time did he leave?" Manny asked Doug.

"Just a few minutes ago. He said he likes to take a long walk on the morning he pitches."

"Really. Well I guess it works for him. What are you plans for the day?" Manny asked.

"Actually, I was going to head over to the stadium early today. I'm supposed to meet a writer that is doing an article on me for some minor league magazine." Doug shrugged. "Reporters are not my favorite thing."

"I'll say. Remember when we got Chip with that bucket of Gatorade?" Manny asked laughing.

"I sure do. Boy, Tom was mad the second time we did that."

"I think he played mad. He was laughing on the inside," Manny said, recalling their conversation in Tom's office.

"Well he looked mad," Doug replied.

"He had to be. The team was giving him a hard time," Manny said. "We've had some good times this year, haven't we?"

"Oh yeah. It's been one of my most memorable seasons yet, and it not even over," Doug said with a smile.

"It's going to get better for you. You'll be with the Sox before the year is over," Manny said, knowing that it really was just a matter of time before Doug was called up. His stuff was too good to be wasted in double A.

"I'm not getting my hopes up," Doug replied.

"Well, my advice to you is to keep a bag packed. You may not get much notice."

"We'll see. Want a ride over to the stadium today?" Doug asked.

"That's okay. I'll find my way over. I'm supposed to call Maria later."

"Okay. Let me know what she says. I'll see you later." Doug excused himself and headed back to his room.

"Hey," Manny called out as Doug walked away.

"What's up?"

"Did Bobby say anything this morning about me? If I said something wrong?"

Doug looked at the ground. "Do you really want to know?"

"Of course," Manny said, curious about what it could be.

"He said he had heard a player on the Barons was suspended for steroids. He seemed to know that you and Zach were friends and asked what I thought about you."

Manny couldn't hide his surprise. "What did you say?"

"I said you were a stand-up guy and the best catcher I ever had."

"Really?"

"You bet. I told him not to believe everything he heard and that he should judge you himself."

"Wow," Manny was taken aback, both by Bobby's question and Doug's response. "I don't know what to say. Thank you doesn't seem enough."

"You don't have to thank me, Manny. I got your back," Doug said and walked to his room.

Manny spent the rest of the morning watching movies and killing time, trying to make sense of what Doug had told him. After Zach was suspended Joe had practically accused him of cheating and now it sounded like other people thought the same thing. He kept thinking about what he could do and almost forgot to call Maria. They talked for a while, and he shared what Doug had told him, babbling on and on until she told him to stop.

He told her that he really wanted her to come up but she was still unsure about coming so he decided not to push it. They still had a few months left in the season to figure it out, so they agreed to put it aside for now. She told him to hang in there and not worry about what other people thought, *easier said than done,* he thought to himself. He usually felt better after talking to her though and today was no different, he would try to put the situation aside and focus on that night's game.

By the time he got to the stadium later that afternoon he found Bobby sitting in Zach's old locker looking at scouting reports for the Pensacola Blue Wahoos. The guy was a pro. He was preparing for this game as if he were facing the New York Yankees. Manny dropped his things in his locker and pulled up a chair. Some pitchers were very uptight before they pitched, and he didn't have a read on him yet.

"Hey, how's it going?" Bobby asked.

"Okay. How about you? Ready for the game tonight?"

"I can't wait. It's been a while. I just hope I don't embarrass myself out there. I'm sure these guys would love to take me deep."

"I don't see that happening," Manny said, surprised Bobby would have any doubts about the game.

"You never know. I'm not really concerned about results tonight. I mean, that sounds bad since I'm sure the guys want to win. There are a few specific things I want to try out. Do you have a few minutes to talk?"

It was total change from the night before, maybe talking to Doug had made a difference. "My time is your time. What do you need?"

They spent the next twenty minutes going over Bobby's inventory of pitches. He had a two seam and four seam fastball as well as a slider and curve. His plan for the evening was to primarily work on location with his fastballs and to mix in a few curves and sliders along the way. He was mostly concerned about location and hitting his spots. He also told Manny to call whatever he wanted since he knew the other team better than him.

"Oh, by the way. I'm going to let a few guys get on at some point. I need to work out of the stretch and practice some pickoffs. Just let me know when a guy with no pop is coming up," Bobby smiled. "I don't mind giving up a few singles, but nobody is taking me deep."

"Okay," Manny said. "I'll let you know the inning before when I see someone." He was impressed that he could give up a few hits to a couple of double A guys and not sound too worried about it.

The rest of pre-game felt like any other night with one exception. Not only was it a packed house, which was unusual for a Wednesday night, there were extra scouts and medical personnel from the Sox in the stands. It made sense. They had a lot invested in Bobby Calhoun and were concerned about his injury.

They didn't need to worry. Bobby was in mid-season form and set down the Blue Wahoos with ease in the first two innings. Manny had heard it said that you could catch some guys sitting in a rocking chair. Well they must have been referring to Bobby Calhoun. His motion looked nice and easy but the ball literally exploded out of his hand. The only person Manny could compare him to, oddly enough, was Doug. They were basically the same pitcher, except Bobby was left-handed.

Before they went out in the third inning, Manny let Bobby know that the first batter up wasn't much of a hitter. He had actually played with him before a few years ago, and he had no power, so he wouldn't be a risk to hit one out. Plus, he was struggling a bit, so a hit off a major leaguer would give his ego a boost.

Bobby was true to his word and left one right over the plate, and the batter responded with a clean single to right field. After a few pickoff attempts he tried to steal second base, and Manny gunned him down with five feet to spare. As they got back to the dugout, Bobby went out of his way to give Manny a high-five and a "nice throw" compliment.

Bobby reached his fifty-pitch count after four innings and came out of the game. He had only given up the one hit and looked like he was in mid-season form. The Barons responded to the big crowd and extra attention and cruised to an 8–1 victory. Manny had two more doubles and three RBIs. He didn't notice it, but the extra eyes in the stands were starting to take notice of him.

Back in the clubhouse the team was excited to find another spread of food, compliments of Bobby Calhoun. It was the same BBQ as the day before, but they didn't mind. Anything was an improvement over the sandwiches they were used to having. Manny looked for Bobby after the game, but he was busy first with the training staff, then team officials and finally the press. Everyone wanted a piece of him, and Manny felt a little bad for him. He probably just wanted to sit down and relax after the game.

Eventually, Bobby made it back to his locker and took a seat next to Manny. "I have to tell you, Manny," he said, "you call a really good game. And you've got some pop in your bat. What's your story?"

"What do you mean?"

"Why are you still in double A?"

"I don't know. It's just never happened for me."

"Your brothers play, right?"

"Right." How did he know that?

"See, it's in your blood," Bobby said. "You don't need any help."

Manny was blown away by the comment.

"Not much for conversation, are you?" Bobby said with a smile.

"What? Oh, I'm sorry. You just caught me by surprise," Manny said. "What do you mean by that?"

"Hey, don't think too much. It just gets you in trouble. I'm just saying, don't take any chances. You can make it on your own."

Manny understood the implication, and it took everything he had not to go off on Bobby. How dare he? Couldn't he just appreciate the way Manny played the game? Did he really think that Manny was on something?

"Let's get out of here. I'm beat," Bobby said, picking up his things.

"Okay." That was all Manny could say right now.

Doug was already in bed by the time they got home, and Bobby headed straight to his room. Manny sat up for a while watching highlights on the MLB Network. He was happy to see

Joe show up on the highlights for the A's vs. Angels game. Not only did he have three hits, he also drove in the winning run with a walk-off single in the twelfth inning. It seemed like his doubts were short lived after all, and he was making it hard for the A's to send him back down to the minors.

Bobby's next start went according to plan, and he went six full innings throwing only sixty-eight pitches. Everything he had was working, and Manny was amazed at his poise on the mound. It seemed like he could control exactly where the other team hit the ball and once again they only got on base when he let them. He only gave up two hits, and once again, Manny threw out both runners trying to steal.

It had been an uncomfortable week, and despite Bobby's veiled concerns about his integrity, Manny felt like he had packed in a month's worth of baseball knowledge into that short time. They had talked about both the physical and the mental approach to the game, and both Manny and Doug had gained a new perspective on what it would take to make it. At least Manny knew now what he would be up against. There were always going to be doubts about him, and he would have to work even harder to make it.

The good news was that he seemed to change Bobby's opinion by the time he left because he made it a point to stop and tell them, "I'll see you both in Chicago before the season's over."

CHAPTER 21

It was funny how the little things could have a big impact on your life. Bobby Calhoun had only stayed with the Birmingham Barons for about a week, but he had made a huge impact on Manny. It wasn't the first time that he had been exposed to someone who had played in the major leagues before. He only had to look to his brothers for that, but Bobby was different for some reason.

Maybe it was just his general attitude or the fact that he stayed with Manny and Doug instead of in a hotel. In could have been seeing how he prepared for the games. They weren't just rehab starts. He took them seriously, like they meant something to him. It could have been any of those things, but it was probably just the last comment he made as he was leaving.

"I'll see you in Chicago before the season's over." So matter of fact, as though it were a done deal. That little comment made a big impression on Manny. He had always thought he had a chance to make it, if he didn't he wouldn't keep playing, but everyone had doubts from time to time. To have someone with Bobby's experience say it, that really helped to keep Manny motivated through the dog days of summer.

July and August were probably the hardest stretch of time for any ballplayer. The initial excitement of the start of the new season, the toll of the day to day routine, and traveling was just starting to catch up to the players. The weather started to change and the games seemed longer due to the heat and the humidity.

Even though they only played for about three hours a day, by the time they threw in the pre and post game time, it seemed like they lived at the ballpark.

By this time of the year Manny had been separated from his family for months and after seeing the same guys day after day he was getting tired of them and longed for something to break up the monotony. If he was lucky, he could get promoted to a higher division, or at least have some new faces join the team at some time. But that hadn't happened yet, and he always finished where he started, and every day began to feel the same.

That's why Bobby's comment meant so much to Manny. It made him think that he could get called up this year. It was not unheard of for a double A player to go straight to the majors, just look at Joe. He had been called up by the A's after the trade and was still with the team. He was hitting a solid .286 with a couple of home runs and looked like he might stay with the club even when their injured left fielder returned.

Manny also knew that Doug was going to be leaving soon. He wasn't sure if it would be to triple A Charlotte or to the White Sox, but there was no point in him staying with the Barons for much longer. He was dominating the Southern League with a 9–2 record, an ERA of 2.12 and of course, a perfect game. The White Sox were trying to stay in the AL West race but were in danger of dropping too far behind to make a run. Their pitching would get better with Bobby's return, but they could still use another quality starter.

Manny was thinking about Doug when he walked into the living room and sat down. "So," he asked, "any news on your upcoming call-up?"

"What are you talking about? I'm not going anywhere," Doug replied.

"You're kidding, right? You know there is nothing left for you to prove here."

"I'm not so sure about that. You can always improve," Doug said with a serious face.

"The White Sox made it pretty clear when you started that game at Wrigley in spring training. You are on their radar. You have to see the scouts that are here for your starts." Everyone knew that the White Sox, and some other interested teams, were always around on days Doug pitched.

"Scouts are always around. That's their job, watching games," Doug replied, mocking Manny.

"Be in denial if you want, but even Bobby Calhoun said it. You'll be in Chicago by the end of the year."

"He was just being polite," Doug said, deflating Manny's ego for a minute. "He's a nice guy, but he's not making the decisions."

"True, but he knows what it takes to make it, and he was watching you pitch very closely." Manny had noticed that Bobby kept an eye on Doug, on the field and off, almost like he was evaluating him for the team.

"We'll see. I was talking to my agent the other day. They are probably more likely to shut me down for the season early to save my arm before they promote me."

"Why would they do that?"

"Teams are doing it more and more now. They set an innings limit for you and shut you down when you reach it. Look at Stephen Strausbug. The Nationals shut him down even though they were in the middle of a pennant race." Doug shook his head in disgust. "I want to pitch as much as I can. I don't want to stop before the season is over."

"But didn't they shut him down because he was recovering from an injury," Manny asked.

"Yes. He had Tommy John surgery the year before, but some teams are doing it with all of their young pitchers."

"Take it as a compliment then," Manny said. "They think enough of you to try and protect you."

"I don't need protection. I'm a grown man," Doug replied.

"True, but they have a lot of money invested in you. They have the right to do what they feel is best." Manny wished the team cared that much about him.

"I guess. It's just hard sometimes when you realize that you don't have much control over your life."

"You get used to it," Manny replied, and it was true. It was hard being a ballplayer, especially one just starting out. You had no control on where you played. In order to get control you first had to make it to the big leagues and then build up enough service time to become a free agent. That is when the power, and the money, came under your control.

"It's just rough sometimes, you know."

"I do. I've been around for a while. This is the hardest part of the year. You just need to grab on to something and use it for motivation," Manny said.

"What do you do?" Doug asked.

"First, I think of Maria and how I'm trying to make a better life for us and the kids. Then I think about my brothers and what they went through, I don't want to be the only one that didn't make it."

"That reminds me, is Maria going to come up?"

"No. We decided against it. It's only a couple of months, and we never got the paperwork set up for the kids to travel." Manny was disappointed, but there would be other years.

"That's too bad. I'm sure you would have liked to have them here," Doug said.

"I am, but we'll see each other soon enough."

"You are always so positive, how to you do it?" Doug asked.

"I'm just a glass half-full kind of guy. It could be worse than this. How many guys do you know that wouldn't want to swap places with us?'

"Very true. I can think of a few," Doug said. "I guess I just need to learn how to roll with it."

"It comes with time, trust me," Manny said. "Tell you what, how about dinner after the game tonight?"

"You know I'm not a Taco Bell guy, right?" Doug asked.

"I won't hold that against you. How about Waffle House?"

"You're on."

"See, things are looking better already," Manny said with a smile.

Manny was sitting at his locker later that day getting ready for the game when Doug walked by with a disgusted look on his face. When Manny asked what was wrong, he said that he had just been in to talk to Tom and was told he was being pulled from his start the next day.

"I told you. They are trying to baby me. I don't want to sit down. I feel fine," Doug told Manny.

"Did you tell him that?" Manny asked.

"Sure. He said it didn't matter, orders from the White Sox."

"That was all he said?" Manny asked.

"Yup. Just like that." Doug sat down next to Manny and put his head into his hands. "I just don't get it."

Manny paused for a minute. "You know, there is another way to look at this."

"I'm not in the mood for a 'the glass is half-full' pep talk," Doug said, lifting his head to look at Manny.

"Too bad, because I'm going to tell you anyway." Manny paused for a minute again. "Maybe, just maybe, they pulled you because they needed you to pitch somewhere else in the next few days."

Doug suddenly perked up a little. "You think?"

"Sure, I've seen it all the time. Guys get pulled because they are getting called up or even getting traded," he added.

"Well, I can do without the trade part, but called-up? Who is pitching this week for the Sox?"

Manny pulled out his iPad. "Let's see. The White Sox are in New York versus the Yankees. Today's starter is Bobby Calhoun, tomorrow's starter is Tom Jefferies, and the next day is TBA."

Doug smiled, "Meet Mr. TBA."

"Don't assume anything," Manny said.

"I won't, but I'd rather think about that than they were sitting me to 'save me.' I'm going to head out to the field. Don't forget, dinner tonight."

Manny felt a little bad. While it was a possibility that Doug was the TBA, it was not a done deal. They could just be saving his arm, or sending him to Charlotte. Oh well, he thought, maybe the prospect of a call-up would help him feel better and get him through the next couple of days. For now it would ease his mind, and that was okay.

The game was nothing to write home about. The Barons lost 7–4 in a poorly played, sloppy game. Manny was 0 for 3 with a walk and two strikeouts. The only time he hit the ball was a weak ground out to second base. Sometimes, things just didn't go his way and tonight was that kind of night. He decided to skip his evening video session. There were only so many times you could watch yourself swing and miss, and he headed to the Waffle House to meet Doug for dinner.

Doug was already sitting in a booth when Manny arrived. They quickly flagged down a waitress and placed their order. "Not much of a game today," Manny said.

"Yeah, we didn't have much life in our bats today, did we? I don't get you hitters. I mean, one day you hit everything in sight, the next day you couldn't hit water if you fell out of a boat."

"I could say the same thing about pitchers. I mean, you guys only play every five days, so you would think you could bring it every time you pitch. You have all that time to rest and plan, but you still struggle."

"Pitching is harder than hitting any day of the week," Doug said in response. "You try getting up there and throwing strikes in front of thousands of people."

It was a familiar argument between hitters and pitchers that had been replayed many times in the house over the months. Manny had a unique perspective because he was a catcher, but he still couldn't help teasing Doug whenever he had the chance. He was about to make another comment when Doug's phone rang and he stepped away.

Manny was halfway through his meal by the time Doug returned. He felt kind of bad that he had started to eat but he was starving and he knew Doug wouldn't mind. Doug had a strange look on his face when he sat down, and Manny asked him, "Is everything okay?"

"What? Oh yeah, it was just Tom."

"Calls from Tom at this time of night? I don't even know if he has my cell phone number." Manny laughed.

"He just called to let me know that the White Sox were calling me up to pitch on Monday night against the Yankees."

"Are you serious? That's great! Home or away?"

"What?" Doug still looked like he was in shock.

"Are they in Chicago or New York?" Manny asked.

"Oh. They are in New York. Can you believe it? My first start will be in Yankee Stadium?"

"I believe it. I've been telling you for weeks that you were going to get called up. When they cancelled your start that gave it away."

"I guess you were right," Doug said.

"Of course I was right. You've got great stuff. Just as good as Bobby Calhoun. I can say that because I have caught both of you now."

"Still. Getting called up and Yankee Stadium to boot." Doug smiled. "And you know the Sox still have to play the A's later this year. Maybe I'll still be around to face Joe. Wouldn't that be something?"

"I'd pay money to see that," Manny said, but he really wished he could be on the field with them.

"Maybe you'll make it up by then," Doug said, looking at his food, but then deciding he wasn't hungry.

"We'll see," Manny said. "There is a long way to go before we go down that road."

"Do you mind if I take off. I've got some calls to make, and I need to start packing. They want me on a plane to New York tomorrow," Doug said as he pushed his plate away.

"Of course. I'm done anyway. I'll meet you back at the house." Manny stood up and gave Doug a hug. "Congratulations. You deserve it."

"Thanks, Manny."

With that, they walked out to the parking lot and made their way home. Doug excused himself to his room, and Manny caught the end of Sports Center. Joe had another big game for the A's, with three hits and a home run. Manny looked around the room and realized that this time tomorrow he would be alone in the house. He was happy for Joe and Doug, but he couldn't help but feel a little jealous. He had been playing for longer than they had, and he had never been called up.

How much longer would he be able to keep this up? How long would Maria be okay letting him leave for six months of the year? He was lucky he had a wife that was so understanding and let him chase his dream. He was getting older though, and he couldn't do this forever. Maybe it was time to sit down this winter and really think about his options.

He was sure he could run the family baseball academy back home. His brothers had told him that many times. It was probably the best thing for him since he could still be part of the game, but he didn't want to feel like he had to depend on his brothers to earn a living. Why did he have to think about this now? Well, one thing he had learned over the years is that every player had doubts, and they usually came at night, when you were alone.

He didn't want to deal with it right now, so he tried to think about the positive. This would be the first time in his life he lived alone. He had always shared a room with someone; his brothers, players, Maria. It would be very different to live by himself. The more he thought about it the more excited he got. Maybe this would turn out to be a good thing for him.

The next morning felt like déjà vu. He stood at the door talking to Doug as he waited for a taxi to take him to the airport. They made small talk and went over a list of things that Manny would take care of for him. Doug wasn't sure if this was a one-start thing or if he would stay up for a while, so they wouldn't send all of his things until they knew for sure.

Doug's cell phone rang to let him know that his taxi had arrived. "Well, I guess this is it," he said.

"I guess so," said Manny, holding out his hand.

"And then there was one."

"Who would have thought that a couple of months ago," Manny said.

"Before you know it, there will be zero," Doug said with a smile. "Believe me, I'm going to bring up your name every chance I get."

"Come on. You don't have to do that."

"You can bet I will. You are the best catcher I have ever played with. You should expect to be up in September."

"We'll see about that," Manny said. "Until then, I'll be watching."

"You better." With that, Doug made his way out the door, leaving Manny alone.

Manny had just finished packing for the upcoming road trip and eating a dinner of frozen tamales. He was settling down on the couch when his cell phone rang. He didn't recognize the number, but he decided to answer it anyway. "Hello," he said picking up the phone and muting the TV.

"How does it feel having the place all to yourself?" said a familiar voice.

"Zach? Is that you?" Manny asked.

"How are you doing, Manny?"

"Okay. I'm just surprised to hear your voice," Manny replied, thinking *shocked* was a better word.

"I know. It's been rough for me. I should have called you before, but you know how it is," Zach said with a sigh. "Talking to you just reminds me of what I left behind."

"I get that, but you know you don't have to go through it by yourself."

"Well, I haven't been the best person to be around lately," Zach said.

"What have you been doing with yourself?" Manny asked.

"Not too much. Just hanging around my mom's house. I haven't felt like going out. I feel like everyone is talking about me."

"I'm sure that's not true," Manny said.

"No. It's crazy. When your name is in the news, people come out of the woodwork. I was getting calls every day for a while calling me a cheater and stuff."

Manny had never considered that before right now. Zach was a professional baseball player, but at the same time he played in Birmingham not Chicago. "Who would do that?"

"You'd be surprised at the number of people that follow the game. Some are locals from around town, but there is an underground group that stays on top of guys that get in trouble."

"Must be people with nothing better to do."

"I try not to judge. I'm really not in position to say much. Anyway, I wasn't calling to talk about me. I just wanted to call and say thank you."

"Thank you. For what?" Manny asked.

"I got a call from Sarah the other day," Zach said, his voice picking up. "She said she had talked to you."

"I saw her at the laundromat. I'm glad she called you."

"We had a nice long talk. I don't know if we can get back to where we were, but I think we may actually have a chance."

"That's awesome!"

"Yeah. She said she had been thinking about me and even though she didn't understand why I did what I did, she knew it had nothing to do with her."

"Hmm. That's a start." If she could get past that, Manny knew that she and Zach could possibly have a future together.

"I was thinking about coming down to Birmingham in a couple of weeks to see her. Since you have the place to yourself, would it be okay if I came and stayed at the house?" Zach asked hopefully.

"Of course, I would love to have you here," Manny said, thinking it would be nice to have someone to talk to.

"You're going on the road now right?" Zach asked.

"Yeah, gone for about a week," Manny said, not surprised that Zach had been following the Barons.

"Well, you keep hitting the ball like you have been, and you may not be there if I come."

"We'll see. It's going to take more than a few weeks to make a difference," Manny said. First Bobby, then Doug, now Zach, he didn't want to get his hopes up.

"The Sox don't have much faith in their current catchers. You better get ready and tell Maria too. I'm sure she'll want to be there." Zach said it like there was no doubt in his mind.

"What about you? Will you be there?" Manny asked and then immediately regretted it. That was not the best thing to say to a guy that had just had to place his dream on hold.

"You couldn't keep me away."

"I'm sorry, Zach," Manny said, "that was a pretty insensitive thing to say."

"Don't worry about it. I made my own bed. I have to lie in it. I'm happy for all you guys. I just wish I could be there with you."

"You'll get another chance. Have you heard anything yet?"

"From the team, no. My agent says it won't be until after the season. Until then I'm just taking it day by day."

"What do you do to keep yourself busy?"

"Not much at first. I mostly sat around and felt sorry for myself. I barely made it out of the house. Every day things got worse."

"Why is that?"

"I don't know. I mean I would think things couldn't get any worse, but every day they did. I think I really hit bottom when Joe was traded and called up, it reminded me of how much I wanted it. To see someone I knew make it just made me want it more, and I realized how bad I had screwed things up."

"But you feel better now?" Manny asked hopefully.

"I have good days and bad days."

"I always told you, you need balance in your life. That's the only thing that will make it work."

"Maybe you're right. I'm going to try. First with Sarah, and then I'm going to do whatever it takes to make it back, even if I have to start all over again."

"That's a good attitude to have," Manny said and he meant it. If Zach could learn from his mistakes and put them behind him he would be better for it.

"I'm not going to say I'm all the way there yet, but I'm trying."

"That's all you can do." Manny spent the next twenty minutes updating Zach on what had been going on with the Barons. It seemed like Zach was feeling better about things. It could have felt awkward, after all, Zach was no longer on the team, but it felt pretty normal. It was good to talk to him and they agreed that they would make it a point to talk more often going forward.

By the time they finished Manny realized he had better get to bed so he wouldn't miss the bus the next day. Since he was living alone now, he didn't have anyone to wake him up if he overslept. It was going to be a short road trip, only five days, and then they had about six weeks left in the season. September was just around the corner, and if what everyone said was true, maybe he would get called up to the Sox. Just thinking about it made him excited and nervous. He had to force those thoughts out of his head so he could get some rest. If it was really going to happen, he needed to produce over the next few weeks, so he forced himself to go to sleep because tomorrow would be here before he knew it.

CHAPTER 22

Manny's days of rooming alone on the road were over. After Zach left he was assigned to a room by himself for a couple of trips, but he knew that wouldn't last forever. His new roommate was Jeremy Donaldson, who had just been promoted from single A. He was supposed to be a hot shot prospect with a big upside. All Manny knew was the kid had endless energy, never wanted to sleep, and when he did, he snored like a buzz saw.

This was a short trip so Manny would only have to deal with him for a few days before he got back to the quiet of his bachelor pad. It would be different living alone, he still didn't know if he would like it or not. They went straight to the field today so unpacking would have to wait until later. The game was uneventful with the Barons losing 6–2 and Manny was 1 for 4 with a double. He was more excited to get back to the hotel so he could see how Doug did in his major league debut.

Doug didn't disappoint. He pitched seven scoreless innings, giving up only three hits while striking out eight and picked up the win in a 6–0 White Sox victory. If he had any pre-game jitters they sure didn't show tonight. Manny sent him a congratulatory text and tried to get some sleep. Jeremy wandered into the room late, turned on the light to watch TV for a while and eventually fell asleep leaving both on. Manny woke up at 2:00 a.m., turned everything off, and tried to go back to sleep.

The rest of the trip was pretty much the same. The Barons lost four of five games, and Manny struggled at the plate finishing 1 for 11 in the three remaining games that he played. He chalked it up to the change in roommates. Jeremy was not an easy guy to be around. Maybe it was because he was young, or Manny was old, but at some point he needed to sleep and he wasn't getting any. He would have to talk to the traveling secretary when they got home to see if there were any other options.

Back at the house things were very quiet. Going from four people living in a place to one made a big difference. The first few days were kind of nice, but Manny was used to having people around. Having come from a big family, he was starting to get lonely. The good news was that since he was getting some sleep again, he was also starting to hit. He had two more home runs in the first four games back, and even when he got out he was hitting the ball hard.

Each year major league teams were allowed to expand their rosters from twenty-five players to forty players on September first. Expanded rosters gave teams more flexibility during the pennant drive and gave teams out of contention the chance to try out some new players to see how they performed. Most minor leaguers looked forward to the end of the season, hopeful that they would get called up to get their shot to impress the big league team.

Manny had never really felt like he deserved a call-up until this year. This was, by far, the best season he had ever put together in his minor league career. He tried not to get his hopes up too high, but it was hard. The White Sox were not really a playoff team. They were eight games out of the division lead and further behind the wild card so they could use this time to try out some players. He had good feedback from Bobby and he was sure Doug would put in a good word for him too. Maybe this would be the year he got called up.

When Tom asked to see him in his office before the next road trip, Manny felt very nervous. September first was right around the corner, and the Barons played their last game on September third. After this trip he would either pack up and go home for the winter or join the White Sox for the next month or so. He tried to lower his expectations. Maybe this was just a "good job this year" talk or something like that.

He got to Tom's office and knocked on the door. "You wanted to see me, Tom?"

"Come on in, Manny, have a seat."

"Thanks," Manny said, picking his usual seat across from Tom.

"Well, the season's winding down, and I'm a big believer in letting guys know where they stand and not leaving them hanging. I'm sure you've been thinking about September call-ups."

Manny smiled nervously. "It has crossed my mind. I mean, I'm not expecting anything. It would be a big jump from double A to the majors."

"Not as big as you think," Tom said. "Just look at Doug and Joe. They are more than holding their own."

"True, but those guys were destined to make it from day one."

"Don't sell yourself short, Manny. You are a talented player and you deserve a shot." Tom paused for what seemed like an eternity. "And you're going to get one. The White Sox are adding you to their roster. They want you to join the team in Chicago after their next road trip. You'll finish up with us and report to them on September sixth."

Manny broke into a wide grin. "Are you serious?"

"Yes. Congratulations. You deserve it. I'm sure it's been a crazy year for you with all of you roommates leaving. You stayed focused and improved your game. You just need to take this time to soak up all you can, and we'll see how things end up."

"Thanks, Tom, you've been great, and I appreciate all your help." Manny got up to leave. He suddenly had a lot of things to do.

"No problem. Good luck. You'll get contacted by the team to help set up your travel arrangements. Until then, I still need you here for the road trip. Let's finish the year strong." Tom stood up and shook his hand. "It's not that big of a jump. Remember that."

"I will," Manny said, hoping he wouldn't be in over his head.

They still had a game to play but he had to call Maria and tell her the news. He found a quiet spot and gave her a call. It had been such a long time coming and they had both sacrificed so much he got choked up telling her. Now she would have to find a way to come up to see him play in a game. They agreed to talk later that night when he had a better idea of his schedule for the remainder of the year.

He then sent text messages to his brothers and other family member to tell them the news. He needed to tell Doug, but it was almost time for the game and he still had a job to do here. The positive feelings spilled over to the game, and he got three more hits to help the team win 6–1. Back home that night he sent out a few more messages and responded to some from his family.

The next week passed by in a flash as Manny packed up his things and got ready for the final road trip of the year. He was able to score his own room for the trip as a good-bye gift from the traveling secretary. One of the clubhouse guys offered to keep an eye on the house until they could get back and pick up their things after the season ended. Everything was falling into place, and now all he had to do was get to Chicago and hopefully get into a game.

Before he knew it he was sitting in front of his locker in the clubhouse of Comiskey Park in Chicago. Hanging in front of him was a brand new jersey with *Dominguez* and the number *41* on the back. He picked it up and slipped it on over his shirt and then put on his hat and stood back and smiled. Right then, he heard a voice over his shoulder.

"Looks good, but I think you are going to need new pants. Those jeans just aren't going to work."

Manny turned around to see Doug smiling at him. "I'd play without pants if I had to," he said, laughing. "I've been waiting for this day for a long time."

"Thankfully, we won't have to see that," Doug replied.

They exchanged handshakes and hugs, and Doug filled Manny in on the clubhouse routine. The rest of the afternoon was spent getting acclimated to his new surroundings. The clubhouse was much bigger than he was used to, and he hoped he wouldn't get lost on the way to the field. He was just getting ready to head out for batting practice when one of the clubhouse guys told him that Andy Pendleton, the White Sox manager, wanted to see him.

Manny made his way to Andy's office and knocked on the door. "Come in," a voice called from inside.

Manny opened the door and was surprised to find a room much larger than Tom's office back in Birmingham. He made his way over to Andy's desk and, after shaking his hand, sat down in a comfortable leather chair. They only had folding chairs in Tom's office, which was so small your knees hit the front of the desk.

"I just wanted to call you in and welcome you to the team," Andy said. "I also wanted to set some expectations around playing time for the rest of the season."

That caught Manny's attention. "Sure," he said, "I'm willing to do anything you want me to do."

"Well, we have about three weeks to go and if we don't kick it into high gear soon we'll just be playing out the string. I'd like you to spend time in the bullpen during the games helping to warm up the pitchers. It will be good for you to learn what they throw."

"I would like that," Manny said.

"I hope to get you a couple of starts this year, probably pairing you up with Doug. He can't stop talking about you by the way. Maybe a few pinch hits along the way. Other than that, try to soak up as much information as you can. I hear good things about you, so I'm looking forward to your time here." Andy stood up, and Manny took that as his clue to leave.

"I'm on board for anything you need," Manny said. He then shook Andy's hand and made his way to the field for warm-ups.

It was an incredible feeling just to take part in warm-ups. Manny had the chance to take batting practice and hang out on the field with the other players. Most of the players were very welcoming and seemed to be excited for him to finally make it to the big leagues. Maybe it was his imagination, but a few guys stopped their conversations when he passed by. It may have just been something private, but it made him feel a little uncomfortable, like the steroid talk Bobby mentioned could be going around the clubhouse.

He spent the first few innings in the dugout talking to Doug and then made his way out to the bullpen for the remainder of the game. He met up with the bullpen coach, who filled him in on how they handled warming up the relief pitchers and how the game was managed from their perspective. He then settled in and watched the game. The White Sox took an early lead, and the game quickly turned into a rout. Around the seventh inning the bullpen came to life and Manny had the chance to warm-up a few of the pitchers.

He could immediately tell the difference between a major league and a double A pitcher. For one, the velocity was much better, and they all had tremendous movement on their fastballs. Throw in a wide variety of sliders, curves, sinkers and change-ups and he knew he was going to have his hands full when he got the opportunity to hit.

The game ended with a White Sox victory and after cleaning up Manny made his way to his temporary home in Chicago. Although Doug had offered to have Manny stay with him, his brothers had insisted on setting him and Maria up in a nearby hotel. He appreciated the gesture. Maria had left the kids and flown up the day before so she could hopefully see him play in a game.

The next few days passed without the opportunity for Manny to get into a game, which was not surprising after his talk with Andy when he first arrived. Although the White Sox fell out of the playoff race, they were playing teams that were still in contention, so it was not the best time to have a new guy make his debut. There were a few series coming up with other non-contenders, and Manny figured he would get his chance then.

The last series of the homestand was against the Cleveland Indians who were also out of the race and a few games behind the White Sox. Manny was in his usual late-inning spot in the bullpen when the call came down to have him head back to the dugout. When he got there, Andy called him over and told him he was going to use him as a pinch-hitter in the eighth inning. Manny took a deep breath and headed down the tunnel to loosen up and take a few swings off the tee.

A few minutes later he was standing in the on-deck circle waiting for his turn to hit. He looked around the stadium, taking it all in. Even though the crowd was small and outcome of the game wasn't in doubt, he was happy. He had worked hard for this moment and waited a long time for it to come. He looked up in the stands and saw Maria sitting there. He smiled and tipped his helmet to her. He was so glad she was able to be there. It was as much her accomplishment as his.

"Now batting for White Sox, making his major league debut, number forty-one, Manny Dominguez." This was it, Manny thought, hearing the public address announcer say his name.

He walked up to the plate, and the crowd that remained gave him a nice round of applause. He was not familiar with the pitcher, but he had read the scouting report on him. He was a veteran that did not have much of a fastball left and relied on a curve and breaking ball. He would try to sneak a fastball in if he was ahead in the count, but for the most part it was junk. Manny would just have to be patient and wait for a good pitch and not chase anything in the dirt.

That was easier said than done as Manny swung at the first pitch, missing it by about a foot as it dropped into the dirt in front of home plate. He stepped out of the batter's box, mad at himself, and looked down at the third base coach who smiled and gestured to him to relax. He was able to lay off the next two pitches that were both outside and low and found himself ahead in the count.

He stepped out again and thought to himself, *What is he going to do next?* He wouldn't want to walk him and was unlikely to throw another off-speed pitch. Manny decided to take a chance and think fastball. He stepped back in, looking for something up and in since he had been working him away so far.

Manny was looking fastball all the way, and sure enough that's what was coming. He waited on the pitch, opened his shoulder up a little, and felt the bat make solid contact with the ball. It flew on a line to deep left center field, and he could tell as he was running up the first base line that it was heading for the wall. He picked up the first base coach, who was waving him on, and as the left fielder picked up the ball and tossed it in he jogged into second base with a stand up double.

Seven years. That was the first thing Manny thought as he stood on second base taking it all in. Seven years he had been waiting for this moment, and he had to admit, it was worth the wait. The White Sox players cheered and Manny saw that they called for the ball so that he would have it to remember this day. The Indians second baseman congratulated him on his first major league hit as he tossed the ball into the dugout. Manny just nodded. He was too choked up to speak.

He was stranded on second base, and as he jogged off the field he looked up in the stands and saw that Maria was crying. He waved to her as he got to the dugout and tried to hold back his own tears. Doug was the first one to greet him when he got back to the dugout, giving him a big hug. The rest of the team quickly followed. They all remembered the feeling of their first big league hit, and Manny took it all in, eventually finding his way to a seat on the bench.

After the game, he found the ball in his locker with the team, date, and pitcher all noted on the ball in crisp black letters. He was anxious to see Maria, but first he had to go and see Andy, who had called for him.

Andy congratulated him on his successful debut and let him know that he was going the start the next day and could expect to start the rest of the games when Doug was pitching. Manny thanked him for the opportunity and after a few minutes of small talk made his way back to the clubhouse.

Manny's locker was next to Doug's, and when he told him that he would be catching his starts for the rest of the year, Doug broke into a wide grin. "That's awesome! I have three more starts, so we'll get a chance to make some waves."

"I think you have been doing fine without me," Manny said. "What are you, four and one now?"

"Only three and one, we didn't hold on to the lead in my last start," Doug said.

"Still, not bad."

"Hey, look at you. Double in your first at-bat," Doug said, picking up the ball from Manny's locker.

"Good guess. He tried to sneak a fastball by me," Manny said, taking the ball from Doug and looking at it.

"There are no good guesses," Doug replied. "That was preparation. There is a big difference."

"I guess you're right," Manny said. "Hey, I've got to get out of here, Maria's waiting for me. I'll catch you early tomorrow, and we can go over the Indians line-up."

"Sounds good. Go out and have a good time tonight."

"Believe me, I will. I've been waiting for this day a long time," Manny said, smiling as he headed out holding the ball in his hand.

Manny met Maria at the restaurant in the hotel, and throughout dinner his phone constantly buzzed with text messages congratulating him on his first big league hit. There were so many, at one point he turned off his phone so they wouldn't be interrupted.

"I am so proud of you, Manny," Maria said. "You had a goal, and you stuck to it."

"I owe it all to you. You were the one that made all this possible," Manny said, holding her hand. "Thank you for letting me chase my dream. I know it's been hard on you being alone so much."

"It was worth it, just to see you out there tonight," Maria said. "But you look like something is bothering you. Are you okay?"

"Never better. I feel like I am on top of the world," Manny sighed, "but I wish Zach had been at the game and I haven't heard from him yet."

"It has to be hard on him to see all of you guys called up. I'm sure he'll come around."

"I hope so. I'm worried about him."

"But you've talked to him recently, right? I thought he was doing better."

"He says he is, but you never know," Manny replied.

"He was talking to that girl, Sarah, wasn't he?" Maria asked.

"Yes, hopefully that will help."

"I'm sure it will. I know you are worried about him, but you know what, let's deal with that later. Tonight I want to celebrate!" Maria said raising her glass for a toast. "To many more nights like tonight!"

"I'll drink to that," Manny said, touching his glass to hers.

The next three weeks passed quickly. Manny started five games, including three that Doug pitched and two for Bobby Calhoun. He didn't know what made him feel better, the fact that the White Sox won all five games with dominating pitching or his own performance at the plate. He ended the year hitting .304, with seven hits in twenty-four at-bats with a pair of home runs.

He made it a point to be available to any of the coaches at any time and quickly picked up a reputation as a hard worker. All the feedback he received from the coaching staff was positive, and although he still felt like some players didn't accept him, by the end of the season he felt like he belonged and he was confident he could stick with the team for a full year if given the chance.

He was still disappointed that Zach had not made his way out to see a game. Manny couldn't help but think that he was having a hard time dealing with the success that his friends were having at the major league level. He was going to have a long road back and Manny was anxious to help, but he couldn't do anything if Zach didn't want to talk. Teammates came and went in this game, and although Manny felt like he and Zach were friends, not just teammates, you never knew what was going to happen.

Doug had finished the year with a six and one record and looked like a lock for the White Sox starting rotation next year. Joe had stuck with the A's for the rest of the season, hitting a solid .293, and it looked like he might have a chance at a starting role. As for Manny, he didn't expect to be a starter for White Sox, but he felt like he had a good chance at a backup role with the team.

Manny had one last thing to do before he could wrap up the season and head home for the winter. He still had some things at the house in Birmingham, and he needed to find out what Zach wanted to do with the Purple Beast. When he pulled up to the house, he was surprised to see that Zach's car was gone. He panicked for a minute, thinking that someone had stolen it, but then he remembered what it looked like. There had to be another explanation. Zach must have come by the house and picked it up.

Why didn't Zach tell him that he was going to pick up the car? Manny was having a hard time keeping up with Zach's mind-set. He seemed pretty positive when they had spoken on the phone a few weeks ago and Manny felt like they would be able to pick up where they had left off. Apparently that wasn't the case or Zach would have been in touch with him to make arrangements for the car.

He sat in the living room and thought about everything that had happened that season. It was always hard when a season ended. You knew the end was coming, but you were never really prepared for it. You always wanted to feel like you had some kind of resolution, a clear ending with a positive outcome, but it never really happened that way. Usually, at least for Manny, every season ended with a bunch of question marks. Where would he end up the next year? If he didn't make another step up the ladder, would this be the end? If it was over, what would he do with the rest of his life?

The good news was that for the first time in a long time he felt like the season ended on a positive note. After seven long years he had finally made it to the big leagues and was actually pretty successful when he got there. He didn't have any grand illusions about his future. He wasn't going to be an All-Star or even a starter. At best he had about five or six years as a backup and then, if he played his cards right, maybe a career as a coach or even a manager.

His one regret for the year was Zach. What a waste. He wished he would have seen it coming. Maybe he could have even prevented it. At this point, there was nothing he could do but wait to see if Zach reached out to him. If he did, he would try to help, but it was going to be up to Zach to make his own future. No one could do it for him. Manny had been around the game for a long time, and as much as he tried to keep in touch with the guys he played with sometimes they just drifted off, and he never knew what happened to them. It was the nature of the game, and it was something he had learned to live with.

The thing Manny loved about baseball was that there was always tomorrow and the future was not written it stone. It could be changed. Every guy that played had the same dream and the same opportunity. It was up to them if they made it or not. He always liked to try to stay positive even when things were not going the way he wanted them to go. He didn't know what tomorrow would bring, but from where he was sitting today the future looked pretty good and he couldn't wait to see what came next.